Cry, Baby, Cry – Heartless

By Don Both and Maria O'Hara

German First Edition May 2019

Contact: https://www.facebook.com/DonBothMariaOHara/

Translated into English and edited by https://buchuebersetzer.webs.com/

Trailer for the book: https://youtu.be/2tQO7kny8wI

Special thanks to Kerstin Patze and Nicole Zdroiek

Cover: Marie Grasshoff

Press inquiries: akreimendahl-a.p.p.verlag@freenet.de

Published at A.P.P.-Verlags GmbH

St. Gallerstrasse 49

9100 Herisau

Suisse

Cell phone: 978-3-96115-714-3

E-pub: 978-3-96115-715-0

Print: 978-3-96115-716-7

Don Both & Maria O'Hara

CRY BABY CRY

A.P.P.
Romance

Summary

For everyone with a broken heart.

And for everyone who continues to fight.

Introduction

ATTENTION!

If you expect me to be one of your beloved bad boys, you'll be disappointed, I am neither bad nor a boy.

I am darkness.

My actions are never comparable to a good man.

I'm not a good man.

I have no soul.

So, if you cannot handle rough stuff, put down the book. Immediately!

Otherwise, you believe you will get to know me, learn to see through me, and assess me, and try to predict what I will do next.

Well, I have to disappoint you, baby.

Nothing about me is tangible, predictable, or familiar.

I am Mason Rush.

And I am a monster.

Don't say I didn't warn you.

Mason K. Rush

Prolog

You are a lost girl. I dragged you down into the abyss.

And I don't intend to ever let you go, Emilia.

Should you manage to escape, I'll come looking for you. And I will find you.

Because you are mine.

You long for the light, but the two of us are darkness, baby.

Fight!

Defend yourself!

Cry!

You will not escape me.

Book 1 – Heartless

1. You Are No Lioness, Emilia, You Are A Lamb.

Mason

You face me and I hate you a little for it, Emilia.

You put on the tight jeans that I told you not to wear. It seems you want the monster in me to come out, Emilia. After all, you're provoking me on purpose, baby.

You've succeeded, Emilia. Not even the three joints I've smoked manage to calm my rage. You chat with two bitches downstairs in my basement apartment. I fucked both, but I will never tell you unless, of course, I want to get you a little excited.

Your hair, Emilia, is still too damn long, but you tamed it into a braid. You wear a black, long-sleeve, off the shoulder top with those shitty jeans, Emilia, simply because you don't want anyone to see the abrasions on your wrists, yet *I* don't care for your exposed collarbone. You put on makeup, red lipstick, and eyeliner. Since when do you wear makeup, Emilia? You didn't even ask me for permission to paint your lips red. Every pisser in the area will dream about those lips around his cock, you know that too well, Emilia.

You're provoking me.

Oh, you will get yours.

But not now, now I have to smoke.

I ash on the floor and the booming bass from the music penetrates my bones. Everyone is stoned except you. Some couples are dancing, others are making out, and the *rest* are talking shit, Emilia. Why are they even here? I'd much rather fuck you right now. I'd like to rip those pants off your body. I only wear jeans, nothing else. Naturally, you hate other bitches ogling my bare chest, Emilia. It eats you up inside. They don't care if you notice them shamelessly throwing themselves at me. And I cannot deny I take delight in your jealous reaction, your eyes sparkling in that particular way.

I sit on the bed with my back against the headboard, one leg bent and a forearm propped on my knee. The joint is between my fingers burning away. I don't know why I keep hanging out with these American Pie freaks again and again. I must be a fucking masochist, though that applies more to *you*.

The parasites didn't take long to make themselves comfortable, Emilia, even in my bedroom. A blonde joins me. Her eyes have that typical cloudiness that says I'm-so-drunk-you-can-do-anything-with-me. "Can I have a drag?" she asks.

I hand her the joint, still quite bored with all this shit.

"Hey," I hear and you grin as you tap the blonde on the shoulder as she inhales while shoving her tits in my face, "don't hog the joint."

I like it when you get bitchy and extend your claws, Emilia. This happens far too rarely.

The bitch raises an eyebrow and challenges you, Emilia. I'm starting to enjoy myself. Maybe I should set up a kiddie pool filled with mud in my bedroom and have the chicks wrestle each other for me.

"Who are *you*?" the blonde asks, annoyed, and blows smoke in your face, Emilia. I don't like that.

"His girlfriend?" She laughs mockingly.

"Like Mason Rush would have a girlfriend. Most chicks here have sucked his cock or enjoyed it in another way." You appear hurt.

I should intervene, Emilia.

You are not a lioness, you are a lamb.

Wordlessly, I forcefully shove the blonde off the bed, making her shriek. I grab your arm, pull you next to me, and lean over you.

"Who gave you permission to wear these jeans?" I ask with you under me. You stare at me with large deer eyes. "Or that fuck-me-lipstick, Emilia?"

Don't tell me you're speechless? After all this time of us fucking, baby, really? But then I love that a bit. You raise your head and whisper directly into my ear to drown out the music, "I put it on for you."

"I want to fuck you, Emilia," I growl and thrust my pelvis against you. "I don't give a shit about the others."

You groan softly. You'd let me do to you as I wish, right here and now, just like a little whore. But then that's you, Emilia, you're my whore. Obviously, you feel how hard I am since I'm pushing against you so you *feel* it.

"Do you want to be fucked, Emilia? Here and now?" You raise your hands and stroke my hair.

"You may do to me as you wish, Mason."

I lower my head to the spot at your ear that smells so fucking good and chuckle softly. You shiver. "Have you considered how dangerous it is to say that to me?"

"I'm not afraid of you. I want you dangerous."

Fuck, baby, I love you. I grab your neck and push you into the pillows. You can't breathe, Emilia, but then you asked for it, right? You want me to take your breath away.

Your hands slide down my back and gently caress my skin as if you're not fazed by what I'm doing to you.

"You're a bit crazy, baby," I say roughly and press my hips directly against the hard fabric of your jeans. Your eyelids flutter and you groan as you lift your pelvis toward me. You rub against me, Emilia, you get hot on my cock, and I have to suppress a moan.

I can't stand it anymore, so I get up and grab your arm. Everyone is too stoned to pay any attention to us as I drag you out of my basement. Nobody sees you the way I see you, baby. I drag you upstairs to my parents' quarters, right into the dining room where I lift you up by the hips and set you on the table. I pull your jeans and panties down with a jerk and open my pants.

You lift your pelvis toward me, Emilia, you little bitch. I grab your ass with one hand and I support myself on the table with the other. Your nails dig into my skin as I penetrate you with one forceful thrust. You also scream quite loud, Emilia. We should be careful not to wake my parents, baby.

I fuck you so hard the table moves while you scream, "God, Mason! Fuck, Mason! What are you doing to me, Mason! "Fuck me harder, Mason."

You are so dirty, Emilia, I love it.

I fuck you harder. It's not like I can deny you. Burying my face in the crook of your neck, I moan against your skin and you hiss when I bite.

Your hands move toward my ass, Emilia. That's not how it works, I tell you what to do with your fingers. I push you back on the table and grab your throat. Again. You love it. Always.

You gasp and bite your lip before your torso rears up. You're almost ready to come, I sense it.

"*Are you fucking kidding me, Mason*?" Bummer, Emilia!

The voice is neither yours nor mine, Emilia. No other voice has any place here right now.

My father is standing next to us! How long has he been there, Emilia? He's regarding us with a dry expression. And his cheek is twitching.

That's never a good sign!

2. You Had Locked Mom In A Basement, Dad

Mason

"Fuck, Dad!" I cry and jump back. I reach for your things and toss them in your lap.

"Fuck, Mr. Rush!" you shout.

"Holy shit, what're you doing, Dad?" He won't let me have a little fun, Emilia. Not even a quickie on his dining table. Why is that, Emilia? Perhaps because I ruined sex for him multiple times and this is his way of getting back at me. I know it.

"Put that cock of yours away before you talk to me, Mason Keaton Rush."

Crap! I quickly zip up as you dress.

"It sounded like someone being murdered," he says. "It also looked a bit like it, Mason."

"Take a hike, baby," I command. "But stay upstairs. You're not to go downstairs without me." You scurry by us, your face bright red, like your ass after I've spanked it, and disappear into the bathroom.

I'm annoyed, Emilia. I was just about to come.

"Dad!" I gesticulate wildly with my hands. "What, no respect for privacy?"

"You were screwing your girlfriend on my table. My dining table, never the less, Mason."

"So, Mom can wipe it off. God, do you only do it in bed or what?"

He raises an eyebrow. "Where do you think you got that from?"

All the blood drains from my face as images flood my mind. *Mom*! *You*! "I want to die. So, where have you two done it? Do I even want to know?"

He sighs, Emilia. He perfected his sigh when I turned twelve. "I don't think you should be privy to that information. Just don't believe you invented this."

Fuck, what is going on? I have a party going on downstairs and you've locked yourself in the bathroom, Emilia. I strongly hope you're not thinking of sneaking back downstairs without me. If so, I will punish you, but then that's what you're trying to accomplish, isn't that so, baby?

I want to get past him to get to you. You and I have to finish this, baby. I'm not one who does things half-assed. But you know that now, right?

Dad seems to have other plans. He grabs my arm, Emilia, if you think my grip is hard, you should feel his.

I glance at him over my shoulder and stare directly into his eyes. My eyes. "What you're doing will not work, Mason."

"What?"

He stares at me intently. I don't like that, Emilia. It is never good when he's this intense. "You cannot keep her tied to you and under control. Eventually, she'll break free."

Emilia, you wouldn't. Never. You love being locked up. You love being in my clutches. You don't want to be without me. You welcome the abysses I drag you into. You crave naughtiness and the darkness. You need it.

"Mom never broke free, did she?" Fuck, Emilia. I can tell by his expression he doesn't like my insinuation. Not one bit! Why can't I ever keep my mouth shut? I want to fuck you, Emilia. You owe me an orgasm.

"*Excuse me*?" he hisses through clenched teeth as his fingers dig into my upper arm. Dad has great self-control, Emilia, always, unless it involves Mom. Mom is his sanctuary. Nothing is more important to him, not even his children. No one.

"I found your journal, Dad." *Why can't I ever keep my mouth shut? Fucking crap*!

His expression turns serious and his grip somewhat loosens, but not enough to break free. I might be strong, Emilia, you know that, but not as strong as he is. From below, I hear the dull bass booming and the laughter of others and I can sense you, baby. I know you're up here waiting for me. And that's the way I want it.

"Where did you find it?" he asks calmly.

"In your office."

"You were in my office, fucking toad?" Damn, now he's angry.

"Why do you always call me that?" I ask, annoyed. "Dad, let go of me. I don't want to get physical." I respect him too much for that, I'm not shitting you. Then again, he's the only one I respect in that regard. No one beats Dad when he gets angry. That's a fact, Emilia. It does not matter how much fucking stronger I become or how many more fights I win.

He narrows his eyes, which is not a good sign, Emilia. And his cheek is twitching again. I don't like it, Emilia. Not at all.

"You will *never* be able to fight me, Mason," he says constrained. "What were you doing in my office? I thought I made myself clear after the last time you demolished my cameras and computers."

He's boring me, Emilia. Right now, I would like to put you on the running washing machine and go down on you. "Yes, you did, but since you took my weed again, Dad, you gave me no other choice. Aren't you too old to play ninja and steal my dope?"

"How far did you read?" he asks. I wonder if that's panic in his voice, I've never heard that tone.

"All the way?" I say ominously, making it sound like a question. I read every line, Emilia. The reason I require more drugs.

"Fuck," he hisses. I'm surprised for he rarely uses that kind of language, actually, never. It seems this is a serious situation.

He lets go of me with a deep sigh and because I'm not a pussy, I won't rub my arm. But damn if it isn't throbbing a little, Emilia.

"Okay, now listen up you little toad." He eyes me sternly. "First, you have an hour to put the book back in the exact spot you found it. Second, your mom is a damn strong woman and I am a man with great damn self-control who can restrain himself. Your little friend in the bathroom is weak, Mason. She's not of your mom's caliber. So no matter what you do, eventually, you will break her. You are an unemployed fool who has zero self-control, who is incapable of keeping the monster inside him in check. I, on the other hand, can."

I laugh dryly. "You are so dramatic, Dad. First, Emilia is already broken. I believe she was born that way, like me. I don't have a monster inside me, Dad, I *am* a monster. I am untamable."

The moonlight shines on him. I notice how exhausted he looks, Emilia, standing here in front of me in his pajamas and bare upper body. I realize how much I put my parents through. I think it's the weed and I'm a little sorry.

"Honestly, you're worse than me," he says dryly, shaking his head. "And I've done quite a few things, as you're now aware of."

"Yes, Dad. You locked Mom up in a basement. That's fucking sick."

"I had to do that, otherwise, she would have hit rock bottom, Mason. She had lost herself and me, but the worst was that I had lost her. I simply could not allow that to happen."

"So, you also believe that the one you love needs to be locked up. Right, Dad, simply because you always mean well?" He just stares at me, Emilia. "I don't trust her, Dad. So, I'll keep hold of her. I will not let her go again. She's sick and the only one who can put up with my crazy shit. She *craves* the monster. I know Mom did not care for you unleashing your monster, Dad. You forced it on her. But Emilia has a monstrous side of her own, one that's self-destructive."

I still don't like the way he's looking at me. I can't stand it. I want to be with you. You all alone in the bathroom makes me nervous for I have no idea what you're doing, Emilia. Maybe you're on the phone with some fucker, maybe even with Riley! Maybe this brother situation has turned you on so much you just can't help it.

"Relax!" Dad growls. Only now do I realize my hands are clenched. "Mason! Breathe!"

I force myself to breathe through the nose before my gaze flicks back to Dad. "I have to get in there now, Dad. Let me go." He stares at me when something beyond my understanding occurs to him and he steps aside.

Fuck, Emilia, I've spent thirteen minutes without knowing what you were doing.

3. You Are A Replacement Drug For A Drug Addict, Emilia

Mason

You are not in the bathroom, Emilia.

I thought I made myself clear.

How dare you disobey me.

I can hardly believe my eyes when I look in the bathroom and find it empty. My hands are still clenched as I turn around and head for the basement. I dash by my father without him trying to stop me. Emilia, you're a little bitch. Purposefully so. You're just out to provoke me. You want me to spank your ass until you can no longer sit. You want me to fuck you until you're sore. You want me to stick him down your throat until you choke. You're such a little horny bitch — you are insatiable. You always want more and more and more...

Downstairs, I push aside whatever fucker is in my way. I hear your laughter before I lay eyes on you. What do you think you're doing, Emilia? You stand at the kitchen window, Emilia, and slap your hand against his chest as you laugh, Emilia. You will die tonight, Emilia. My legs start to move as if on their own while one hand is still clenched. That son of a bitch facing you receives a punch right on his ugly nose so that his head slams against the kitchen cabinet. He definitely didn't see it coming. He squints as he stumbles backward into a group of women who scream as their drinks spill. You just stand there and utter, "Oooops..." With your eyes sparkling, your lips turn into a smile, Emilia.

"Out!" I hiss at the other hunks. No one is stupid enough not to listen. A few guys need prodding and 10 minutes later, everyone has exited my apartment. Naturally, you are still in the kitchen, Emilia, and appear relaxed as you down your drink. A non-alcoholic beverage, of course, for you can't handle booze.

Am I no longer intimidating, baby, or does my jealousy and overprotectiveness turn you on so much that you don't care about the consequences? Whatever, Emilia, you were seeing my brother at the time we hooked up. I don't trust you, probably never will, and you're not doing anything to make it better. On the contrary, you love to play with fire, with madness, with the monster inside me.

"I've told you *not* to touch other guys. I've also told you *not* to go downstairs into the basement alone, Emilia. But where are you *now*, in *my basement* still wearing *your fuck me jeans*."

I do not give you an opportunity to answer.

The entire night.

***

Just in case, Emilia, I brought your cell phone along. You are still sleeping and that's fine since I worked you over until five this morning — hard and everywhere, Emilia. Even I'm sore this morning, though relaxed and satisfied. Earlier, I had no problem letting you fall into an almost comatose sleep. You were a good girl last night after first being bad. Sometimes I wonder if you're doing that for me or yourself? Do you want to be punished or do you want to relieve me of my constant tension and anger? I've never been so relaxed. It's only since you've been constantly by my side. You are like a substitute drug.

I make it upstairs. Today is a warm day and the sun shines into the house. Everything is clean. Mom probably had another one of her cleaning frenzies and has been up all night. That only happens when Dad is in the house. The house seems different when he's not around. Shit, I don't want to know what goes on up here that requires such a thorough cleaning afterward or is it *part* of the cleaning. From what I've read about him – which I'm still digesting – I believe anything is possible, Emilia.

Speaking of the journal, Emilia. When I see my father and now in a sober state, I recall a few things I read yesterday. Disgusting things.

Mom is busy making pancakes, giggling, Emilia, and Dad is standing next to her with a spatula. What am I to make of that? Why is this family so nuts, Emilia?

"Stop, not so much flour, Olivia!" he says. Mom makes a strange sound as he slaps her ass with the spatula. Firmly.

Fuck, I want to turn around and erase that image from my brain, but Dad says, "Good morning, fucking toad," without looking at me. "Isn't it a bit early in the day for you to be up, huh?"

"Shit, Dad, put that thing down, please!" Dad smacks Mom's ass again, who is bright red and squealing.

"Keaton, please! Not in front of the children!"

"If you only knew what they're up to, Olivia!" He gives me a distinct look, a rather disgusted one.

"I don't want to know!" The pan starts to sizzle as she pours batter into it. "Where's Emilia?"

I smile smugly. "She's in a coma." My father rolls his eyes. I set the cell phone on the table and take a seat.

"What are you doing with her cell phone?" my father asks.

"Uh, so she can't make a phone call when I'm not with her."

"You locked her in the basement and kept her phone?" he asks, blinking.

"A familiar scene, right, Dad?"

Mom's head whips around, her eyes huge. "Keaton!"

Mom's cell phone rings upstairs, just in time to save Dad. "It could be Amber, baby, you better get it!" he whispers to her and Mom appears overjoyed at having a reason to leave the kitchen.

I sit at the table with my fingers laced behind my head, grinning from ear to ear. "Amber, huh? Aunt Amber? *Really*, Dad?" I recall everything I read about what my father did to Aunt Amber. He wrote it all down in his notebook, Emilia. Why did I read it all the way through and not burn it, Emilia?

Dad's expression darkens. "Stop it!"

"By the way, who's *Leila*?" I can't help it.

"If you mention that name in front of your Mom, I'll make you disappear, Mason! Don't you dare!"

I raise my hands in a noncombative gesture and shrug. "Don't you think we should talk about what I read in your journal, Dad? It was a bit disturbing."

"I'm also disturbed by you, Mason, which is going on twenty-four years now."

Mom returns with her phone. I hear her say, "Yes, it would be wonderful if Cherry came along, Amber. Oh, don't worry. Him? He's got a girlfriend now, so it'll be fine!" My ears perk up and I glance at my father, who's staring at me threateningly, Emilia.

"Don't even think about it, Mason!" Mom ends the call and comes back into the kitchen.

"Cherry is back?" I ask, obviously to provoke my father some more. If he gives me grief, I'll say the name Leila and quickly leave the room. It feels great to finally have something on him, and, oh boy, do I have *plenty* to choose from, Emilia.

"She's finished with boarding school in Switzerland, so Amber wants to bring her along for the summer." Both my parents stand tall before me with their hands propped on their hips glaring at me. They resemble mafia parents. I don't need a gangster boss as a father with a mom like mine.

"What did I do to deserve that look?" I ask innocently. "And when am I finally going to get a cup of coffee? On a side note, Mom, your pancakes are burning. Please, not again." She hurries to the stove while Dad continues staring at me.

"You will leave Cherry alone, you have Emilia now, understand! Once you finished your fun with her, Amber had to send her to a girls' boarding school, Mason. Think about what that means!"

"It means I'm an incredibly corrupt bastard, Dad." I recall my time with Cherry, Emilia. She is Amber's daughter and the only child of a single parent turned into a tiny drill sergeant. She's tough, cheeky, confident, quite unlike you, and four years younger than me. We grew up together, Emilia. I deflowered and ruined her. At least, that's how Aunt Amber sees it. I haven't seen her for quite some time, though in earlier years, we hung out a lot. She's the redhead in the pictures that hang in the hallway. Everyone is on their guard, anticipating Amber's revenge. But then Aunt Amber is someone special. She's worse than Aunt Penny — and she really hates me. I'm glad Aunt Penny moved away a few years ago. With her around, it was always stressful for she always turned Mom against Dad and me, whereas Riley was always the golden boy.

"One more thing, Mason, Riley is coming too. It is going to be a family vacation and you'll just have to do your best to deal with it. I don't care what happened between you. You are brothers. Because of the deal, he will stay in New York, which is ongoing. Nevertheless, he can visit us any time he likes, which he won't since he wants to avoid you, but during the vacation, you two will tolerate each other."

I raise an eyebrow knowing my gaze can be piercing. "If you think I'll let that fucker near my girl, think again. I'll kill him the next I see him, Dad. So, don't do it or you'll end up with only one son."

"You little shit! Now you listen to me, fucking toad! Get over yourself, you arrogant ass! You two quarreled over a girl and you won, he ended up with nothing! You will be civil to him. I'm not asking you to make-up and be friends and have pancakes together. Just stay out of his way. He will do the same!"

"If he looks at her even once, Dad, I'll prick his eyes with a fork or, if need be, use my fingers."

"God, we understand, you big macho man!" Mom comes from behind and sets a stack of pancakes in front of me, then ruffles my hair. I hate when someone messes up my hair, Emilia, except you during sex. She even plants a kiss on my cheek, like all the touching wasn't enough.

"Oh, I'm so looking forward to our summer vacation." Mom is already in her cotton candy family mood. I don't have a good feeling.

4. You Are The Bullet And I Am The Barrel, Mason.

Emilia

Hot breath constantly blowing in my face wakes me up. I stretch slowly for I'm sore all over. Thank you, Mason. Still, I love having sex with you. It's like a drug, I crave it every day. Like the feeling of being under your control, only then can I let myself fall.

I open my eyes. They burn, I'm still so tired. Missy lies next to me. She positioned herself to catch the one ray of sun shining into the basement. Her head rests on my arm, her black fur shimmering in the sunlight. Nowadays, we're friends, Mason. In the beginning, she regarded me as competition, but now she protects me, even from you. You could say I've become her master. I snuggle with her thick soft fur, to which she groans happily like a foghorn. She wags her fluffy tail, tickling me.

I hear your footsteps and pretend to be asleep, taking care to wipe the stupid smile off my face. This is the happiest I've been down here in your basement in months.

"I know you are not asleep, Emilia! Here's your cell phone." I feel it land on the bed next to me and Missy jumps down. *Hey, stay here*, I think. The mattress compresses and your big warm body pushes up next to me. A tingling sensation immediately overcomes me. I hear footsteps pacing one floor above and know it's time to get up to start a new day. Why do nights fly by so quickly?

"Open your eyes, Emilia." Obeying your command has almost become a habit, so I open my eyes and grin at you. You look so incredibly good, Mason Rush. Every morning, you take my breath away.

"Hi!" I whisper and you smile. You're not a person who smiles, Mason, so the few times you do, it's special. Basically, you only smile for me and Missy because we're special to you.

"Hi," you say with a roll of your eyes. Only now do I see the plate you brought along. I see fluffy, lightly burnt pancakes, a tube of chocolate sauce, despite sauce being already on the plate, and juicy green grapes. My stomach growls. You dip your index finger into the sauce and brush it over my lip before kissing me, intimately, intensely, intoxicatingly. The way you always kiss me. You taste of chocolate and Mason. I could kiss you all day. You also don't kiss enough, Mason. Whatever affection you give me is in small doses, though increasing. You were never in love and now that I know you, I can say the same about me. You also never told me you love me, but you let me know in so many different ways as you are not a man of words but actions. You brought me breakfast, Mason, and coffee. You lean over me as you help me up into a sitting position. I immediately bury my fingers in your hair since I want you again even though I'm sore. And as I'm getting turned on, you pull away and stop kissing me, Mason. I'd cuss you out if you weren't Mason Rush.

Then you rip the blanket from my torso and your dark gaze takes in my curves. Just that makes my nipples harden. You brought along chocolate sauce, Mason, a whole tube of it. I believe it's my reward for last night. You don't spoil me that often and we have rough sex, but I believe today I'm going to be pampered.

"Don't move, Emilia," you bark as you spread chocolate sauce over my body. It runs over my breasts and its coolness gives me goose bumps. It oozes down my belly and puddles in my navel. My neck hair stands on end and I have to restrain a groan. You grin, get up, grab your cell phone, and take a picture of me.

I feel like begging you.

You grin even wider. Abruptly, you toss the cell phone aside and lean over me. "You're such a dirty girl, Emilia. What am I supposed to do with you?" you ask roughly before you lick from my abdomen to between my breasts. Then over to my right nipple, which you close your lips around and gently suck on. I moan and arch my back.

Your fingers slide unerringly between my legs and feel how ready I am for you. I push my pelvis toward you as my hands claw at the sheet beneath me. You continue to lick the chocolate sauce from my body as your fingers slide in me and I have to bite my lip.

"You must not come, Emilia," you whisper directly at my lips before kissing me again. Your fingers grow more urgent, more assertive. I melt on the inside in sync to the sauce on my body. Soon after, my muscles tremble. As punishment last night, you also forbade me from coming. Now I can't take it anymore. You can tell and immediately pull your fingers out.

I whimper.

You raise an eyebrow. "I told you not to come. Can't you ever listen, just once, Emilia?" Your fingers gently stroke my pussy without entering me. It's pure torture. I feel like I'm about to burst!

"Mason, please, you're the devil," I whisper shakily.

You get into position between my legs, "I know, baby," and push your cock inside me.

I groan and try to dig my nails into your skin, Mason, but you hold my wrists over your head. "Do not come, Emilia," you say again and fuck me with your tip, making me want to die. Honestly, die.

I throw my head from left to right while I squeeze my eyes shut. The way you tower over me is too sensual of a picture. You have new tattoos, Mason, whatever new ink makes your body only more desirable.

"I can't go on," I whisper as you slowly push all the way inside me. You are so rough that I have no chance, which you know. You regard my face intently as I explode around you and you inside me.

Panting, you lower yourself onto me and I feel your hot breath on my skin. You cup my face in your palms. I love the weight of your body on me, it seems to devour me.

"You're such a bad girl," you whisper. "You simply cannot listen, can you?"

I chuckle softly in your hair while you kiss my neck. "You are mine, Emilia. Never forget that."

* * *

I'm under your spell, Mason. Always.

You're lying on the bed, the sun shining through the small window directly onto your bare stomach. Your boxer shorts sit low on your hips, your tattoos shimmer seductively. You are so beautiful. I know you'd never use that word to describe yourself, but that's what you are. You *are* beautiful. The way your dark hair falls across your forehead, the way your eyes always shine a different color, your striking facial features, and rough cheeks with two-day stubble. You possess a strong aura, no one is immune to it.

Freshly out of the shower, I dress in only baggy clothes because I know we're just going to hang around the house. My wet hair tumbles over my shoulders as I towel dry it on my way into the room.

You stare at me. You always look at me when I enter a room, Mason. Your attention is always one hundred percent directed at me. Every time, your gaze makes me shiver. I know our relationship is not quite normal. We never reached that level, just skipped right over it. I had normality with Riley, but I'm not cut out for it, Mason.

The two of us, you and I, are like a tsunami that sweeps away everything its path. The two of us are a force of nature. An earthquake that shatters everything. We can seriously hurt each other since we're in tune with each other. We can love each other so passionately because we are interdependent. We are not healthy for each other, I know that, Mason. It's like you're the bullet and I'm the barrel. You the junkie, I the drug. When one of us moves, the other's eyes are glued to them. Like two magnets. I understand why you don't trust me, Mason. How could you? I don't even trust myself. But I'm good with all of it; the pain, the jealousy, the distrust, the anger. You go through all that just to be with me and that is the only thing that matters. You make me sick, Mason, and vice-versa. But then you're also my antidote, my medicine. You are angry, always so angry. You have so much hatred inside you, that's why you're taking it out on me. I know what you need. And you know what I need.

"You are staring at me, Emilia," you say matter-of-factly and place an arm behind your head. You are so *hot* when you do that. I know not knowing what I'm thinking is killing you. I also know I'm messing with your mind when I look at you without saying anything. You are the jealous type, Mason. You always worry I'm thinking of other men. The truth is you're the only one who haunts my mind all day long.

I sit on the edge of the bed and drop the towel. With the help of your mother, we renovated the basement that you demolished. I know it will happen again, but that's okay. We restored it to its *former* glory. After all, that's your taste. It took time to convince your parents. Regardless of what I thought, I have a good relationship with your father. I assumed he hated me, Mason. Maybe he does, a little, at least for what I did to Riley. I cheated on him with you, his brother. But since that one night where we talked openly, it feels like we've established some kind of relationship.

Your mom first had to see how broken I am before she accepted me again, to some extent. She had so much hate for me, at first, she didn't even want me living in your basement, which I understood. Considering everything that happened, she stayed loyal to Riley. Besides, she was torn up when she found out about what happened between him and me in New York. It was eating her up inside.

It took quite some time and a lot of patience before she finally said hello to me again. Your father probably had a hand in it. Ultimately, she gave me a chance and we had a long heart to heart between women. I was open with her, Mason. I told her *everything* and explained my feelings for you. I look up to Olivia, she's a wonderful woman, and I know I'm never going to be as strong and confident as she is. We sat upstairs on the couch and once I told my story, the two of us cried our eyes out.

Recently, your father took me aside, Mason, it's the reason we're having this conversation now. It is inevitable and I know you won't like it.

"You're still staring at me, Emilia." You raise an eyebrow, your eyes show skepticism. What do you think I'm thinking about, Mason?

"I'll never get used to how hot you are," I say, grinning. I have no confidence, Mason, which you know. I'm not good at asserting myself and when a dominant person such as your father enters the room, I immediately feel intimidated. With you, however, at least in some situations, it's easier.

You place a hand on my knee and lower your head. I love it when you look at me like that, Mason. "There's something else, Emilia. What's going on? And don't lie to me, understand?" I love the hardness in your voice. God, I'm a real mess.

"I just wanted to ask you..."

"What?" you growl.

I take a deep breath. "It's about college. Mason, I'd really like to get a degree and perhaps, it's time for you to continue your studies. I...I don't know, but we can't just loll around the basement every day, can we?"

Shit.

I'm sure you didn't want to hear that, Mason. I hate confronting you with something you don't to hear. You're unpredictable and get so angry. I can tell when you're in a mood to smash furniture or when I can jump you and fuck your brains out.

You narrow your eyes and regard me for a bit. I feel empty when you remove your hand from my knee, Mason. I love you touching me, whether it is in an innocent or absolutely dirty way, the way you like it.

"Why would you want to do that, Emilia?" you ask softly, though with a threatening undertone. "Go to college and get to know other people." *Shit. Shit. Shit.* You pace back and forth like a caged tiger and it's obvious you're restraining yourself so you won't break anything. Your muscles twitch and you clench your jaw. "So you want to get out of here, huh? You're no longer satisfied down here? Are you bored?

Maybe you're longing for a different cock? Fuck!" You kick the nightstand and it almost topples over. Missy, who was on the bed, basking in the sun, jumps up and hurries away with her tail between her legs.

"It's not like that!" I quickly say and stand up. I want to calm you down even though I know I should keep my distance right now. "I'm only thinking of us, Mason. We could learn something useful...which is important for our future, right?" I stand in front of you and, if you're angry or not, place both hands on your stubbly cheeks, attempting to make eye contact. You are so tense, Mason. Your hands are clenched and you're rapidly breathing through your nose. "Hey! I'm only thinking about us, baby, okay?"

You stare at me appraisingly before you pinch your eyes shut. Just as I'm thinking you've somewhat calmed down, you push me away. "It'll never happen, Emilia. Do you have any idea what goes on at college? Do you think I'd let you parade around in front of some bastards like you're fair game? You'd be the reason I turn into a killer and end up in prison. Forget it!"

Fuck!

I guess I had better not mention that your father already registered me at the university where you study, or used to, a couple of weeks ago, Mason. I was supposed to convince you and we would start this autumn.

But now I don't even know what you will do to me or him once you find out.

5. You Want To Make A Killer Out Of Me, Emilia

Mason

Fuck, Emilia. Are you trying to turn me into some shitty murderer or what? It certainly seems so. It's like you want me to fucking freak out. I can't help wonder why you're doing this, baby. By now you should know me. You should know that I would never let you go to some fucking college. Do you have any idea how many horny guys you'd cross paths with? Do you have any idea how many would come onto you? I don't trust you, Emilia. Perhaps you'll find a better cock! Maybe mine is now boring! I understand I'm robbing you of the opportunity for higher education and development, but I don't want you to flourish, Emilia. Then we would no longer fit together and you'd really see how fucked up I am.

You come and stand in front of me, your eyes are big, your hair wet, whereas your tight top is accentuating and lifting your perfect breasts. Your eyes betray your fear. Still, you're facing me, though chewing your lip as you make eye contact.

"Forget about going to fucking college," I hiss and you exhale frantically.

"Okay, calm down, Mason. I was merely sharing what was on my mind. Imagine the two of us studying while living in your penthouse."

"Never!" I growl, wondering if you've lost it, Emilia. Do you want me to act like Riley for you or what? That's never going to happen. You and he lived in that place, even fucked, showered, and ate there. I don't want to be near that place regardless that Dad is trying his best to get me to move in there. He invested eighty grand in renovating the place and it's completely unrecognizable. But then my demolishing it had the same effect. Still, I don't want to live in it.

"Shit, Emilia, you're so sick," I snap and run a hand through my hair. "You want me to clean up, go to college with you, preferably in matching clothes, and live with you in the apartment where you fucked my brother? You can't be serious? Fuck."

Your eyes widen as it dawns on you what you're asking of me. "Okay, maybe moving into the apartment isn't such a good idea. But please, just think about it..."

"No!" I'm angry again, Emilia. "Drop it or I might end up demolishing everything including you!" You flinch and exhale in frustration.

"Okay, forget it," you say, defeated, and your shoulders sag and your head drops. I don't care, Emilia, go ahead be sad, what you've dreamed of will never happen. I'll never parade you around in front of vultures. I'm just going to end up beating everyone's face in. Is that what you want?

"Good," I say. "Never ask me shit like that again."

* * *

I'm so fucked up, Emilia, it's the reason I grab your wrist and drag you upstairs. You know, Emilia, right now I'm so pissed off, I don't want you around me. I want to be alone. However, I won't know what you'll be doing, Emilia, and I don't trust you — remember, I can't reiterate that enough. That's why I'm not leaving you in my basement without me be your side.

Today is Saturday, an oh-so-typical day here. Mom is busy vacuuming with the radio in the kitchen turned on high. The sun shines in, illuminating the little, disturbed dust particles dancing in the air. Missy joined us upstairs once she recovered from my little outburst. She's known me for a long time, Emilia. Still, she startles easily, like you

She's happy to see Mom, like the last time was years ago. Meanwhile, she's shedding her long black fur everywhere. Just like you, Emilia. You two must be related. With summer approaching, her new fur is coming in and Dad is freaking out. He hates animal drool and hair. That became clear with our former bitch. Her name was Rosie, she was an English bulldog, Emilia. But I don't remember her all that well. She was 12 when she died and we buried her out in the garden. Mom was heartbroken and didn't want another dog, but then one day, Dad came home from work with Missy. Actually, she was trained to be a police dog, but on duty, she was always too friendly. Missy is more bark than bite. At some point, you noticed the same and became less afraid of her. When I kept handing you her leash to take her on walks, you always seemed panic-stricken, baby. Nowadays, you two are inseparable. Now she's more loyal to you than me, Emilia. But that's okay. With you, I don't mind.

Still, I'm fuming.

How could you make such a shitty suggestion to me, Emilia?

Mom greets us briefly as she kneels in front of the couch, vacuuming underneath. She shoos us out of the room but not Missy. The furry shedding beast is allowed to stay.

Dad is probably up in his office. Who knows what he's doing in there, Emilia, but then I don't actually want to know. Considering everything I read in the journal, I wouldn't mind a strange case of amnesia. I look at Mom again, her hair is up, she's sweaty, red-faced, and kneeling on the floor, and I wonder how it would affect you if I did to you what Dad did to her.

The good thing about you, baby, I don't have to break you anymore. With Mom, it seems he wasn't too successful, otherwise, she wouldn't be such a strong woman who constantly stands up to him.

I sit you down at the kitchen table and say, "Stay put, Emilia!"

Missy joins you and settles in next to you. You sit there waiting with an unreadable expression on your face, and then you both lower your heads. You remain quiet, so I leave you there and walk toward the stairs. The vacuum cleaner falls silent.

"Hey, mister!" Mom calls out, "Where do you think you are going?"

"I have to talk to Dad," I growl.

"He's busy at the moment!" Mom puts a hand on her hip. Her shirt is soaked with sweat. "Doing something for work, Mason. Speaking of work, it would do you good." I hate it when she acts like Dad, Emilia. She's so much cooler when he's not around.

I moan in annoyance. "I have to talk to him!"

"Mason!" She calls after me too late for I'm already past her. I purposefully approach his office door and open it without knocking.

My father is never startled. I'd love to see him lose his composure, but he just slowly looks up from his new monitor and sighs in annoyance when he sees me.

"Well, hello, Mason. Come right in, it's not like I'm busy. Certainly not. Hey, grab a seat and join me as I watch porn."

I make a face even though I know he's being sarcastic. Just in case, I sneak a peek at the monitor since you can never be too sure, but all I see is text and charts.

"Ha-ha, Dad, not funny." I shake my head in an attempt to suppress the mental image that popped up.

"What do you want, toad?"

I roll my eyes, Emilia. I'm getting so tired of being called fucking toad. He's been at it for the past year.

Though I have to say this about Dad, I love that he always gives you his full attention. And I mean, always. Whenever I approach him for a talk or to clarify something, he sets everything aside and sits there patiently, looking at me. He also never interrupts. Granted, he *does* interrupt me because I'm the exception. Besides, I'm pissed and it shows.

He sits up straight in his armchair with his forearms resting on the armrests, his head is a little lowered and he's frowning. "What is it *now*?"

"*You* manipulated Emilia into thinking she should get a degree," I state dryly.

"Yes, I did." I thought so, Emilia. Somehow you two became allies and I don't like it one bit, Emilia. He doesn't even appear remorseful or whatnot.

"Dad, why are doing that shit?" I roar. "Are you trying to separate us?"

One of his eyebrows shoots up as he clasps his hands. "Excuse me, Mason?"

I'm so pissed off, Emilia, so angry, I actually brace my hands on his desk. "Do you know how many dicks there are running around a campus, Dad? She'll be totally in her element there, join a sorority, go to parties, meet some Romeo faggot, and realize how fucked up I am!" I growl.

"Well," he replies dryly, "I'd like that for the girl. Better than you continuing to roll over her like a tank." I can't believe my ears, Emilia. I forcefully breathe through the nose. The last time I freaked out you told me to continue to breathe as calmly as possible. I do that now, Emilia, and it's not helping because I'm too upset. What is he saying?

"Dad," I growl, "Never manipulate her like that again. I don't care if you are my father or the president. I damn well will not let her..."

"Blossom?" he asks soberly. "Find herself? Let her live her life? Get an education? Earn good money? What is it you don't want her to do, Mason? When you love someone, you only want what's best for them. You don't keep them under lock and key. Now don't start with your mother. That was something completely different. Once I was finished with her, she was doing interior design instead of cleaning toilets, Mason. That's called selfless love."

I snort. "Emilia can't survive in a world like that, Dad. If the wrong guy approaches her..." He starts to laugh, but I ignore him. "Or if someone talks her into doing drugs or slips her a mickey...then uses and abuses her. Can you imagine what I would do?" I'll end up in prison, Dad. Is that what you want?"

He shakes his head. "You are too paranoid, Mason. You'll be there studying *with* her."

"But. I. Don't. Want. To. Study," I growl.

"Then live with her going back to school. You can't control everything, Mason."

I angrily push myself away from his desk. "I can. I have. And I will."

Unimpressed, he regards me before shaking his head and making a dismissive gesture. "Then do what you want, Mason. But it will land you on your ass."

"Fine!" I hiss. "I'll keep her with me."

Dad is stunned. "It must be love, right?"

"My kind of love," I say and leave. That should clear things up.

College, Emilia.

Sure.

6. You Should Not Wait For Me, Riley

Emilia

I know what you're doing upstairs, Mason, I just hope your father keeps our little secret. If you find out I'm already registered for the fall semester, all of us had better quickly hide to get out of harms' way.

Your mom is immersed in her housework. Still vacuuming, she keeps shooing Missy away, then feels bad and calls her back again to give her a hug, so the cleaning takes twice as long. I watch her play with Missy. She's too cute, Mason. It is perplexing to me that she's your mother. She's so blonde, bright, radiant, an actual glowing light in the darkness. For you *are* darkness.

You didn't remember to take my phone along, Mason, and you usually take it when you make me wait somewhere for however long. I now feel it humming in my pocket. I have no idea who's calling. I'm immediately panic-stricken. I want to ignore it but my curiosity gets the better of me.

I'm not familiar with the number. I swallow hard and stand. Your mom is not as attentive as you are. She obviously does not believe I need supervision. I quickly glance at the staircase when I hear you cursing. You're still preoccupied, so I enter the bathroom and gently close the door.

"Hello?" I answer softly while covering my mouth with a hand. My heart is racing. I hope it is a wrong number.

I face the mirror and regard myself. I look like a deer caught in the headlights, Mason. My eyes terrified, skin pale. When I recognize the voice on the other end, I grow even paler. You will kill me if you find out, Mason.

"Finally, I thought I'd never reach you, Emilia!" Riley Rush says. Fuck.

I continue staring at my horrified reflection and briefly consider hanging up. Hearing his voice brings back a flood of memories of our relationship and its ugly ending. I forgave him, Mason. He's not a bad person, besides, he has done his best to make up for it. Every time he and your mom spoke on the phone, he inquired about me and every time you freaked out. He was worried that his behavior in New York or the other thing he almost did, left scars. He merely regrets it.

My eyes well up with tears. "Riley?"

He sighs. "I'm so glad to hear your voice. How are you?"

I can barely hear myself over the blood whooshing in my ears. "Uh...good? And you?"

"I'm okay. I've settled in and work keeps me busy. It's different in the city, which you know. I miss my old home, but I'd rather go to hell than home. It's enough that everyone is getting together for a vacation. I merely wanted to call and check that you're okay. Mom never lets me talk to you since she's worried Mason might freak out if he finds out. I tried a few times before, but he always answered. I find that more than odd."

Okay, that's too much information, Mason. Riley called to speak to me and you didn't tell me. You didn't even give me a hint. But I know why, after all, I know you, I get it. But seriously, you could have at least told me. And why is he talking about a vacation? With everyone? I don't want to feel embarrassed and admit that you didn't tell me anything, so I simply keep my mouth shut.

"Yes, I believe you have a good idea of why he doesn't want us to talk, Riley."

"Oh, come on," he says derisively. "In the end, he took you away from me, not the other way around, Emilia."

"*I chose him*!" I say firmly. "He didn't *take* me away. I'm not an object, Riley."

"To him you are," he replies nonchalantly. I flinch since he's right. I stare at my mirror image and see my eyes flash combatively, ready to step up to defend you, Mason, but I can't. Not right now, right now, I have a lump in my throat.

"Are you calling to tell me he's an ass?" I ask. "If so, I might as well hang up."

"No, sorry!" he quickly apologizes. But it sounds forced. I am stunned since I'm not used to him apologizing for something he said. You'd never do that, Mason. It completely escaped me that it could be different. "Emilia, honestly, I'm simply calling to find out how you're doing."

Despite everything that has happened, his concern soothes me somewhat. "I'm fine," I say. "Really."

He takes a deep breath. "Why don't I believe you?"

"I don't know, Riley. You've never believed me when I said so. You've always tried to make me feel better even though I was already feeling fine."

"Then you wouldn't have cheated on me, Emilia." I have the feeling he needs this conversation for closure, Mason. "Don't get me wrong, I'm not calling to blame you or me. I just know it's going to be difficult seeing you again so soon on this shared vacation, so I wanted to talk to you without Mom or *him* present." He finally confirms my suspicions. It reminds me of why I liked him in the first place, Mason. He's always so sensible and empathetic, Mason, a trait you've completely lost if you ever possessed it. I am still clueless about the vacation he's talking about. Anyway, it's not important now.

Sighing, I sink to the floor with my back against the washing machine. That washing machine on which you whacked my ass and did so many other things to me while Riley sat in the dining room announcing our engagement. God, he didn't deserve that. And then everything he did afterward, how mad he was and how confused, I get it. I know his soul. It is unblemished, Mason, like your mother's. You, on the other hand, are probably more like your father.

"Okay," I say. "What do you want to talk about, Riley?"

"I don't know, Emilia. Maybe I want to hear that I didn't destroy you and you have gotten over everything that happened between us. Maybe I want to hear that I have no blame for you choosing him. Or that I'm not responsible for you rushing toward your doom. And maybe I want to hear that you actually loved me once and that you'll never forget our time together. Or that it wasn't my fault that you cheated on me, Emilia. Everything that happened fucked me up. To be honest, I constantly think about all of it, no matter what I do or how long ago it happened."

I'm moved by his words, Mason. I even feel a tear building in the corner of my eye.

"I loved you and will never forget our time together. It wasn't your fault that I cheated on you. You were perfect, too perfect for me. Mason offered me something you never could, Riley. Darkness and hardness and... but you...you are light, warmth, confidence. I really don't understand myself. If I did, we wouldn't have broken up. I don't know, Riley. Please, don't blame yourself. Whatever happened, I've already forgiven you. You hurt me, I hurt you. Physically, mentally, whatever. I know you were desperate and I know you regret it. I don't need to know more. Please, stop feeling bad. Okay?"

Shakily, he exhales. "You have no idea how much I needed to hear you say that." Now I burst into tears, Mason, because I realize what he has been going through these past few months. "Do you think we might have another chance?" he asks. "Perhaps once you've found yourself and that phase is over? When you need something other than darkness and pain? Something good for you and you know I'm good for you. I've always tried to make you happy. We would have had a wonderful future here in New York, Emilia. You deserve it even if you don't believe it."

I choke down the lump in my throat as I recall our conversation, Mason. How little you want me to grow or be *me*. You shape and push me in whatever direction you want without regard to what I might need or want and I love you so much I don't care.

"I love him, Riley," I say hoarsely. "Even if common sense tells me you're the right one for me, my heart keeps yearning for him, and I don't believe that will ever change."

"We'll see," he replies. "I'm a patient man, Emilia, you know that. I can wait."

"But don't wait too long," I mutter. "Please."

"Forever."

"I have to hang up now. If he finds out I've been talking to you, he'll kill us both."

He laughs dryly. "Let him come, this time I'm prepared."

"Don't say that, Riley. I'm hanging up now."

"Okay...and thanks."

"Bye." I move the phone away from my ear and end the call. I stay put for a moment and digest the conversation.

"Shit, what was that?" I whisper to myself.

"That was you, Emilia. You in action. *Slut!*" you reply, Mason.

7. You Go Down With Me, Emilia

Mason

You've betrayed me, Emilia. I knew it would happen sooner or later.

With him!

With him!

With! Him! Emilia!

I overheard every word, Emilia. I was standing behind you the entire time, but you were too engrossed in your conversation with sunny boy to notice, Emilia. *You even cried, Emilia*! *You said that you loved him, Emilia, and you won't forget your time together, Emilia*!

That he made you feel good, Emilia. You even said he was perfect, Emilia!

You're standing before me, your eyes wide with terror, lips shaped in a silent *Oh*, and pale face. You are so shocked, you drop your phone.

I still see him kissing you and his hand wandering over your body. I see you moaning for him and calling his name like you did on the phone howling.

I grab your cell phone and hurl it forcefully against the mirror. "*You little fucking whore*!" I shout as I approach you, Emilia. I don't care if I hurt you. No, actually I *want* to hurt you. Trembling all over like I am, you back away from me, your eyes looking fearful, Emilia. I'm going to take this whole shitty house apart and drag you down with me, Emilia!

I grab your throat and push you back against the tiled wall so the back of your head smacks it with a dull thump and all air whooshes out of your lungs. Your breathing is erratic as you gaze at me terrified. Oh, yes, baby, you should be afraid right now because right now, I feel like taking your breath away, his too.

I hear a scream from behind me, from Mom. "Mason!" she yells and pulls on my arm. "Let go of her! This instant!" She's trying to separate us, Emilia. No one will ever separate us. I fling her off me and she slams against the bathroom cabinet that's beside us, spilling her perfumes and cosmetics onto the floor.

As soon as I see my mother stumbling, my anger gives way to ice-cold horror. Then everything happens quickly. Someone grabs my shoulder, whirls me around, and I feel Dad's fist in my face before I find myself falling to the floor. I still hear you and Mom screaming, but it sounds far off, and as I hit the floor hard, everything goes black.

Keaton

Olivia, I thought things would be easier with Riley gone and that he ended up with the girl. Granted, his outbursts have grown less frequent, Olivia, but he has read my journal and is using his newfound knowledge to blackmail me. To me, it seems as if he twists everything around to excuse his urges. You are so different from Emilia Sullivan, baby. You could not be broken, whereas she was already broken. Granted, you were a bit tamer, but only at certain moments. This girl, however, is so messed up, Olivia, a man like Riley would actually be good for her. But, she went ahead and chose Mason. I already know how this will end.

The little toad just left my office without bothering to close the door, Olivia. He doesn't want her to go back to school. I knew he wouldn't, which is why I already registered her at the university. Obviously, I was watching her closely beforehand and even asked about her preferences, desires, and talents. Next, she tells me she would like to be together with Mason. I swear that girl clearly doesn't know what's good for her. Certain people require a little prodding. We've practically adopted her, Olivia, so it's only natural I feel responsible for her even if that was never the plan. But naturally, shit eventually has to happen, so now I worry about her and about what she and Mason are doing, which is nothing. They don't work, they don't learn anything, heck, they don't even go outside. All they do is hang around his basement and do who knows what. All day, every day, Olivia. I'm actually glad there are no more cameras and don't have to witness what goes on down there.

I hear Mason screaming downstairs and my head snaps up.

"*You little fucking whore*!" echoes loudly through the whole house. I jump up from my chair and hurry downstairs. Olivia, when will it finally end? When will I no longer have to shove that little toad onto the floor or against a wall for him to calm down?

"Mason! Let go of her! This instant!" I hear you yell. Baby, I thought I told you to stay away from him when he's like that. So. What. Are. You. Doing. Down. Here?

My heart starts to race even though usually his little outbursts don't faze me and I'm calm as can be. I have to be, one person should always be calm.

I enter the bathroom and see him pressing Emilia against the wall by her neck. You're hanging on his arm, trying to pry him off her when he forcefully shoves you so that you crash into the bathroom cabinet, Olivia. There is a clatter and a crash as the bathroom items hit the ground.

Now I know how Mason feels when he has an outburst.

I can no longer control myself.

I'm next to him in three steps, spin him around, and ram my fist into his face. He collapses.

Nobody touches you, Olivia.

I leave him on the floor. Nobody touches you without your consent. I don't give fuck who. I go to you. With wide glassy eyes, you stand next to the cabinet and hold your cheek in shock. If I had a heart, it would break now. I know I should check you out and assess the seriousness of your injuries, but I'm totally beside myself, breathing heavily and shaking all over.

I hear Emilia sobbing behind me. She has dropped to her knees next to him, talking soothingly to him. I can't stand any of this anymore.

Abruptly, I turn and go. He has finally managed it.

My self-control is in pieces on the floor just like your perfumes.

8. You Should Put Up A Fight, Emilia

Mason

My whole face hurts as I carefully open my eyes.

The first thing I see is you, Emilia. You lying little bitch. You're kneeling on the floor next to me, tears running down your cheeks as you cradle my head in your lap. You run your fingers through my hair.

I taste blood in my mouth, my nose hurts like hell and I briefly see black as I try to sit up. Groaning, I drop back down onto your damn lap.

I throw an arm over my eyes since the light is blinding. I might have had a lot of fights in the ring, but I've never been laid low with one blow. I always knew never to mess with Dad, Emilia. So far, I've only had the pleasure of meeting his fist once before. That was also about Mom. He only freaks out when it is about her.

"Piss off!" I moan painfully.

"Mason, please. Let me explain. It's not what you think, I..."

"Get out, Emilia," I say forcefully. "Now!" It seems you hear something in my voice that finally awakens your fucking instinct for survival. You sob as you gently lay my head on the tiles and get up, you bitch.

"Never touch me again!"

You leave. I lie here, unable to move or breathe properly. Or think.

I hear soft footsteps approaching and moan again. "Fuck off, Emilia!"

"It's me," I hear my mother say. Immediately, everything inside me contracts. I squint and see her sitting down next to me with bandages.

"Mom," I say weakly yet repentantly. Her cheekbone is a bit discolored and that's your fault, Emilia. Why did you do that? Why did you provoke me like that?

I raise my hand and gently stroke her cheek. She twitches a bit at my touch, but she knows what I'm trying to express. Mom always knows what I'm going through.

She takes my hand and kisses the palm. "I know," she says. She wets a washcloth and gently dabs the blood from my face, lip, and nose. I try not to groan in pain.

"What happened?" she asks carefully while rinsing the washcloth.

"She talked to Riley on the phone," I say roughly.

"Oh, no," she sighs. "I explicitly told him not to call her. But when does anyone here actually listen to me?"

"I'm going to kill her, Mom."

She laughs dryly. "And then what, Mason? Are you going to continue hiding out in your basement while entertaining one girl after the next because they don't give you what she does? Besides, you know she's unique. Like she was made for you."

I try to frown and immediately flinch since even that is painful. "Dad says something else," I say quietly. "I thought you two always agreed."

She explains while she skillfully bandages my nose. "Your father may know everything she went through, but he doesn't know how it made her feel. She's stronger than he gives her credit for. Besides, I firmly believe she's strong enough to make it by your side."

"Humph! I don't want her by my side, I simply want her to do as I say. Don't forget, Mom, she's a little slut."

"Mason!" she chides angrily. "Whatever she may be, please don't call her that. Never. She already has a low opinion of herself and you aren't helping." She pinches my nose, Emilia, and I flinch.

"Ouch!"

"See how it is?" she says. "That's how it feels to her too."

"I don't trust her."

She smiles mildly. "To trust someone takes time, believe me, I know what I'm talking about." Oh, Emilia, I recall the journal and immediately feel sick. I squeeze my eyes shut. I'll definitely not mention that to her. That's not something you talk to your mother about. Besides, it would feel like I was betraying Dad.

"I don't know if I can ever trust her again. I was gone for only a few minutes and she phones him. Why? What could he want from her now? Does he still love her?"

She strokes my hair. "Who cares what he still feels for her. The only thing that matters is what she feels for you. Besides, she loves you, I know that much. Mason, do you think any woman would put up with your kind of a relationship? Most wouldn't even last this long. Think about it the next time you feel like killing her."

I hate when Mom is right, Emilia.

But she always is, that's the problem.

* * *

Emilia

I put on a pair of jeans, put Missy on a leash, and walk haphazardly down the streets with her. It is already dark and smells of summer. The air is balmy and a shirt suffices. I miss the summer nights and the warm air on my skin, Mason. I long to do something and we only hang out in your basement. But I guess I can forget about that for the moment. You hate me because I spoke to him on the phone. How could I have been so stupid to even answer the phone? The number was unfamiliar to me. I should have just disregarded it. You gave me clear instructions and I know what happens when I don't follow them. That's when you hurt me — in some way. I usually like physical pain, Mason, but I'm afraid eventually, you'll break my heart with your angry behavior toward me. I can bear the physical pain, I even enjoy it, but I'm vulnerable when it comes to mental pain. Missy seems to sense my weary mood for she keeps nudging my hand with her cold wet nose, wanting me to stroke her head. It does not matter how far we walk, something inside of me continues to crave you, the monster, so eventually, we turn and head back. It is a clear night and the stars are shining brightly. Everything is so peaceful, at least it appears that way. When it comes to us, I don't think it'll be ever peaceful again.

From afar, I hear the bass echoing through the garden and wonder why your father is letting you get away with it, but then I realize the house is dark and both cars are gone. I leave Missy upstairs in the empty living room and walk downstairs to your basement apartment. It still doesn't feel like ours even though I've lived here for so long. As soon as I open the door, a thick cloud of smoke wafts towards me and the music thunders in my stomach. There are people here I don't know, Mason, and I don't like it. I don't like it at all. Strange men make me so nervous — usually. I need to know that you're looking out for me. My eyes search for you.

You sit in your battered chair, Mason, and you knew I was coming or you wouldn't be doing what you're doing. Claire is sitting sideways on your lap, one of your hands on her hip. I lost touch with her because of you, Mason. I cut her out of my life because I wanted nothing more to do with her, but now she's here in your basement, on your lap.

There is a variety of emotions brewing inside me

Anger.

Hate.

Indignation.

Disappointment.

Grief.

Pain.

Why are you doing this? You haven't laid eyes on any female since you brought me back from New York. I was wrong to assume it would stay that way.

Now what?

Now Claire runs her index finger across your – as is common for you – bare chest. You're smoking a joint and your arm is casually laying across the backrest. Your nose is bandaged, your upper lip split, and you seem broken, beaten.

All the smoke in the room burns my eyes, so I rub them as I approach you. I would like to act like women in movies do and fling her off you and scream at you. You admire them and tell yourself to think that you are as confident and strong as those women, but the truth is I feel completely overwhelmed and would rather run away crying.

You stare blankly at me.

My stomach knots up and I feel quite nauseous.

So I simply retreat without saying a word. My eyes stop burning as soon as I storm up the stairs and disappear into the guest room with Missy. I have no desire to see you again today, Mason – and that has never happened to me.

You do with her as you please.

I lay with Missy on the bed and cry into her fur.

***

The sun has already risen and is shining in my face as I emerge from a disgusting nightmarish sleep. You woke me up because you came in. Now you're standing in front of my bed and your face looks horrible. You've been in those fights again. I tried to stop you once before, but as usual, you didn't care. Your eyebrow is split, you have a shiner, and blood is on your white shirt — probably another man's. You haven't gone there much lately, but when you did, you always look brutal and radiate something animalistic and hard as if you left the last spark of your soul behind.

I can't breathe when you look at me like that, Mason.

So piercingly. Now I recall that Claire sat on your lap and I feel like jumping out of bed. I have to get out of here, as far away from you as I can, but your hand automatically reaches out and pulls me close until we stand next to each other. You regard me intently from the side. "I told you before, you'll never be able to run away again, Emilia!" you say tonelessly before you abruptly push me back onto the bed. Missy is in flight mode again. Shortly afterward, you lean over me and pull your shirt over your head in one fluid motion.

"Mason, go away!" I have no idea where that came from, but now it's out.

You freeze and all your muscles stiffen.

"What did you say?" you ask with your head tilted. I'm immediately intimidated again and can't make a sound. My throat is dry. You smell of blood and sweat, Mason. So, I use my body instead and raise my arms, tentatively putting them on your chest to push you away.

You raise an eyebrow and now your eyes flash dangerously. "What are you up to, Emilia?" you ask quietly and open your belt. “So, you want me to leave?” You pull my t-shirt roughly over my head. Now I’m topless since I didn’t bother to put on a bra. You pinch my nipple and watch my eyes for any reaction of pain like an eagle does its prey. “Go on, Emilia, fight back if you don’t like it. Fight!” You slowly twist my nipple until I cry out. Your eyes burn more intensely. “Scream at me, hit me, tell me to stop, or I’ll do whatever I want with you!” You finally let go of my nipple and slowly and pointedly open your zipper. I am almost melting, but I’d like to punch you in the face at the same time. Again. As if enough people haven’t done that already.

“Claire!” I utter for whatever reason.

You smirk. “You bore me, Emilia!” You shrug and I punch you in the chest. For a moment, you seem as stunned as I am. Startled, I stare at you.

“Anything else?” You provoke me. “Yeah, I want to slap your face!” I roar. Again, you seem taken aback before your eyes darken. I had no idea it meant that much to me, Mason, but you did tell me to let it all out. You clench your teeth, apparently having a difficult time digesting it.

Again, I punch your chest. It probably hurt my hand more than it did you.

“Go on!” you growl tensely, as if you’re hypnotized.

“You chained me up in your parents’ living room!” I punch you again.

“Go on!”

“You choked me so hard and for so long, I thought I was going to die!” I can’t stop hitting you. You no longer react to it and just hold still. “You messed around with other women in front of me! Right there for me and everyone to see! And just to hurt me! You blackmailed me! And why Claire?" Now I push against your chest. You do not resist as I spin you around so you land on your back with me on top of you. I hold your face in my hands and kiss you. As soon as I taste blood, I bite your lip extra hard to cause you pain. You hiss but don't push me off you, instead, you grab my butt firmly and pull me against you. Your fingers dig into my bare flesh since I'm only wearing panties.

"So, now what, Emilia?" You are beneath me, looking complacent, beautiful, and so dangerous, and you are mine.

"I hate you, Mason Rush!" I push my panties aside, take your hard cock out, and lower myself all the way onto it.

"You've been fucking me for too long, now it's my turn!" I don't know what you've unleashed in me, but it feels good and you don't seem to mind, not at all. You grit your teeth as you feel me. I claw at your chest to support myself, arch my back and toss my hair at the same time, and give in to lust, anger, hatred, and love.

You straighten up so that our bodies press against each other and grasp my neck with one hand. "I didn't fuck her, baby, I only fuck you!" you growl and kiss me. My lips are wet with your blood and your dirty hands claw my thighs, my ass. I scratch your back, inflicting more wounds like you did to me, and claw your hair and pull on it while biting your neck. You drop your head back with your eyes closed and put your arms back to prop yourself up while I run my fingers over your sweaty flexed bicep.

"Baby, I'm coming soon. If you want to come with me, fuck me harder!"

I rise up until I only feel your tip inside me. "You'll come when I come, Mason Rush. Right now, I'm still too angry!"

"You little bitch!" you whisper directly against my lips, grab me tighter, and jerk me back down onto you. We both groan and I throw my head back. I slide my hands over my shiny, sweaty upper body as I close my eyes and let my pelvis do what comes naturally. In exactly the way that feels good to me. I feel you growing harder

"Oh, fuck!" you utter hoarsely. I love the despair in your rough voice.

No one has ever been allowed to control you like I'm doing now. It is exhilarating.

As I feel you start to twitch – this time, apparently you didn't want to warn me – I quickly rise up again and hear you swear loudly.

"Are you kidding me, Emilia?"

I smile slightly. "I don't know why, but I don't want it to end yet. You deserve a little punishment too, Mason. I have a lot of crap stored up."

An hour later, we are worn out and I let you come, Mason — with me. Our orgasms are so intense and loud, I'm glad your parents aren't home. We lean our foreheads together. This was by far the most intense orgasms we've shared. At the same time, we open our eyes and look at each other. You stretch out your hand and with your thumb wipe your blood from my lip, just like you did with the raindrop at your grandmother's funeral.

I believe that was the moment I actually fell in love with you.

You grin and your eyes show you're at peace. Thank God. "I can go for that kind of punishment more often, Emilia." I smile shyly before I bury my face in your neck.

"We'll see," I merely whisper and feel your arms wrap around me.

9. Shit, Emilia, I Still Like Her

Mason

We have a tradition in our family, Emilia.

Dad insists on it.

You are not allowed to know about it since we didn't go last year because I wanted you in my basement.

And the year before that, Riley went without you because he wanted to keep you a secret from me, Emilia. That worked really well, *Emilia*.

Missy is panting on my neck from the huge cargo area of the Range Rover. It is Mom's by the way and though she might not require so much space, Dad wanted her to drive a safe car. I wanted to drive my Mustang, but Mom said it would be a waste of fuel. However, I know about her little plot. She wants Dad and I trapped together so we will talk, Emilia. We haven't talked for three weeks, all because of you, Emilia.

Riley will also be there, that little parasite. If he looks at you the wrong way, he'll be eating mush because I'll knock his teeth out, Emilia.

Incidentally, this also applies to you.

I am worked up just thinking about it and grab your hand too tightly. You flinch. "Mason!" you whisper. Dad peers threateningly at me through the rearview mirror. Don't worry, Dad, I'm not freaking out again!

You are not allowed to pee, Emilia. Just thinking about it pissed me off. You're sliding uneasily around on your seat because we're on the road for three hours and I haven't allowed you to stretch your legs.

Mom is singing happily along to some ancient country song that's playing on the radio while hugging Dad's arm. She's trying to engage him to sing along with her, but he just rolls his eyes. He knows what she's up to.

She's trying to lighten the mood.

"Oh, I'm not in the mood!" I abruptly moan and you flinch again.

"Oh, come on, it'll be great! We always have so much fun! The day we spend at the beach and then, in the evenings, we all have drinks outside on the patio! Remember, Amber is always so funny when she drinks!" Dad is still giving me the evil eye through the rearview mirror since he knows I know he used to fuck Amber. I grin from ear to ear at him. Mom knows too, but it would probably be fatal to bring it up.

"Are you looking forward to seeing Aunt Amber too, Dad?" I wink at him and he narrows his eyes. I love non-verbal communication, Emilia. Even though Mom knows about it, I know what happens if I bring it up or mention the name Leila.

"Mom," I turn to her, "If you'd had a girl instead, what would you have named her?" Dad steps on the gas. I don't know if we'll survive this ride, Emilia, but any reaction is better than this shitty silence between us. I hate it when he doesn't talk to me.

"Perhaps a name that starts with *L* would have been nice." You look at me doubtfully from the side and Mom turns her head to me. Like I give a fucking crap about kids' names.

"Are you pregnant, Emilia?" Mom asks and you turn bright red.

"No! Mason!" you hiss at me and I put an arm around your shoulder.

"What do you think of the name *Leila*, Mom?"

Dad slams on the brakes, which is not good since we are driving down the highway. We all snap forward, including Missy, whose head is suddenly between ours. She's panting in my ear and Mom is pale.

She stares at my dad. "I hate that name. Why, Mason?"

"Oh, I just find it rather exotic. A name suitable for a strong woman." Mom's look could cut diamonds.

"Mason, what the hell are you talking about?" you ask, anxiously eyeing Dad. He just sits there, clutching the steering wheel with both hands, probably imagining it's my neck. Then he accelerates like a maniac and I know there will be consequences.

"Oh, nothing, baby, nothing at all."

Mom gives Dad the evil eye for the rest of the trip.

***

After driving for about fifteen hours, we arrive in the early morning hours. The only time Dad pulled over was for Missy or when Mom was hungry. Then he couldn't find a gas station fast enough, Emilia. He just ignored me when I was hungry and kept on driving. He was also too stubborn to give up the driver's seat to Mom or me and simply stayed behind the wheel the entire time. Dad hates losing control, Emilia, whereas I love it. That's the difference between us.

And the reason I enjoy life more than he does.

The sun rises above the sea and reflects off the surface, which is the same color as your eyes. I hate your eyes. They're everywhere.

We drive down a gentle slope to the cottage that belongs to Amber. It stands deserted by the sea. We could have flown, but then I would have had to leave Missy somewhere, or worse, transport her in the cargo hold, but I would not do that to my baby. I'd rather do that to you, Emilia, to punish you for whatever it is you've done.

The house stands on stilts and has a bright white front with light blue trim around the windows. On the windowsills are light blue vases with tiny flowers. I hate flowers, Emilia.

Dad parks in the wide driveway, opens the roof cargo carrier, and immediately starts barking orders.

"Get the dog out of the car, toad!" are his first words to me after three weeks of silence, Emilia. I believe we're making progress.

Missy immediately runs into the water. She loves it here because she can run around all day wherever she wants. There's no one else around for a two-mile radius. The property is huge and fenced in.

I carry your bag, Emilia. My legs feel like lead, a bit asleep, and are not working properly. Still, I'm going to fuck you before we catch a little nap. Mom and you rummage through the roof storage box while giggling. You girls seem to be in a good mood and pointedly don your sunglasses. I enter the house, rolling my eyes. The coolness of the house feels good and I feel like a little boy again as soon as I enter. I used to play here and later, I did other things...

I head toward the stairs to get to the room I always stay in when my eyes wander through the living room and perceive something outside on the porch.

I freeze and drop the bag I was carrying. "Shit!" I swear softly.

I knew she would be here too, I just had no idea that she had turned into a woman, Emilia.

She wears a white and red polka dot bikini top with a loose C-cup, Emilia. She has a narrow waist, round hips, and a nice tan. Back in the day, she was always as white as a sheet. She has taut long legs and is a head taller than you. Her ass is simply...*damn!* I like asses, Emilia. Yours too, of course, baby, so don't worry. Her curly hair hangs down to her shoulder blades and parts on the side. A shimmering bright cherry red in the rising sunlight. Actually, she looks like Amber, only younger and hotter, though Amber is quite hot. Her lips are full and painted a dark red. She is standing in front of the railing, leaning on her arms, looking out over the sea. A light wind blows her hair from her face.

Cherry.

She's already here.

"Mason?" I hear you ask from behind me and flinch.

"Oh, there's Amber!" Mom calls and loaded with bags, disappears up the stairs. Dad is still busy emptying the car for I hear him swearing since Mom brought so much stuff along. Missy runs to a smiling Cherry.

"Hey, sweetie!" I hear her say as Missy jumps up on her and licks her face.

"Mason," you say a little louder and I quickly turn to you.

"What?" You stand in front of me loaded with luggage.

"Which room should I take this to?" you ask. I aggressively rip the big bag off your shoulder. "Let me have it," I growl. Then I stomp up the stairs and you follow, uncertain.

Why do you always have to be so insecure, Emilia?

I know you can do better.

Is there a reason you're insecure? Huh?

I carelessly toss the bags into the room while you look at me helplessly.

"Change your clothes, freshen up, and come back downstairs!" I bark and disappear.

"Mason?" you call after me, but I keep walking.

Shit, Emilia.

I'm fucked — and not in a good sense.

***

As I am about to welcome Cherry on the patio, her mother pushes herself directly into my path and gives me a wide smile. But it's more like the grin of a psychopath.

"Hello, Mason! I heard you brought your girlfriend along. I'm very happy about that!"

"Hi...Aunt Amber." I indulge her kissing my cheeks and she whispers in my ear, "If you so much as touch Cherry again, I will kill you, Mason Rush!"

Shit, I believe my balls briefly shriveled up, Emilia. Unfortunately, she should know her words only spur me on. I put a cigarette in my mouth and one hand in my pocket and casually stroll out onto the patio.

I stop right next to her. "Hey, Cherry, baby!"

She doesn't grin or so much as look at me, but her cheeks redden. I like that, Emilia. She has freckles on her perky nose and her dark brown eyes are as deep as abysses.

"Hello, Mr. Rush," she says with a smirk and finally looks at me.

Shit, Emilia. I have completely forgotten how pretty she is up close. I'm speechless for a few seconds. I lean on the railing with one elbow and take a hit of the cigarette, but blow the smoke away from her. Although she smokes too, she doesn't like smoke in her face. That happened once – okay, it was on purpose – and had dire consequences.

"And? Did your mother finally take you out of that institution?"

"The one I had to go to thanks to you? Of course, Mason," she whispers.

"I didn't put you in there."

"You stuck *it* in me, which is why she put me there." She's tough and snotty, Emilia, and believes she has it all figured out.

I laugh, just like she does. "And? Was it worth it?" I raise an eyebrow.

"Oh, yes, every second, Mr. Rush." Her eyes twinkle challengingly.

"And? Have you had anyone else?"

She smiles. "No, I have not. After all, I'm not a slut, Mason."

"What are you trying to say? That *I'm* a slut?"

"Yes, that's it!" She giggles again and I grin. Shit, Emilia, I like her — still.

I didn't think any woman could still attract me in any way when you're nearby and you're *mine*. Up until now, every woman has been a pure turn-off because you're my grenade, baby. You are mine. But, Cherry... Cherry and I have our own history that I've never told you about, though it is immortalized by the tattoos on my body. She got under my skin, Emilia, and me under hers.

My neck is tingling and as I turn around, I see you standing in the open door. You look so lost, baby. Your shiny black hair is down. You are wearing an airy white summer dress that accentuates your tanned skin and perfect breasts.

You're the most beautiful woman I've ever laid eyes on, even next to her, but that's not the issue.

I can tell by your eyes that you overheard us and next to me, Cherry is making herself small.

"Hey, baby!" I say loudly and grab your arm. You stumble a bit as I pull you to me. You don't complain, instead, you give me the evil eye. Cherry would have immediately slapped me. She used to slap me a few times, Emilia.

"So, you must be Emilia?" she asks nicely because that's her nature. I know you want to hate her, Emilia, because you saw us laughing together and know we're close, and probably because you overheard exactly what was said. You will see that you don't stand a chance at hating her. That is impossible.

"Yes, hi," you answer numbly and I feel a bit weird, Emilia, like I'm cheating on you. I feel lousy, like my stomach is turning.

"This is Cherry! She's Amber's daughter, as you can see!" I babble sheepishly because I feel the need to explain myself for something that didn't happen.

You are slightly pale, Emilia. Do you feel ill?

"Oh, it's so nice that Mason finally has a girlfriend! I only know him as a man-slut!" Cherry says with a grin. I roll my eyes whereas yours widen hearing someone bold enough to speak to me like that. I casually take a drag from my smoke. I'd like to remind Cherry that she enjoyed my slutty side a lot, but I don't. You already seem troubled enough, Emilia.

"So, how long are you guys staying?" Cherry asks and with her elbows, leans on the railing. Fuck! Look at her tits, Emilia. I'm desperately trying to look elsewhere, though the more I try, the more I stare at them. You notice me staring and I'm waiting for you to get angry, go nuts, and punch me. What more needs to happen, Emilia? I am a total asshole!

"Two weeks," I say casually and you look like you wish you'd never come here.

"Two weeks?" you ask, shocked.

"You didn't tell her how long you're going to be on vacation? Mason, you are such an ass! She should know that too."

"Why?"

"God, you truly have no empathy!" Cherry rolls her eyes, grabs my cigarette from my fingers, and takes a drag. You stare at me like you expect me to freak out. I'm staring at her cherry lips sucking on the filter, Emilia.

"I'm a realist, Cherry!" Just then, I see a taxi pulling up, Emilia, and tense up. We're one person short and I wish he hadn't made it. Riley!

He gets out of the cab. I hate him! Because you called him three weeks ago, I almost killed my mother for that, Emilia. When you see him, you pull away from me and take a step away. I don't think I am seeing right. So, I grab your arm and pull you back to me. I know my grip is too tight. Cherry raises her eyebrows as she looks at us You can feel it, which is why you glance at the floor Are you ashamed, Emilia?

Riley, the pisser, brought along a suitcase and a laptop bag, Emilia. What's he going to do with a fucking laptop on the beach?

He grins at you and then he sees Cherry and me. He was probably hoping I'd finally had enough of you, especially considering that he knows how Cherry and I are together. He strolls toward us with one hand in his pocket, his hair slicked back, and that greasy arrogant smile.

"Damn, I hate that guy!" Cherry mumbles and flicks away whatever is left of my smoke into the sand. Emilia, we had better not tell her that you used to fuck him. Cherry has never liked my brother and always takes my side. That's what you should have done instead of talking to him on the phone behind my back.

He's closing in to greet you when I take a step forward and give him a determined look with one eyebrow raised. Mine, stay away!

He stops in time and rolls his eyes. "Nice to see you, Emilia!" he says in your direction.

"Bitch!" He nods to Cherry.

"Bastard!" He nods to me.

"Fuck you!" Cherry and I mutter in unison. I give her a conspiratorial wink, which she returns.

"So, when you've had enough of this primitive idiot, my room is two doors down from Mason." Riley grins at you.

"You little..." I'm about to charge him when Dad grabs my arm and holds me back. Where the fuck did that old fucking ninja come from?

"Riley, go inside!" he says sternly.

"I want a peaceful vacation! No jealousy dramas, no whining, no sex! I don't care if you dry up! Everyone stays in the bed they share with their fucking fuck partner! Emilia, should I catch you with Riley, I'll cut off his balls! And you, Mason, should I catch you with that red-haired vampire, you'll take your last breath! My hatred for you is at an all-time high, so don't fuck with me, Mason, and leave your brother alone – best – leave everyone alone. Understand?" He doesn't wait for my answer, but turns and follows Riley.

You made yourself very small while Cherry is grinning at me. "Wow, that was some announcement. Has someone been naughty, Mason Rush?"

"It's a long story!" I make a dismissive gesture and pull you close.

I have to fuck you, I'm hard.

10. I Was Not Allowed, Cherry

Mason

The bedside lamp is broken on the floor, Emilia. You lie exhausted and sweating beside me, breathing as if you'd just run a marathon. Your hair is all sticky, Emilia. It smells of sex and sweat in here and I don't think I've ever – ever – fucked you so hard. Against and on every surface I could reach. You wipe your sweaty face and stare at me.

"What was that, Mason?" you ask, breathing heavily.

"I don't know, has to be the ocean air," I reply monotonously and roll a joint. Obviously, I'm *well aware* of what spurred me on. I'm angry at myself for still finding her so damn hot. The problem with her is that it's not only her appearance that's hot. I hate to say it, but she has it all — sex appeal and the body to go with. Besides, I've known her for a damn eternity, since I was still shitting my pants. She too knows me well. Apart from Mom, she's the only woman who knows the real me. You, on the other hand, don't know shit about me. I light the joint and blow the smoke in your face.

You don't even blink, although I know you hate it. But you just put up with everything I do, right?

Slowly, you straighten up and fish around for your bra. You pull it over your shoulders and slightly turn to me as you close the clasp. “So, have you and Cherry known each other for a long time?” you inquire softly. Your eyes flash uncertainty and pain. I love it when they look like that, Emilia.

“Yes, a while.”

“Be more specific,” you say.

“She’s four years younger than me. I’ve known her since she was born. You know my parents and Amber are close friends.” I take another hit and enjoy the sluggishness that spread through my mind. The main thing is not to think.

“Aha,” you say and nod. I know you want to know so much more and you’re so jealous that you want to yell at me, slap me, and cry, but you don’t, Emilia. You would never do that. That one outburst about Claire in my parents’ guest room was all I received from you about that.

Instead, you dress and walk to the door. “I’m going to check on your mom,” you tell me. “Maybe she needs help.”

“If you so much as look at him, I’ll fuck you to death, Emilia,” I say lazily before you leave. I can’t get up yet, Emilia, my boner is still too damn hard. I could have fucked you for another four hours and I still wouldn’t have gotten rid of him.

I used to push Cherry into the mud. She was that little stalker every guy has at some point when he turns twelve. With her gaping teeth and stupid red hair, she showed up everywhere I went, Emilia. She announced from small on that she would marry me and made huge plans because Cherry is that much of a megalomaniac. Just like me. I could never stand her, she was so annoying, Emilia. Every summer I had to put up with her.

When she turned 14, she grew tits and a bombastic ass that made her so much more feminine.

When she turned fifteen, Emilia, she started to put on makeup and got familiar with how to use her feminine charms.

When she turned 16, Emilia, I grew a boner just looking at her. Even the guys in the neighborhood started staring at her ass, Emilia. I didn't like that. At that point, I liked her around me, not those jerks. When we smoked pot and drank together and then made out – without sex. She remained a virgin. To this day, I still remember our first kiss. We were stoned and laughed our asses off. Then we stuffed ourselves with chips and toast with Nutella. She had Nutella in the corner of her mouth like you always do, Emilia. I wiped it off her lip and at that moment, I knew I wanted to kiss her, that I had to kiss her. But she leaned forward first and beat me to it – blowing my mind, Emilia.

Eventually, summer vacation was over and we went our separate ways again.

Amber was against us seeing each other outside of summer vacations. She knows the kind of guy I am.

The next summer she was 17 and the most beautiful thing I had ever laid eyes on. I stalked her the entire vacation, obsessed with her, Emilia. I knew she was into me. I gave her my cock – wrapped with a red bow on it – for her 18th birthday by lying naked on her bed with a boner. That's when I deflowered her. I was careful and gentle. Our second time I was not and she loved it. She has always challenged me, talked back, and at the most inopportune times, showed me she was not wearing panties, like when we were dining with our parents. Oh, she loved me, Emilia. But her mom told me to keep my hands off her and I pushed her away. After all, I was not good for her. I would have ruined her. Without me, Cherry had a chance to actually live her life the way she deserves.

That's when Amber carted her off to a boarding school and I did not see her for two years. But now she's here, Emilia, at the worst inopportune time, and I'm fucked. We're fucked. Everything is fucked.

"Your girlfriend is pretty," a sensual voice rips me out of my reverie and I glance up. Cherry stands in the doorway, her arms crossed, pushing her tits up even more, her gaze gliding pleasurably over my body. My cock may be covered by the thin sheet, Emilia, but it twitches treacherously.

Crap!

"I know," I say. "You know I'm not into ugly women." I make no move to further cover up my cock. She walks into the room with her hips swaying, looking confident, as if the world belongs to her, and plops down next to me. I pass the joint to her wordlessly. She takes a long drag and drops her head back. I cannot help but stare at her elegant neck and watch the smoke escape from between her lips.

"She's shy," Cherry states. "Is that your doing? Did you scare her, Mason Rush? Don't do that." I grin without remorse.

"You know I don't give a crap about what one should or should not do, Cherry-Baby."

"Oh, yes, I remember. That was something." She passes the joint back and I give a silly grin like I always do when she's around. She makes it so easy, like breathing, Emilia, yet with you, it is as difficult as trudging through a blizzard.

I trust her, Emilia, one hundred percent. She could walk around in whatever she wanted and not show any interest in other cock if she were together with me. She'd just laugh at whoever tried. That's how she is, Emilia.

"You hurt me quite badly back then, are you aware of that, Mason?" she says and I immediately know what she's referring to.

"I had to do it, Cherry. You're better off without me. I'm an asshole, a wreck, yet you…" I fall silent because I can't find the word for what she is to me. Or did. I don't know, Emilia.

"I could have decided what's good and not good for me, that decision was not yours to make. You hurt me greatly, Mason."

"I know," I say quietly, feeling as nauseous as I did back then.

"Do you love her? Your friend Emilia?" she asks and props herself up on her elbows next to me. She doesn't care that I'm naked, Emilia, or that my cock is getting really hard and lifting the covers like a tent pole. Or that the situation is becoming more and more dangerous. Regardless, I don't have to think twice about the answer.

"Yes," I say straight away and Cherry lowers her gaze.

"Did you love me?"

"Yes." Again, I don't have to think twice about it. She looks up and I'm mesmerized by her brown depths.

"You never told me that, Mason."

"I wasn't allowed to, Cherry." My voice sounds harsh.

She swallows. "So now you're over me?"

I stay silent since I can't bring myself to say the words, Emilia. Fuck!

I remain still as Cherry leans forward and gently brushes her lips over mine. So light, as if it didn't happen. I can no longer breathe. I don't react until she shrinks back with a knowing smile on her lips.

"Good to know," she says, gets up and leaves.

"Fuck!" I swear loudly and fall back into the pillows.

11. I Am Losing You, Mason

Emilia

I don't like the way you look at her, Mason, or the way you say her name, and tonight was the first time you turned your back on me. You've never done that.

I was in the kitchen with your mother and Amber when I saw her go upstairs. Thinking of you and her alone together made me feel like I was suffocating. I don't even want you looking at her, let alone be in the same house together.

I was so sick I couldn't even eat or talk that evening. You sat next to me, yet the entire time you seemed so far away. You and Cherry talked about old times and laughed a lot. Usually, Mason, you never laugh, but yesterday, you laughed more than the entire time I've known you.

I want to get out of here. Now.

Naturally, I remain silent. I cannot even talk with your mother about it. Whenever I say something, it becomes reality. Or maybe I'm imagining it. Maybe my jealousy is unfounded and you're merely childhood friends. Riley gives me a look like he knows something I don't. He's been doing that since last night's dinner, though he hasn't spoken to me. I think he could tell I wasn't feeling well.

We ate breakfast and again, you were laughing the entire time. Your father was quite tense, Mason, I know for now I can interpret his expression and sense his moods. It was the same look he gave you when Riley and I were over for dinner. It's the way he's looking at Cherry now.

Am I paranoid, Mason?

Is this the woman who broke your heart and sent you into a downward spiral? Or were you already spiraling downward and it was you who pulled her along? Eventually.

You are so different around her than when we are alone.

I'm confronted with a completely new person that makes me want to crawl into a hole — and never come back out again.

Amber and Olivia are clearing the table while you two are still sitting there, deep in conversation. You don't even notice when I get up and leave, Mason. *You!* Usually, I cannot even make it to the bathroom without being watched or accompanied by you, yet here you don't even look up when Riley starts to follow me. I cannot take it anymore.

He's following me, Mason, yet you remain completely unfazed!

I go down the stairs leading to the beach knowing Riley is behind me. I don't care, I want you, Mason, not him.

I plop down indiscriminately in the sand so that waves roll over my bare feet as the sun beats down on my legs. I'm wearing a short yellow summer dress, but you didn't say anything about it. *Riley is here and I'm wearing a short summer dress, Mason*!

And you don't say anything!

In a totally romantic setting, we sit on the beach and you still don't say anything!

What's wrong with you?!

"Hey," Riley says. I see him out of the corner of my eye. He's wearing loose-fitting, white chinos and a dark blue shirt that tightly hugs his chest. Apparently, he has been working out for his muscles are more defined. His hair is a bit longer than usual and still unkempt, falling loosely over his forehead. Back in the day, I used to brush back his curls or pull them long to make them bounce. Today, I barely pay attention to them. My eyes well up with tears as I look into his familiar dark eyes. I quickly glance away to the horizon in the distance.

"How are you?" he asks and brushes my long hair back to get a better look at my profile.

I only shake my head because anything I say would only cause me to burst into tears.

"I knew her being here would not go over well," he murmurs. "Actually, I should be ecstatic, but I'm not."

I swallow in an attempt to choke down the lump in my throat. Clear, bright laughter can be heard coming from the house followed by a darker one. It's like being slapped in the face, Mason. Why are you doing this?

"What went on between them?" I ask softly without looking at him. I know what I would see in Riley's eyes and right now, I couldn't handle it.

"Well," he sighs, and out of the corner of an eye, I see he's also staring ahead. "She was Mason's first great love." Ouch. It feels like Riley punched me in the stomach. Now I feel sick, but I suppress the urge to throw up. My head seems foggy and the rushing in my ears is louder than the waves breaking. The cold waves roll over my feet and the salty water assaults my nose and throat. It feels like I'm suffocating.

"They've known each other since they were little, Emilia. Such a bond is hard to match. You better believe it when I say that I don't envy you, although one might think it is karma. But you don't deserve to be treated like shit by him. You never did." Really, Mason? Don't I deserve the way you treat me? Maybe yes. Perhaps it's what I deserve. Perhaps I'm not good enough for anything or anyone and never will be. Never enough, not long, not deeply. Always superficial because apparently, I have a world-class pussy. That's it. I try to recall if you ever sat with me at a table for that long and just talked. I also try to recall when you last laughed so loudly with me or gave me such a soft longing look. But I can't, you never have.

"Am I losing him?" I ask monotonously.

"I wouldn't know," he replies. "Cherry always has had that effect on him. With her around, he can be the normal positive person that he can never be at home. He was always crazy about her and vice-versa. The summer vacation three years ago, they constantly hung out together until Amber told him he wasn't good enough for her and he stopped pursuing her. He left her for her sake, you understand, that way he didn't pull her down like he's doing with you. Emilia. Look at me." I can't, Mason. I might die if I look at him, really. It hurts so much. Yesterday, on the way here, you held my hand and everything was fine. How can something I believed was so strong break so quickly?

Riley lightly takes hold of my chin and turns my head so I face him. Now I'm lost, for his deep dark eyes peer so softly and lovingly at me. No matter what either of us did, he's still clean and brilliantly white to the core, Mason. Why can't I hold onto things and people that are good for me? Why did I push the angel away and invite the devil to bed?

"You are the most beautiful woman I know. Cherry has nothing on you, Emilia." I don't see it that way, Mason. She has that certain charisma and look. That's worth more than any good looks. All I have are my looks.

"You're vulnerable," he says. "You require protection. No one's heart should be toyed with like that. It is barely holding it together as it is."

"What do you mean?" I ask shakily. He's still holding my chin. Maybe you are watching us from the veranda while having a smoke. Or maybe not. Maybe you don't care.

"What I mean is that I can tell you've been through something horrible. I could always tell it's just that I didn't want to pry. After all that we've been through, with everything I know about you, and after meeting all those faces of yours...and when you chose Mason, Emilia, and the shit that happened in New York, it made me think and I believe I know what's going on. But I won't push you to tell me. I never have and never will because I respect your boundaries, Emilia. I almost did it once and I still regret it."

Shit, Mason. I wish you would look me in the eyes the way Riley is doing right now, even once.

He drops his hand and looks at me. I look back at him. It seems Riley and I have a bond. We were in a relationship, Mason. For two years. We shared a bed, grief, even made plans for our future. We planned to marry. And now, after all this time and heartache, I'm sitting here staring into his eyes and they're the only things that are keeping me from taking off my dress and running straight into the ocean to never be seen again.

I notice he's leaning over and I realize, in my desperation, that I am doing the same. It would be so easy if I only loved him as much as I do you. At the last moment, I avert my face. His breath burns hot on my skin. His lips are so close. I smell him, but he isn't you.

Riley pulls back and sighs. "I'm sorry."

I just smile. Why apologize to me? I too leaned in. "If you want to talk, you know which room is mine."

He leaves and I find myself alone on the beach.

I sit staring out the ocean for what seems like hours. I'm sure my face is burned by now because I didn't put on sunscreen. But I don't care. I feel empty, Mason. How can it be that you love someone so much, but leave them because they are better off without you? I thought we were sharing that kind of love. I thought the two of us were special. But maybe Cherry and you are special and we were simply passing time?

"What are you doing here?" I hear your voice and goose bumps crawl up my arms, which do not feel exactly pleasant. My eyes well up with tears again. Dammit! I quickly wipe them away with the back of my hand.

"Are you crying?"

I shake my head. I can hardly stand it when you sit down on the sand next to me, legs up, forearms on your knees, and look at me from the side.

"Emilia," you say demandingly. "Look at me." Your brother just used the same words, Mason, yet he delivered them so much more tenderly. Why do you hate me so much?

I shake my head again.

Abruptly, I'm flung on my back and you're leaning over me. You're blocking the sun, Mason, and your shadow makes me shiver.

"Are you jealous, Emilia?" You eye me seriously and push me into the sand. I'm so cold, Mason. I feel so alone even though you are here. Oh, how I would like to tell you everything I'm feeling. But I can't.

Just then, I can no longer hold back the tears, which roll hot down my temples into the sand. I cannot lose you

You look me in the eyes and right then, an expression crosses your face that's not seen often. "Fuck," you whisper.

I am so sad, Mason. I believe my heart broke a little. It hurts so much and there's nothing I can do about it. All I can do is lie here.

"Emilia, please stop crying," you say sternly. I cover my face with my hands so you won't see me.

You grab my wrist and pull one hand down, then do the same to the other.

You link our fingers and press the backs of my hands into the sand. "I cannot stand seeing you like this, Emilia."

"I'm sorry," I say. It feels wrong.

"Stop apologizing. Fuck." You lower your face to me and press your forehead against mine. I breathe your breath, I smell your scent, and feel your skin. It relaxes me.

"I need you, Emilia."

I almost want to ask, *Are you sure you want me, Mason?* But I don't. You pointed out numerous times to me that nothing is going on, Mason. So now you are here, aware that I'm jealous, but all you've said was that you cannot stand seeing me like this. That's because unlike me, you don't lie.

I turn my face just enough to kiss you. Desperately so, because I know I'm losing you.

You kiss me in the same manner, Mason. When did we arrive here? I want to scream because I can't hold onto you. Regardless, I try with my body, my lips, my tongue. I'll use whatever it takes but it won't be enough. It's all I've got. I don't have a lively intellect. I cannot joke around with you because my heart races a mile a minute when you're near. I also cannot talk about my feelings because there are no words to describe them.

I love you so much.

And yet I'm losing you.

12. I Hate Myself Right Now, Emilia

Emilia

That evening, everyone is sitting in the living room. Amber and Olivia have been giggling like young schoolgirls the entire time. Olivia has already had quite a few drinks and is red in the face. They've been having a good time talking about the old days and are laughing at themselves as they imitate Keaton's bossy voice.

"Bring in the girls! Get me a new shirt! Stop laughing. Laughter is evil, Olivia. Fun is evil, Ambaaaaaaaaaa!" Amber says, mimicking Keaton. They're laughing so hard that they can't breathe. I wish I could be like them, so easy-going and carefree. I'm not feeling well, Mason. The windows are open and a balmy salty breeze is blowing in. Everyone is gathered around the coffee table, everyone found a seat. I took a seat next to your father since I simply feel comfortable in his presence. I move as close as possible without actually touching him. And he allows it. Missy is comfortable in front of our feet, sighing contently. She had a busy day. We threw sticks into the water for her and even after two hours of retrieving, she didn't want to stop.

Riley sits across the room with Amber and your mom and rolls his eyes at the women. He seems tired for he too has had a few too many, just like everyone else — except me because you always forbid it and your father because he hardly ever drinks.

You, Mason, commandeered the armchair. Your hands are clenched, Mason. Cherry is sitting on one armrest. Why are you so tense? Don't you trust yourself?

I cannot breathe, Mason, can't you see that? We spent the afternoon together at the beach. I put sun lotion on you and then we had sex. Afterward, I almost began crying again.

Right now, I'm wearing your t-shirt, Mason, with shorts underneath. Yet Cherry is wearing a sheer top that shows her bra and silk shorts with embroidered hems that stand out nicely against her tanned skin. Her medium-length, dark-red hair is curly from the sea air and covers shoulders. She is not wearing any makeup and still looks breathtaking. You two look so good together, like you were made for each other.

"Ambaaaa! We are not talking about this in front of the kids!" Olivia shouts while pointing an outstretched index finger at us. She's laughing so hard, she almost slips off her chair. Next to me, Keaton moans in annoyance and I smile a little.

"Hey, hilarious moms! Don't you think it's time to go to bed? You're disturbing the young people!" Cherry calls out while raising her perfect eyebrows in amusement. She has such a sexy voice, Mason. If I were a man, I'd probably fall for her the first time I hear her speak.

"God, why now? Or do you want to do something you wouldn't or shouldn't do otherwise?" Riley asks annoyed while eyeing Cherry.

I almost expect you to say something in her defense, Mason. Your mouth even briefly opens before closing again as soon as you glance in my direction. Keaton notices it too because he looks at you in the same way, Mason.

The mothers activate the music on their cell phones and start to waltz through the living room. Then they pull Keaton up onto his feet and force him to dance the lambada. He rolls his eyes in my direction and I giggle a little. Olivia drags Riley to his feet while Amber continues dancing with Keaton. Riley sighs and imitates John Travolta's moves perfectly for Mom until she cracks up with laughter. So much happiness, Mason, yet in my head, I'm at war with my heart. I am so sad and just want to be alone. Simply run away.

Suddenly, you are in front of me and I glance up at you. You eye me sternly, as always. A little uptight, a little tense. Finally, you pull me to my feet with one hand. My heart flutters, Mason, as I feel your hard naked torso and warmth pressed against me. We are so close, I smell you. You keep one of my hands pressed against your chest and I feel your heart pounding faster than ever before. Your other hand is on the small of my back. I love your strong arms around me and your eyes on me. The way you look down at me. I lean my forehead against your clavicle and inhale your scent like an addict while I touch your soft skin with my lips as I breathe kisses on it. The laughter around us seems far away. Now there's only the two of us, the two of us against the rest of the world. I'm overcome with too many crazy feelings, too many contradictions, too many fears and longings. I cannot lose you and I cannot hold onto you. That is entirely your call.

Apparently, Cherry chose a new song called *Cherry* by Lana Del Rey, yet you continue leading me, Mason.

I said real love, it's like feeling no fear
When you're standing in the face of danger
'Cause you just want it so much
A touch
From your real love
It's like heaven taking the place of something evil
And lettin' it burn off from the rush

I move my nose further up and feel your warm breath in my hair. Your lips are on my temple and I wish we could dance like this forever, holding each other close like this.

You cannot laugh with me, you cannot talk to me, but our bodies have found a language that nobody but us understands. I know you feel it too, Mason.

Darlin', Darlin', Darlin'.
I fall to pieces when I'm with you, I fall to pieces.
My cherries and wine, rosemary and thyme.
And all of my peaches are ruined.

I love you so much it is tearing me apart, Mason. I simply cannot help but feel that it will soon be over. That you will slip away from me. Right now, I'm still holding you, I'm still in your arms, but perhaps as soon as I let go, you will be gone forever.

"Mason?" Cherry calls to you and you turn your head in her direction. From behind me, I hear growling or some guttural sound. Startled, I turn around and see Keaton glaring at Cherry.

Then I glance back at you and then her. Mason, you're still holding me but you're looking at her. She asks you something and says, "Come take a look!"

You look at me and I think, *Please don't*.

Your expression seems determined. You take my hand, turn around, and pull me upstairs.

I swear to God, Mason, my heart is racing a mile a minute. Everyone's eyes pierce my back and but it is much more important that I feel your hand in mine.

We go to our room and you close the door. We sleep under a sloping roof and the moon shines right in on the white floorboards. The waves break and I smell the soothing salty air. There is continuous laughter downstairs. Your mom laughs so loud, it echoes throughout the house. You put your hand on my cheek and brush your thumb over my chin as if I were made of porcelain. I see in your eyes that you find me beautiful. Slowly, you lean down and put both of your big hands on my cheeks, cradling my entire face. Your lips find mine without having to search for them. Even darkness cannot separate us, Mason. At least I hope so.

You push me onto the bed. As you lie down on top of me, your weight makes me feel safe for a few minutes.

* * *

Mason

Three days have passed, Emilia. And I'm constantly fucking up. My father is staring at me. He knows what I'm going through. Luckily, Mom and Amber have been drinking the entire time, providing Dad with some amusement so that he wasn't solely focused on me.

Now I lie awake and watch you sleep, Emilia, which I do often. Obviously, you don't know that. We've had a lot of sex over the last few days since I'm constantly turned on, Emilia. And not only because of you.

There, now it's out in the open.

Fuck!

I can still remember how Cherry's pussy felt. I still remember everything, Emilia. That's the truth and it makes me feel like shit. That's why I locked us in here for the last three days like I do at home in the basement. You see, Emilia, being around other people never works out. They are dangerous, Emilia, we are only safe when we are alone.

Fuck!

Fuck!

Fuck!

Fuck!

I hate myself right now. I had not planned to meet her again, and of course, I know running away is also not a solution. Baby, I don't want to hurt you. I don't want to be the reason you cry like you did four days ago at the beach. That tore me apart, Emilia. I've never felt so helpless, it's not like I could break something or beat someone's face in.

I don't know how to behave when you're so vulnerable. After all, I only use sex as a distraction or solution. I'm not the kind of guy who'd pull you into an embrace and comfort you as Riley would. I'm too selfish, cold, and sick to ever do that.

You're lying on your stomach facing me, as always. These last few nights you've held my hand while you slept, Emilia. Like you're afraid I might leave if you let go.

Your long, wild hair is fanned out everywhere and your eyelashes cast short shadows on your cheekbones. I lean over and smell your neck as I brush my nose across it and feel your calm beating pulse under the skin. I would love to grab you and drive home, then lock us up in the basement and live with you like that until the end of my life. However, another part of me longs for something completely different, Emilia.

Everyone is asleep. Actually, this is our time, but these last few nights have taken a lot out of you. You are too exhausted and don't have enough energy to stay awake because I had to let it out. Because the monster inside me is currently taking up more space than it ever did before.

I lie back on the pillows. Your fingers twitch slightly in mine and I squeeze your hand. I'm here, baby, at least physically.

The door opens quietly and I already know who it is before seeing them. A small crack of light spills into the room and my stomach knots up since I don't trust myself, Emilia. I mean, who knows what I might do.

She sticks her head in and her hair falls across her cheeks. She glances at the bed and eyes me, Emilia, and I notice myself letting go of your hand, baby. Slowly, so you don't wake up. Meanwhile, I feel like the greatest traitor the world has ever seen. I try not to look back at you as Cherry beckons to me. I sneak out like a thief, which in a way, I am. I know your heart is in my hands and that I'm about to break it into a million pieces. But that's typical of me, Emilia. I'm a fucked-up fucker.

She's only wearing a baggy black shirt that barely covers her ass. Her red hair is damp and falls loosely over her shoulders. Today, I watched her at the beach, Emilia. Then later, I fucked you so hard, I'm still sore. I hate myself so much, Emilia.

She takes my hand and I notice she's carrying a bottle of gin in the other. She loves gin. Yet I have no idea what your favorite drink is, baby. Do you even like alcohol if I did not forbid it? That time we were on the train tracks, you said you didn't care for it — because of your father. Is that so? Or was I so stoned I made it up?

Her hands are slimmer than yours and her nails are long and painted red, yours are chewed. I feel them poking my palm as Cherry leads me downstairs. The steps creak and she giggles. By God, I actually smile even though I don't want to. I don't know what it is, Emilia, but she gets to me in a different way than you do. Her way is more dangerous than yours because I don't stand a chance against her. She won't let me get the upper hand.

We leave the house, cross the patio, and sit under a palm tree in the sand. It is the spot where we've spent many hours smoking and drinking the night away. Whenever I cannot sleep, I often think back to those times.

"Shit," Cherry whispers and slides around in the sand. "I have sand in my panties, Mason."

"I'd check on it if I weren't taken," I say, feeling really proud of myself. She rolls her eyes, opens the bottle, and takes a swig. I watch as a drop of gin runs from the corner of her mouth, down her pointed chin, down the gleaming skin of her long neck, and down into the neckline of her shirt.

I clench my hands and tell myself that it wouldn't be right. What am I doing here in the first place? Why am I not lying in bed next to you? Why is it no longer enough now that I've seen her again?

She hands me the bottle and I'm only too happy to oblige. "Do you remember that night with the shooting star, Mason? When we were laying here all night counting them? We were so stoned, in the end, we didn't even know if it actually happened."

Recalling the time makes me laugh and I push and twist the bottle into the sand. The gin burns my throat and I feel its affect along with the three joints I already finished.

She looks at me from the side with her head tilted and a trusting smile on her lips. Her dark eyes even sparkle in the darkness. "I've missed you," she says.

"Me too," I reply without thinking.

She runs her index finger over my arm, Emilia, up to my shoulder and along my neck, when I grab her hand.

"Cherry, what are we doing here?" I ask her almost imploringly, hoping she'll give it a rest for I'm not sure if I'm strong enough to stop her, Emilia.

Abruptly, she leans forward and presses her lips to mine. I freeze briefly. I'm fighting an inner battle to push her away. Finally, I manage to pull back.

We look at each other, Emilia.

I don't want to do it, Emilia.

But I can't help myself, Emilia.

This time, I lean forward and press my lips to her mouth. Not timidly, not carefully. Without any restraint, I kiss with the passion that has been pent-up for years and suck out her moans.

Fuck!

I push her down on her back. She tastes like gin and Cherry, as she always did. And she smells as sweetly as she always did. That fact alone brings me to my knees.

Emilia, I'm sorry!

I feel the heat from her body flowing seamlessly over me and memories flood my mind like a wave. The two of us out here in the ocean, naked, in the middle of the night. Our lips. My teeth biting her skin. Her fingernails clawing my back. We share so many memories she will always be part of me, Emilia. And most of them are good. Not like our story, which is clouded by darkness.

Cherry was and always will be my light.

I slide her panties aside as she unzips my pants.

Our fingers are frantic and shaky. With you, Emilia, my fingers never shake.

And as I enter her, it feels like coming home.

13. Did You Cheat On Me, Mason?

Mason

I just came inside another woman, Emilia.

I just cheated on you.

I kissed her and fondled her breasts.

I also felt her contract around me.

I'm the greatest bastard on earth, this makes it official.

I don't feel well when I return to the house. Instead, I feel like there is a huge rock in my stomach crushing me. You were lying up there sleeping while I was in another. Cherry is still at the beach. Afterward, I just got up and left without saying a word.

I'm so lost in my thoughts, it's not until I'm in the living room that I notice someone sitting on the couch. For a second, I worry it is Dad, but seeing it is just the fucking pisser, I immediately relax.

He looks different than last year, not so much like a damn fagot anymore. However, his eyes still flash the same old hatred as he gets up and looks at me. My hair is still disheveled from her fingers and her sweat is still on my skin.

He seems tense. His muscles flex menacingly and I find he looks much more fucked up than previously. He is unshaven, has bags under his eyes, and his hair is unkempt. Did you have your fingers in them, Emilia?

I have seen him watching you the past few days and simply didn't freak out because I was distracted. I can't freak out around Cherry.

"So, you finally did it?" he asks roughly.

"Riley, what do you want from me?" I ask.

He comes at me slowly, Emilia. "What do I want from you?" He raises an eyebrow, then swings and punches me full force in the stomach where the stone is. And I let him. During the next two punches, I don't raise an arm once in defense or attack because I deserve it, Emilia, and we both know it.

"If you hurt her again, Mason, you'll never be able to fuck anyone after that." He walks by me and bumps my shoulder hard before heading out onto the porch and disappearing down the stairs to the ocean.

* * *

I'm fucked up in the head, Emilia.

I don't sleep all night and I don't come to your room. I showered for an hour and then wiped out a pack of smokes outside on the patio. Now I sit here on the steps, elbows on my knees, watching the sunrise, as I used to do so many times with her. She's not here because she knows we fucked up. That's probably why she went upstairs. Our bottle is still under the palm tree and the summer wind has wiped out any trace of us. But when I look, I can still see it down there in the sand. How I gazed into her eyes and seemed to find all the answers to all the questions in them while I slowly moved inside her. Slowly, Emilia. Not hard and fast. I think I'm drowning. I want to break the curse that shadows me. It started with the cherry red lips and the cherry red hair, and I don't know how it's going to end. Fuck, Emilia! Why do I feel like our time is up? And it's my fault. I destroyed everything I found in you. Suddenly, it all seems so wrong. It felt so right when I was inside her. There was no hatred, no jealousy, no resentment, and no addiction to another. It was just... I can't even name it.

Shit!

I flick my last butt far away into the sand and get up. My ass is numb from hours of sitting. I'm so tired yet unable to sleep because I can't stop thinking.

Shit, Emilia.

I fucked another woman.

I fucked Cherry. Still, I'm not sure who I cheated on because you, Emilia, should know that part of my heart will always be in her small red-painted fingers. You are my poison whereas she seems to be the cure.

I'm your darkness, your ugliest side, whereas she is my light, my most beautiful side.

It took me a long time to forget her, Emilia. I was somewhat successful when you made an appearance. You were so broken, so vulnerable, so fascinating, and with the wrong guy. I knew I had to have you, feel you. I had to feel who you are and who you want to be. I wanted to possess you with my body and subdue you with every fiber of my being.

Fuck, Emilia!

I don't function without you. I don't think I will ever be ready to let you go. That is my biggest weakness. I need it, Emilia. A little light. A little peace. A little less stress. A little less jealousy. And it was so easy to get it from her instead of you.

I start running with Missy right on my heels, even as I run faster and faster. At some point, I don't know if I can even stop running.

FUCK!

* * *

Emilia

You're not there when I wake up, Mason. The mattress next to me is cold. You've been gone for some time. And I don't just mean in this bed. The last few days haven't been too bad. But there was still that look every time she was in the room with us. This tension that came over me. God, Mason, I'm so on the edge. I felt that sharp feeling in my stomach before I even left the bed. I want to cry because everything feels so wrong. I'm powerless and I don't know why. It feels like something has changed since we arrived here.

Especially since last night because apparently, you weren't here.

Where were you, Mason?

Why didn't you say anything to me?

We always spend nights together. Nighttime is our time.

I get up and slip into my loose-fitting red dress. It is airy enough for this heat. It is the dress I wore the evening Riley announced our engagement. Somehow it feels like a lifetime ago.

Barefoot, I walk downstairs and discover a quiet kitchen. It's a morning that feels like a breakup. Like you've just been dumped and wake up alone. Realizing it wasn't a dream. Like the morning after a night of drinking. Like the eerie calmness that arises when there is something in the room that should not be there.

I swallow and shake my head in an attempt to dispel these thoughts.

It is still early. The sun is just starting to rise. It is a fiery orange ball on the horizon reflecting off the calm turquoise blue ocean.

I look out the window and see Riley on the patio. He wears loose hip huggers and no shirt. His hair is a mess. He is holding a cup of coffee, his forearms resting on the railing.

I'm drawn to him, Mason, no matter that you don't want that. But you're not here and I'm afraid to be alone.

Therefore, I go outside. Riley doesn't turn around as he says, "Did you sleep well, princess?" In the early days, he used to call me that often. It always made me feel special. Riley is the first and only man in my life who could make me feel that way. Back before that shit with you happened,

Mason. Back before I became ungrateful and cocky. Back before I became a liar and a cheater.

I stare at his spine, tanned skin, and broad shoulders.

"Riley, have I ever apologized to you?" I ask.

He turns his head to me in astonishment and I see dark bags under his eyes. His curls fall over his forehead. He looks the way he always does when he just got out of bed.

"You don't have to," he says, nodding to himself. "Come look at this."

I take a deep breath. The salty air clears my head and I go to stand next to him, so close that I feel his warmth and our bare upper arms touch.

"Isn't this perfect?" he asks softly. For some reason, maybe because I'm such a mess, I lean my head against his shoulder like I've done a thousand times in the past. Maybe all I want from him is a bit of his strength, a bit of his confidence, and a little of his…luck?

"It is beautiful," I say softly and fall silent.

I don't even say anything as he puts his arm around my shoulders and his cheek on my head. I have no idea how long we stand like this, though it feels like an eternity, like back before it all became so terribly complicated with you. You know, Mason, I was starting to become a better person before I met you. Riley had pulled me out of the deep black hole that used to be my life and you shoved me right back in — even deeper than before.

"What the hell do you think you are doing?" you growl behind us, sounding tired. My heart immediately starts to pound. I have no idea what we're doing either, but I do know how it makes you feel.

"Crap."

I abruptly pull away from Riley and whirl around. You stand five steps away with your hands clenched and nostrils flaring. Your eyes seem so different. You take a step toward me and your hands reach out for me when Riley's broad back moves directly between us. Now my heartbeat actually skips a few beats.

"No!" he growls as gloomily as in New York when we argued. "Keep your hands off her!"

You raise your eyebrows as if you did not hear him correctly. I place a hand on Riley's arm before the situation escalates. "Riley, please, it is okay." He actually checks you out first to see if I'm right before he steps back and I move toward you. As soon as I'm within reach, you grab my arm hard and drag me into the house. You remain quiet as your firm grip says it all. I am in a trance as you drag me through the whole house.

In our room, you throw me on the bed and ask, "Are you fucking him?"

"Where were you this morning, Mason?" I reply monotonously and feel something change in me, Mason. This is not good. Me questioning you actually takes the wind out of your sails for a few seconds before you shake your head briefly.

"I don't answer to you, Emilia!" you bark at me.

"But I have to answer to you, Mason?" My voice trembles. Even though I feel a little insecure, the words spill out of my mouth without hindrance. Again, you stare at me flabbergasted.

"I asked you if you were fucking him, Emilia," you repeat more softly and forcefully.

"Of course not, I'm with you, Mason, I've told you I love you a thousand times. Once in my life, I cheated because I *love* you and because I'm crazy about you. But I would never cheat on you," I say while looking in your eyes. But you look away, Mason. Why are you looking away?

"Mason?" I ask softly. My pulse pounds in my head. I even feel it pounding in my forehead and temples. I can barely open my mouth and I feel paralyzed. You're still not making eye-contact and are clenching your hands.

"Mason!" I repeat emphatically. "Did you cheat me, Mason?" Now you look me in the eyes and say, "No."

With that, you turn and leave the room.

14. Why Do We Have Kids, Olivia?

Keaton

Why did we have children, Olivia? I can't stop wondering about it. Maybe if we had no children we'd have had another threesome with Amber, Olivia. Or I would have screwed you at the beach. We would have done something useful, Olivia, instead of having the shit pile up over our heads again.

What the hell…

We are sitting at the breakfast table. Amber is still out jogging. She keeps herself physically fit while on vacation, clearly, she's mentally disturbed. You're sitting next to me – while the devil's brood surrounds us. I regard each one over the rim of my coffee cup.

Riley is to my left. This morning he has dark bags under his eyes and appears to be pretty pissed off, Olivia, the way he glares at his little brother. Last night he hit Mason, I saw it. Nevertheless, I keep the reason to myself for it would break your heart — again.

Next to him sits a rather introverted Cherry, staring at her plate. I can tell just by looking at her face what she did last night with whom, Olivia. The chair next to her is empty. It is Amber's seat.

And then there's Emilia, little, sweet, damaged Emilia. She slept in, but I can see in her eyes how much she has cried the last few days, always when he wasn't around. I know where he was when he wasn't with her. He's still going to get it from me, but last night, Riley took over. Besides, I heard and saw Cherry and him sneak outside with a bottle of gin, completely uninhibited like the children they once were. I meant to go after them but I saw Riley come out of his room and follow them, so I went back to bed.

Then on the next chair over sits the nation's greatest fucker, our son, Olivia. He seems pissed off, angry, and totally guilty all at the same time. His face is pale and it is obvious he hasn't slept. I glanced out the window at six this morning and saw him sitting on the patio steps. I hope he never gets any sleep again and his guilty conscience ends up killing him. He also has dark bags under his eyes and his hair is disheveled. He also went running and reeks of sweat. He'll realize soon enough that he cannot run away from his actions – I had to learn that too – but by then it surely will be too late, providing the girl has any backbone whatsoever. I know she idolizes him, Olivia, but sometimes love isn't enough.

Cherry is to Mason and Emilia what Leila was to you and me — only I never loved Leila, but Mason loved Cherry. She was always the one who made him laugh when we were here, who made him forget how bleak his life was, who showed him that things could be different than what he was used to. There's no question she's good for him. As good as Riley is for Emilia. Do you believe Mason and Emilia are right for each other? They're not. They'll destroy each other, eat each other up, and then spit each other out all over again.

Mason could never do that to Cherry or Riley to Emilia.

I wonder what good this vacation will bring.

"And?" Riley asks and everyone jumps — everyone including you, Olivia. You have a hangover, baby, damn, were you hot last night. I love it when you're inebriated. That's when you completely lose control of yourself and do exactly what I say. "Did you sleep well?"

Mason regards his brother sullenly and Cherry's eyes widen while trying to make herself even smaller.

Emilia frowns and you reply, "Yes, thanks for asking." You blush a little, Olivia, for you didn't get much sleep last night. You kick my leg so I'll stop staring at you, Olivia. I grin and bite into my croissant.

"I also had a good night's sleep," Riley says. "Though at one point, I woke up to what sounded like someone sneaking down the hallway." I look at Riley and ask him non-verbally if he really wants to open Pandora's box. Mason is obviously running out of patience.

"What crawled up your butt that you're pussyfooting around like that? Everyone just wants to eat their shitty meal, you bastard," he snaps and Riley merely smirks.

"I see someone got up on the wrong foot. What's bothering you, bro?" He sounds quite provocative, Olivia. What has gotten into him? I like his attitude.

"Don't call me bro!"

"Oh, I thought you like it because that's what you always call me. Okay, forget it then." Riley also takes a bite of his croissant. Then he points to all the goodies on the table in front of him and addresses his former fiancée. "You should also eat something, princess, you've gotten too thin.

No, Olivia.

How so?

"Mason!" I yell even before he moves, only to be ignored as he jumps halfway across the table, toppling his chair in the process.

Oh, no, Olivia. Why did we get out of bed? We should have had breakfast in bed. I would have licked jam off your body and you would have licked it off my certain part. However, now we're here with this madman going crazy, Olivia.

I swear to you, if you interfere this time, I'll kill him or I'll kill you, but definitely one of you two.

"Mason!" I hear a voice I didn't expect. Cherry. She grabs his arm and looks ruefully at him, Olivia. She doesn't even appear to be afraid of being hit since he would never do that — to her. "Mason, what do you think you're doing? We're having breakfast. Get a grip. Enough! Get back in your seat and eat, for Christ's sake. God, the people at this table are hungover, show them a little consideration." Mason snorts and sinks back into his chair. Everyone's a little baffled, even me.

"So, can we eat now?" Cherry asks. "Or does anyone else want to jump over the table?" Everyone starts picking at their food again, only Emilia gets up without saying a word and walks to the front door without reacting to Mason's harsh voice, "Baby, wait!" and disappears outside But I saw the tears in her eyes, just like you, Olivia. You put your hand on my leg, my cue to go after her.

I'm on my way out when Mason attempts to get up and is stopped by a warning look and deep "No!" from you.

He actually listens to you. Sometimes he's not so stupid.

***

Emilia

I breathe through my nose several times, trying to suppress the nauseousness, but I am unsuccessful. I lean against a palm tree next to your house and throw up. When I finish, someone wordlessly holds out a handkerchief to me. It is Keaton.

"Oh God, now I'm embarrassed," I whisper hoarsely and dab my mouth. "I'm sorry you had to see that."

"I've seen worse. Let's take a little walk." He starts walking and I quickly fall in step, glad he's here. By now, he has become an actual father figure to me. We go down to the beach and walk in the still cool sand. I'm barefoot – like the last few days. In my head, I see how she touches you all the time, how she looks at you, and how strong the connection is between you two. But you assured me you didn't cheat on me. Did you really look me in the eyes and lie to me or am I reading too much into it?

"You are not overreacting, Emilia. I would do the same if Olivia's ex was here and I saw them sharing such familiarity." I'm a little surprised by Keaton's candor and wonder if I accidentally spoke out loud. We sit down on the jetty that extends far out into the ocean. The air is fresh and blows through my hair.

I close my eyes. "What am I supposed to do?"

"Run away," he replies matter-of-factly. "You should have run away much earlier. You are not good for each other. More precisely, Mason is not good for you!"

"But I love him," immediately bursts out of me.

"I know, but sometimes the things we love are detrimental to our well-being. Sometimes they even kill us — like drugs, cigarettes, or whatever addictive substances. We actually love everything that harms us."

"What am I supposed to do without him?" I ask, trying to imagine my life without Mason. My eyes instantly well up with tears again.

"You have to find your path yourself, Emilia. Don't be dependent on others."

"I don't want to be without him, but I can't be with him either. I think he loves Cherry."

"No, you're way off!" Your father immediately sets me straight. "He loves the thought of her. He loves the Illusion of their past, but that will fade as soon as this vacation is over and he will regret the way he behaved. But don't run back to him like a little puppy dog, you must show him you've had enough. He needs that or he'll never respect you."

"I'm afraid."

"Fears are there to overcome."

"But if I..." I can't even say it, "leave Mason...I'm all alone!"

He smiles softly. "Of course you won't be! In our hearts, Olivia and I have already adopted you, otherwise, I wouldn't care what Mason does to you. After all, that's your business."

I smile weakly and say, "Thank you."

We fall silent and just sit there looking out at the ocean. Today, the water is rough and stormy, really restless — like I feel.

15. Fuck, Emilia

Mason

Fuck, is an appropriate word for my life. I have no idea what just happened, but somehow things got out of hand.

I fucked Cherry.

You were watching the sun rise with Riley, Emilia. What's with that shit? Who does shit like that, Emilia? However, Cherry – somehow – managed to calm me down. I know it must have affected you because you left. With Dad! Who is more your dad than mine now and my dog who is more your dog than mine.

Shit, Emilia!

I am still sitting at the table, although Mom and Amber are already clearing it. Amber just arrived. Fortunately, she was spared the drama this morning. Riley disappeared into his room and Cherry is sitting, looking at me looking at her. It was less than seven hours ago when I was inside her. The way she's looking at me makes me think she's thinking the same thing.

Emilia, I would be lying if I say I regret it. I cannot explain to you what Cherry means to me. I mean I cannot even explain it to myself why I am and always have been attracted to her. I'm sorry that *you're* the one who will be hurt the most once everything is said and done. I really didn't mean for it to happen, baby. I never did. I don't like it when you suffer – at least not in this way – and especially not because of me.

You return home and seem resolute, your gaze fixed forward. You walk past us and disappear up the stairs.

You seem so determined, Emilia.

Are you leaving me now?

I don't finish the thought and push the chair back, breaking eye contact with Cherry. I hurry up the stairs after you. Since knowing you, this is the second time I've run after you, Emilia.

You are in the room.

You left the door open, anticipating my arrival. You heard me.

You sit on the bed with your hands folded in your lap. The red dress flows over your tanned body and your hair is gathered loosely at your neck. You wore this dress when you and Riley announced your engagement and your move to New York a year ago. I remember it like it was yesterday when you were sitting at the table across from me.

I stand in the doorway and stare at you. You sit there and stare back. We stay like that for a while, simply staring at each other without exchanging so much as a word. I feel the tension in the room, Emilia. Actually, it is coming from you and directly flowing toward me. I remain in the doorway, blocking your way because I would never let you leave me. I'll never let you go, I warned you, Emilia. I am fucked up and you said you were aware of it.

I foretold that we would ruin each other, Emilia.

Now you see what I was talking about.

"You missed your opportunity to run away," I say.

"Who says I want to run away?" you reply quietly.

"So what is it you want, Emilia?"

"I want you to tell me the truth, Mason, please." Fuck, don't look at me so imploringly. I cannot breathe when you look at me like that, Emilia.

I'm not willing to do that to you, baby. No way. I step into the room and close the door behind me. "The truth is that you are mine, Emilia."

"And who do you belong to, Mason Rush?" The look in your eyes makes me nervous, Emilia. I've never felt that way before. It speaks of a newfound determination and I don't like it at all.

"Baby, I belong only to myself, you know that."

"I thought you were mine. You told me that." You get up, Emilia, and approach me. You stop short when our bodies are almost touching and stare up into my eyes. What has gotten into you, Emilia, why are you so challenging?

"Was that a lie, Mason, when you said you were mine?"

"I'm not answering when you're so pushy!" I shove you away with one hand because you're making me nervous. You stagger, quickly find your balance, and look at me.

"You know what, Mason, if that's the case, we have nothing more to talk about."

"Emilia, I don't think I heard you correctly. What's gotten into you?" God, I swear, just thinking about losing you is driving me crazy, Emilia. I'm losing it before I even realize what you meant.

"I guess after the vacation, we'll have to figure out who belongs to whom?" You actually want to get past me and leave the room, Emilia. What did my father, who you were with earlier, put in your head? Get rid of me and everything will be fine? You'll never make it without me. You need me, Emilia.

When you open the door, I block your way by slamming it with an outstretched arm right in front of your nose. You flinch.

"You're not going anywhere!" I say distinctly. You stand there with your back to me. I step closer and hiss in your ear as I grab your arm, "I'm telling you this for the last time, Emilia, you can't and won't run away from me." I open my pants slowly, letting you feel what I am doing. You tense up but stand your ground. You also don't object. However, from the corner of an eye, I see you closing yours as I push your dress up. "It is too late. Do you understand?"

You turn your head and glance over your shoulder into my eyes. Your gaze is as vacant as it was when you entered my basement for the first time. Back then, you had courage, now it doesn't seem so, Emilia.

I push your panties aside and abruptly thrust into you. I have to feel you. I have to feel your presence. But as I enter you, I see Cherry's face — the way she looked at me while I was on top of her.

I'm fucking you hard in order to drive the image away. You gasp my name, but in my head, it is Cherry who moans my name.

"Fuck," I swear and lean my forehead against the back of your head. You smell so good. You are my girl. I cannot stop thinking about everything I did to you and what is still to come.

I fuck you even harder, more aggressively, you whimper.

"I hate you, Mason Rush," you murmur weakly.

I cannot do this.

"Fuck, Emilia!" I abruptly pull my cock out of you that was in Cherry earlier and zip up.

I have to get away from you, so I push you out of the way and storm out the door. I also hate myself, believe me.

"You may hate me, but you're staying."

I'm in charge, Emilia, never forget that!

***

Emilia

Mason, you were gone two out of the last three nights. You probably think I'm asleep, but I'm awake, Mason. You know I'm a night person, that I'm chased by my own demons and unable to sleep. Why are you leaving and why am I letting you? Why don't I grab hold of your hand and prevent you from going when you're about to sneak away? Why don't I hold onto you?

We haven't had sex in three days! That has never happened before. Usually, you can't get enough of me. Last time, we didn't even finish. You just took off. Besides, your touches aren't what they used to be.

Is it because another took my place?

Today is another sleepless night and I decide to knock on Riley's door. I'm fed up with sneaking around to see Riley while you and Cherry sit somewhere, laughing and talking about old times. I quickly slip into a white tank top and black yoga pants and step out into the hallway. I cannot help it and press my ear to Cherry's door only to hear nothing. Then, I tentatively knock on Riley's door and hear him grumble, "Um, what? Who? Why?" I grin and open the door a crack. He's always so cute when he is sleepy.

"I can't sleep. Do you want to go for a walk with me?" I ask. Abruptly, his head pops up as he sits up in bed like a ghost. His hair is disheveled and he's only wearing pajama bottoms that ride low on his hips. I see his skin shimmering even though it is dark in the room.

"What's going on?" he asks sleepily.

"Oh, I just can't sleep."

"Where's Mason?" He turns on the bedside light. I shrug and try not to show how greatly disappointed I am by your actions, Mason. Where are you now? Do I even want to know?

Riley moans in annoyance and whispers, "Freaking bastard!" and he effortlessly swings out of bed. I've always admired him for ignoring his handicap.

"I'm up for whatever." He salutes. "What time is it anyway?"

"4:20 a.m.! You must be dead tired. I'm sorry I woke you," I say, but he merely shakes his head and indicates for me to take the lead.

"You always were a night owl." We go downstairs and he stops off in the kitchen. "Hold on, I believe we could use something to drink, right, baby? Uh, shit, Emilia, I didn't mean that. Sorry, it must be due to a lack of sleep!"

"Oh, forget it and grab that bottle of good wine! I believe your father keeps it stashed where nobody will see it!" It's good to get my mind off things and not think about you, Mason. Even if it's only for a few minutes.

"Yes, ma'am!" He briefly disappears and comes back with a bottle of wine that he uncorks before we head outside. It is a cloudless night and the starry sky shining over the ocean seems particularly intense. A warm breeze blows through my hair. I am so miserable, hurt, and numb. When I wake and find you gone, Mason, I pretend it does not affect me, otherwise, I'd break down. I don't even think about your whereabouts because deep down, I know what you're doing and I don't need confirmation. Did Riley feel like this?

"Riley, how did you feel back then?" I ask and take the offered wine bottle as we stroll along the beach.

"I'd say I felt like you're feeling now," he says.

I look at him wide-eyed. "Do you think he's sleeping with her?"

"Emilia, don't involve me in your affairs," he replies harshly. "But I'll be there for you no matter what happens. I'll be whoever you need me to be." My eyes well up with tears since I cannot shake the feeling that Mason and I are over. Then I ask myself if I will ever feel the way I felt with you again? And if not, is that good or bad? God, I don't want it to be over. But it's like racing toward a wall at 300 mph, towards the inevitable end — with malfunctioning brakes.

I take a sip, as does Riley. It's been a while since I've had alcohol, Mason. It's been a while for many things.

"Are you happy in New York now?" I ask Riley.

"Emilia, I thought New York had captured my heart, but it only felt that way because that's where we met. The place is not the same without you. I would have come back already if it were not for Mason waiting for just that and Dad expressly forbidding it. But I don't think I'll stay away much longer." His words fill me with hope and I take another sip. Maybe it will help me forget certain things. Right now, Riley is the only hope, the only light, then again, in a way, he always was.

We continue strolling down the beach. The moon is shining brightly enough to see. The slowly rolling-in surf continuously crashes against the shore.

"If it were up to me, I'd never go back," I tell Riley.

"We could stay here, forever. I could rent the place from Amber, after all, she adores me, unlike Mason, but then no one does."

"And, what would we do here?"

"We'd get up in the morning and start the day by drinking coffee while watching the sunrise. Then we'd hop into the ocean for a morning swim, naked of course, since no one lives nearby, followed by fabulous sex on the beach. If it were a cool stormy day, we'd stay inside and get comfortable in front of the fireplace. We'd make hot chocolate with the marshmallows that you love so much. Does he know you love those things in your cocoa? Or that you're only ticklish under your armpits?" He pinches me and I jump back screeching before he continues to daydream about our future. "We'd just loll around on the couch and exist. If you wanted to we could go into town and buy you the most beautiful clothes they had or we could go to a library and get whatever books tickle our fancy. Do you still read, Emilia? What was the last book you read?" Astonished, I stare at him when I realize I haven't read anything in half a year, because he still knows me so well, and has described my perfect day.

I sigh. "It sounds perfect and that troubles me, Riley, I'm not perfect. There are a few more skeletons in my closet that you don't know about and probably never will. Like Mason, my inner monster may come out and its self-destructive nature will pull me down even further."

"Emilia, I'm the hero in this story. I can handle any monster. It was you who never fully committed to the relationship because you believed I couldn't handle your baggage. Mason sensed your weakness and took advantage of it like a vampire. So now your life essence has been sucked out of you, Emilia. I don't even recognize the person I once knew. Yes, you were always shy, but you also had another side and quite often gave me your opinion. Now all I see is a tiny frightened doe caught in the headlights unable to move out of the way. You are running on empty, he's sucked you dry. And now, when there's nothing left for him to take from you..."

"So now what?" I ask anxiously.

"How would I know, you tell me?" Riley comes to an abrupt stop and looks at something behind me. "Fuck!" he whispers. "Let's turn around. It's not nice here; I don't want to continue anymore!" he babbles and reaches for my hand, trying to pull me along all at the same time. I don't budge since I've already turned my head to see what he was looking at.

I'm frozen in place.

The bottle slips out of my fingers and my world shatters.

16. I Love You, Emilia

Emilia

There you are, Mason.

Under the jetty.

Her back is against a pylon and her legs are wrapped around your waist. Your pants are slightly down...

Her fingernails dig into your back as you bury your face in her neck.

You hold her so tightly, Mason, like you want to reassure her you will never let her fall. Her hair sticks to your sweaty body.

You groan her name.

I exhale and clutch my stomach. It is as if you've reached under my ribcage and ripped out my heart. I reach for Riley for help and he immediately catches me before I fall.

"Shit!" he whispers. "Shit! I didn't want you to see that, Emilia." You hear that, Mason. You turn your head and I see your lust-veiled eyes. We stand there staring at each other for what seems to be an eternity. I cannot breathe.

"Riley, I can't breathe!" I gasp as if I'm dying.

"Shit!" he whispers again. You step away from her in shock and pull your pants up over your hips. You stare at me with such horror in your eyes, you could say you woke up to find yourself in a nightmare. I feel Riley's arms holding me as my legs buckle.

"Emilia!" you say softly as if spellbound and take a step toward me.

"Don't even think about it! Stay where you are or I swear I'll kill you!" Riley explodes next to me and you freeze, visibly shocked. I'm unable to walk, so Riley lifts me up into his arms and carries me away. My legs feel like they are no longer part of my body.

"Fuck!" I hear you roar and something breaking.

Mason, what have you done?

***

Riley takes me to his room, not yours. After all, there is no longer an *us*. He sets me down on his bed. I'm shivering all over. All I can think about is you and her, and how you looked at her. How you buried your head in her neck and held her while her legs wrapped around your hips and her fingers clawed your back. I feel so sick, Mason.

"Riley!" I gasp, "I think I'm going to throw up." He quickly hands me the trash can to throw up in, but the only thing that comes out is wine. I have hardly eaten anything during the past few days. Riley holds my hair, which reminds me of when you held my hair some time ago in another world.

Exhausted, I plop back and sink into the pillows. I don't want to see those images anymore, please...

"*Fuck, Emilia*!" suddenly roars through the house. "WHERE ARE YOU?" I look wide-eyed at Riley.

"Stay here. Don't you dare come out! Stay put!" Riley says firmly and stands up. He leaves the room and shuts the door. I roll onto my side, clutching my stomach, feeling like I've been ripped in two, and you did it, Mason.

"Let me see her right now!" I hear you outside the door, followed by a loud bang.

"Take another step and I'll push you down the stairs so you break your neck!" Riley replies and...

"What's going on here?" Keaton.

Thank God!

Your father continues, "Shit. Let him go, Riley!"

"Uh...Emilia and I caught Cherry and Mason having a nice romantic midnight fuck on the beach."

"And, what were you doing there with Emilia?" you growl.

"She came to me because you weren't around, asshole!" he snaps.

"I'll kill you!" you reply.

"Is that true, Mason?" Now your mother speaks, the noise must have woken her. "How could you?"

"Shit, let me see her now or I'll kick the door in. Mom, get out of my way!"

"If you hurt her again or so much as get too close to that girl, I swear I'll throw you out myself, not your father, understand, Mason Keaton Rush?" Olivia says in an authoritarian voice that does not tolerate backtalk.

"Get out of this house and be quick about it," I hear Keaton say. "Before I get my hands on you, Mason!"

Everything is silent for a few moments before you shout, "*I love you, Emilia*!" And the last part of me shatters.

17. I Cannot Breathe Without You Around, Emilia

Emilia

I spend the whole day in Riley's bed in the exact position I was in yesterday. Everyone leaves me alone. Olivia tried to get me to eat but left again when there was no response from me. I could hear Keaton swearing all day. Amber and...*she*...left this morning.

Bitterly, I wonder if Mason gave her a dramatic goodbye kiss. Today, Mason, *you* become *him*. From today on, you are no longer a part of me.

There's so much anger inside me, I want to scream it out.

I hate him.

All the feelings I've suppressed so well in recent years creep back to the surface. I'm again angry with all the men in my life and especially with myself for always picking such men. There is no reason for me to be here, so I should leave.

I gave him everything I had. It may not have been much, I know that, but that's all I had, which obviously wasn't enough. Men like him are never satisfied, no matter how much you give of yourself. They always want more and more and more, until eventually, there's nothing left of you. Riley had it right.

Keaton promised to drive me home today. Olivia is packing my things, yet from *him,* I haven't heard a peep. He's probably given up or caught a ride with her. I don't really buy his *I love you*. Someone who loves another does not treat them the way he did me. Someone who loves another also does not stray and resists temptation no matter how tempting.

I rock back and forth in a futile attempt to ease the pain that has taken hold of me. I feel it everywhere, my legs, stomach, head... Everything throbs. If I had my way, I'd walk into the ocean without ever getting back out again, but Riley won't allow that. He keeps busy somewhere in the house and checks on me at regular intervals. I wouldn't want to see anyone else, especially not *him*.

It seems he doesn't care what I want because I hear the window opening and know it's him before I see him. I sit up abruptly and yell, "Go away!"

Mason freezes in front of the window.

He's wearing the same clothes he wore yesterday when he fucked her. The same sweatpants. His hair is disheveled and his arms are scratched up. From her long red nails. I *hate* red nails.

"Shit!" he whispers and steps towards me.

"Stay where you are or I'll scream for help!" I explode. My heart pounds wildly and my hands shake.

"Emilia!"

"Don't ever say my name again!" I snap. "Don't even look at me. I can no longer stand looking at you, Mason! You're a lying, cheating pig!" He actually appears shocked because I've never called him that, no matter what he did to me.

"Listen to me, Emilia."

"No, *Mason*!" I say in the same tone. I inch toward the headboard sine he continues forward. He circles me like a tiger and I follow his movements with my head.

"Shit, what's wrong with you? Just listen to me!"

"Hell no! I don't want to hear shit from you. Hearing you moan her name yesterday was enough!" He flinches and stops dead in his tracks. Though I see despair in his eyes, I don't let up. "How many times did you fuck her while I was asleep in our bed?" I have no idea why I changed my mind.

He remains silent.

"*Tell me, Mason*! How many times? Where? How? I want to know everything!"

"Don't make me tell you, Emilia."

"Do you think it'll hurt me? Can't you tell you robbed me yesterday of everything I need in order to feel, Mason Rush? Do you actually think I care about in which hole you fucked that little redhead slut?" His eyes widen. "God, you disgust me. How could I ever kiss you, let alone touch you?"

"Emilia, stop that!" His eyes darken warningly. I was actually intimidated before by his glare, now I find it laughable.

"Had you already fucked her when you said you hadn't? Answer me, Mason!" I say as harshly as he usually sounds. If I had the strength, I would grab him by the throat and shove him against the wall and make him answer, however, that's wishful thinking. I know this conversation will leave me drained once the adrenaline rush runs its course.

"Yes!" he says.

"Very good, Mason! You actually looked me in the eye and did not lie to me." I clap my hands sarcastically. I feel so empty.

"I didn't mean to hurt you!" he says.

I laugh mockingly. "Oh, no, of course not! You might have succeeded if you had kept your cock in your pants, Mason, but you didn't. Why? What does she have that I don't? Please, enlighten me." He swallows, obviously at a loss for words since he is unused to me being like this. "Was it because you deflowered her ages ago or because cheating gives you that extra kick you crave, Mason?" He seems flabbergasted. "Be that as it may, it no longer matters, we are through, done, finished, in case you hadn't noticed."

"I say when we are finished!"

I laugh. "Okay, try and stop me from leaving. By now, your father has my luggage in the car and is waiting to drive me to my new home that you will never find." I rise slowly so he can't get any closer and I walk backwards to the door like I'm sneaking away from a wild animal.

He presses his lips together and his look is piercing.

"Emilia. Don't!"

"I don't give a shit about what you want, Mason Rush!"

"Don't!" I continue to back away.

"Emilia." Panic flares up in his eyes and he breathes faster.

"Will you freak out again now, Mason? Well, do as you please, I won't stick around to witness it! Maybe *she* can calm you again." As I open the door, about to step outside, he falls to his knees in front of me, clutching my hips and pressing his forehead against my belly. "Don't leave!" he says hoarsely. I can feel his hot breath through my top. Oh, my God, Mason Rush is on his knees in front of me, however, it no longer affects me.

I grab his arms and pry them off me.

"It's too late," I say and step back.

"Emilia! I cannot breathe without you!" Now he looks at me with tears in his eyes.

"Well, I can breathe easier without you around, Mason!" I reply softly. I step backward until I bump into someone. Riley.

"Let's go!" he says quietly. When Mason sees Riley putting his hand on the flat of my back and leading me downstairs, he roars, "NO!" He's about to come after us when Olivia appears out of nowhere and blocks his way. She reaches for his cheeks and my eyes moisten at the sight.

"Calm down, baby, look at me." Olivia frantically gestures for us to leave as she stands her ground between us in the narrow hallway.

"Emilia, please!" He sounds quite desperate and does not look at his mother. "Please, baby...don't go!" Riley and I continue down the hallway. It's taking everything I have not to turn around and walk into his arms. "I honestly meant what I said yesterday! Emilia, I love you!"

I hesitate, but Riley pushes me toward the stairs and down and out the front door.

The door shuts behind us and I hear his desperate roar.

17. It'll Take A Lifetime To Get Over You, Emilia

Emilia

Numb, I sit in the back seat, staring out the side window without noticing the passing scenery. It's like I'm no longer complete, like he kept a part of me. Replaying his last words in my head is still tearing me apart. I'm so messed up because the truth is, even now, I'm still willing to turn around, get on my knees, take his face in my hands, and kiss and cry with him.

However, we've been on the road for an hour and Keaton stares intently through the windshield. He calls Olivia every 15 minutes to ask if she's okay and if Mason has lost control. She is fine. Mason is still sitting in the hallway, staring at the front door. She is leaving him alone.

I hate how he must feel right now. I hate that I saw those tears in his eyes. So many feelings I never expected and the worst part, I can't even believe them.

Riley came with us. I guess he's afraid I might do something stupid if left alone. I have to say, he might be onto something. I don't want to be alone, be without him. Right now, nothing of whatever determination and confidence I had remains. Feelings of emptiness are growing stronger the longer we are on the road.

Keaton will return to the beach house once he drops me off. He says the farther apart we are the better it is for Mason, so they're going to stay a few more weeks. I don't think this is how Keaton imagined this vacation, but neither did I. This was my first vacation and I never want another.

When I think of his name, it tears me apart. When I think of his eyes, I want to cry. All the moments we've spent together shoot through my head. How I hate that my brain only shows me the beautiful things. How he sometimes smiled at me. How gentle he could be when he wanted to be. When he'd run his fingers through my hair when he thought I was asleep. Sometimes he'd take my hand when we went for a walk. When he'd get in the shower and hold me from behind in his arms. The two of us under the splashing water, no sex, just him and me. When he sat next to me on the porch swing and we remained silent in the dawn. Or when he brought me back from New York and washed me and put lotion on me. The way he looked at me, like he had to protect me, like I was worth it. The two of us on the train tracks, how he held me, his fingers on my neck, and he listened to my story without judging me. Our first encounter in the cemetery when I sat on his lap in the rain and he looked at me as if I was his lifeline. How I sat here with Mason and snuggled in his arms, how he held me while I slept and drooled on him. And how he kissed me on the head when he thought no one was watching. I can still smell his scent and feel his fingers on my body.

Did we share all those experiences only because he was trying to get over *her*? Was I merely the notorious rebound-girl! A little, cute, hot distraction so he wouldn't have to deal with his true feelings? Yet it felt so real, so intense and deep. I was under the impression he was as smitten as I.

Silently, tears run down my cheeks. I barely notice until Riley wordlessly hands me a pack of tissues, which I accept and blow my nose loudly.

However, he did leave me something good for now I have a father and a mother. Let's see if things stay the way there are now that he and I are finished.

When I glance up front, I notice Keaton watching me through the rearview mirror.

He takes a deep breath. "This is better for you. Eventually, you'll realize that."

"I cannot breathe without him and I believed he couldn't breathe without me." My voice is hoarse, barely like me.

"You can breathe. You've been doing it the entire time," he says. "And you will keep on breathing. Right now, you may find it difficult, but over time, it will become easier and easier."

"It doesn't feel that way," I reply and glance out the side window to watch the other cars race past us. I envy anyone who does not have to feel this pain. It is so overwhelming that I start to close myself off.

Just like when I was a kid.

"I know it doesn't feel that way right now. I'm sure it'll take a while for that to happen. But one day, you'll wake up and realize you're fine." I love Keaton. He's an incredible person, though a bit strict at times. However, his heart in the right place and Mason lacks it often.

"My father always said I wouldn't amount to anything and would end up in the gutter where I came from. He told me that I was to blame myself for everything that I experienced in my life." The thought of him lessens my anger toward Mason because if ever there was a bigger monster than him, it was my dad. He didn't deserve the quick death his pancreatic cancer brought along.

"It seems your father was also a dickhead," he notes dryly. "People who do that to their own flesh and blood have major psychological problems and are basically full of shit." Riley briefly looks at me, confused, like I am after hearing Keaton's statement. I don't think Olivia has told him anything, but then again, Keaton Rush usually knows everything.

"I hate my life," I mutter dryly and lean my head against the soft leather.

"Riley will stay with you as long as you hate your life," Keaton states in a voice that doesn't tolerate contradiction. "To watch over you. You will not contact Mason, do you understand me, Emilia?"

God, the thought of not being able to contact him whenever I feel like brings me down even more.

"I only want what's best for you. If you were meant for each other, your paths will eventually cross again. But the way you are now, there will always be new pain."

He's right, I know, but I hate to accept those words.

"If you're tempted, talk to Riley or call Olivia or me." He gives me a meaningful look through the rearview mirror. "Do I make myself clear?"

I nod.

He has. I think I'll actually do as he says.

Now it's time for a fresh start without Mason Rush.

* * *

Mason

I sit here like a dog, staring at the front door, Emilia, with Missy's head on my lap and my hand scratching behind her ears. I'm on the hard tile floor, though by now, my butt is too numb to feel discomfort. I haven't felt my body for a while, which I think is for the best.

I keep seeing my mother's legs walk past me, but I never respond. I cannot. You are gone, Emilia, with Dad and Riley. You took off. I told you I love you and you simply left. And I honestly meant it. Fuck, baby, what have we done to each other? What have I done to you?

I try to recall the moment I woke up.

I suddenly realize it was the moment I was inside another woman and you stood there staring at me...at which point, the woman meant nothing to me anymore. She faded and suddenly wasn't what I thought all that time. She was one of many, Emilia, which became clear to me when I saw the

ONE standing there, looking broken and hurt as she fell into the abyss that I had just shoved her into. My knees almost buckled under me and I found myself falling too, baby.

Emilia, it took me forever to win you over yet only a week to lose you. Now I can spend my life trying to forget you, which will only work once I've taken my last breath. I'm sure I'll still be thinking about you and your ocean blue eyes and long black hair on my fucking deathbed, Emilia. Are you aware that you are a goddess? I'm the fucking pilgrim who adores you, yet never showed you who you turned me into. I regard you with such awe it was oftentimes too much to bear. I would have loved to put you in a gilded cage and keep you just for myself. That way, only I would see your beautiful laugh and unique way of sitting, lost in thought, on the swing. Or the sensual way you move, which is so unlike your insecure, screaming for protection look that you always give me, Emilia. Your look can drive men crazy or mesmerize men and topple kingdoms. But you are unaware of it. You also have no idea of the power you have over me, Emilia. I was too much of a coward to admit that to you.

I don't want anyone else to see how special you are.

I don't want that. I couldn't bear it.

I'm such a dumbass, why couldn't Dad do me a favor and beat the crap out of me.

I pushed you and Riley was there to catch you. Now I hate myself for it, Emilia.

If only I could to explain to you how rash and stupid I've been and that it was a one-time thing. I was drunk and not in control of myself...but that would be another lie, Emilia. I knew exactly what I was doing. I wanted it and went for it. I was adamant about it. I deluded myself into thinking that she was the one I actually needed; open-minded, confident, sexy, sensual, and strong. I regarded her as the light like Riley is to you. But it turns out I was wrong and rather stupid, Emilia. I don't love Cherry. Maybe I did in the past. Or my testosterone and infatuation made me believe it was love. She was quite hot and so different from all the other women in my life. How could I be so stupid and throw away what I had with you? It was so intense and real. We didn't even need words for our bodies had a language of their own, like our souls were connected — in a way not visible. Throughout my life so far, you've been the only one who's gotten under my skin, Emilia. Cherry does not even come close, regardless of how self-assured she acts.

Please, come back! Just open this door and step back into my life.

I'd do anything for you to forgive me, Emilia. Without you, I feel incomplete, I don't like that one bit.

I suddenly become aware that I will never encounter someone like you again, someone who adapts so easily and naturally to me so that we connect and became one. But now we've been torn apart so painfully that I will never recover, Emilia.

Book 2 – Fearless

18. When Your Hair Was Still Long, Baby

Mason

Three years later

I lean against the toilet stall wall while the hooker I brought in for questioning kneels in front of me. She gives great blowjobs, Emilia. It doesn't take long before I come in her throat while pressing her head forward. I like it when they choke, Emilia. That hasn't changed, never will.

I close my jeans and the bitch on the floor is almost drooling as she checks out my body, her gaze wandering over the white shirt under my bulletproof FBI vest, then on to my gun that I slide back into its holster. I took it out to avoid an accidental blowjob shooting.

"Let's go," I say lazily and pull her along by the handcuffs. Finally, I can officially use my handcuffs, Emilia. Anywhere, just like that. I don't think my father really thought it through when he gave me such a position of power. He forced me to finish the FBI academy and work for his department.

Now my dad is also my boss, Emilia.

It's not as fun as it sounds.

I've been here for half a year and still get the shitty cases. And he still calls me *fucking toad* in front of our colleagues! They get such a kick out of it, they turned it into a drinking game, which is why some days, they walk around the office pretty toasted, Emilia. It's not as serious here as you might think unless there's a special operation or big case that requires everyone's involvement and focus. I hate focusing, Emilia, I'd rather let myself go. However, I've learned to keep my shit together at work since I'm responsible for human lives, which should not be fucked around with.

Nowadays I have responsibilities, Emilia.

I *hate* responsibilities.

I don't care for it at all.

I sigh as I pull the hooker behind me and leave her with Mike for interrogation.

I enter my little room, which dad refers to as my office. I believe it was a broom closet before it was called my office. My father says I shouldn't expect any privileges simply because he's the boss here and I should work my way up, Emilia, so that I can take *his place* at some point and know what it really means to have worked for it. I'm approaching 28 and I'm not in the mood to work. Who wants to work voluntarily, Emilia? Really.

Every day, I wonder how you are doing, baby. The bit of surveillance I do by locating your cell phone no longer suffices. I need to know how you're doing. For the past three years, I have wondered about that first thing each morning. You moved to New York, Emilia. I knew you would. But you're not living with Riley. You remained *friends* and get together twice a week. How can people who had regular sex end up as friends, Emilia?

You share a dorm room with another student and in two more semesters, you will earn your degree. I'm proud of you, baby, honestly. But I hate that you're living on campus, Emilia. I check your daily posts on *Instagram.* I also know you are aware of it. Are you trying to irritate me, Emilia?

Every weekend, parties and drinking games. So much alcohol is not good for you.

And what's with the pictures of shitty looking broads sitting next to you.

You even have to post pictures of yourself studying in the library, Emilia.

And Central Park at night and your *Starbucks* coffee.

You've turned into a real New Yorker, even wearing your hair shoulder-length. What's it all about? You wear makeup every day, Emilia, and your clothes are much more modern and, unfortunately, more revealing.

You also adopted a German shepherd, Emilia. You named her *Venus*, like the Greek goddess of love, and she is white. The main thing it is not what I have, is it, Emilia? As long as it's the opposite.

I sit in my broom closet and scroll through your Instagram profile like I do every day.

You seem much more carefree now that you are free from me, right?

You're laughing in every picture and your eyes shine. No pain, no fear, nothing.

You're over me, Emilia, yet I still sit here thinking about you.

Suddenly, I see you've uploaded a new picture and I stiffen.

You titled it, *Summer in New York*, and drew one of those *hearts*. I hate those red hearts.

You are not alone in the photo, there is also a man, Emilia. He has blue eyes, black hair, and two heads taller than you. You gaze up at him as he hugs you from behind with his chin on your head — and you laugh. Why the fuck are you laughing? Why did you never laugh so much, so warmly, so real with me?

You follow him, Emilia. His name is *Seth*.

I visit his profile. Oh, God, he's a tattooed photographer, probably from your class. He looks fucked up, Emilia. But then you're into that, plus you already uploaded several pictures of the two of you, Emilia. You seem happy in every single one.

Are you merely pretending for my sake, Emilia?

Or are you actually happy without me?

I'm not a man who wants to see you happy when you're not by my side. I hate seeing you happy without me. Knowing you found someone you deem worthy enough to include in your posts is truly fucking me up.

As is often the case, my finger hovers over your name in my phone list, directly above the notorious green button. It happens every day, actually, but I never press it, Emilia. The last time we exchanged words was at that damn beach house in Virginia.

I hate *Virginia Beach*.

"What are you doing?" Someone barks behind me and I whip around, startled.

"Fuck, Dad! Do you always have to sneak up on me? How about you knock for a change?" The ajar door slams against my desk, Emilia. The place is pretty tight, especially when my father barges in. It is never a good sign. Seeing how angry he is, makes it even worse.

"Mason, how many times do I have to tell you: You can't fuck the hookers you arrest!"

"She offered, Dad. It's not like I forced her," I say, recalling how I held my FBI badge intimidatingly in front of her face so she would blow me.

"That is abusing your authority, which will get you thrown in jail!"

"Only if someone files a complaint, which no one ever does, Dad. No way. The last one offered to pay me money to do her again."

Annoyed, he groans while massaging his slightly graying temples. "Move your ass, Mason, we have a meeting. Have you prepared your documents?" he asks monotonously.

"Um, no?"

"Mason, you had four days."

"I had important things to do, Dad," I answer, raising my hands defensively.

He pinches the bridge of his nose and barks, “Rodriquez, get your documents, now!” and rushes out of the room as I close the phone directory.

There you are, baby, as my background picture. You look at me with a little smile while lying on your side in my bed. You lie naked on the side of my bed, the blanket pulled over your chest, my tattooed hand resting on the side of your head.

Back when your hair was long and you still loved me.

Fucking crap, I wish I could go back in time.

19. Oh Shit, Mason

Emilia

The sun burns my skin as I step out onto a typical small New York balcony and breathe in exhaust fumes. I wear one of Seth's t-shirts and it's already too hot for that. It's only seven o'clock in the morning and it is as bright and dazzling as if the sun was high in the sky. Seth is still lying on his huge mattress in his loft. Last night, I wore him out pretty good — and vice versa.

Soon, we have to leave for classes despite very little sleep and I contemplate playing hooky and staying here with him, in his studio apartment with A-frame roof beams. I stretch leisurely and squeak. Out of nowhere, Venus comes running to check on me and I pet and reassure her that everything is fine. I lean on the railing, look down, and watch the yellow cabs snaking through the heavy traffic and angry New Yorkers as they meander through traffic. It's loud and full of rats, but I don't care.

It was three years ago that I went with Riley to New York. Keaton had my class credits transferred from Chicago to New York. Initially, Riley and I lived together – merely platonic – but following a devastating night, he confessed he couldn't go through that pain of losing me again. So, to make it easier on him, I moved into the dorm. Otherwise, I'd only be using Riley, without whom I would not have taken this step to begin with in order to get over Mason. Without him, I would have never made it. Riley carried me safely through the critical times like a huge steamer through a stormy sea.

At times, it was crucial.

However, that was the past and not worth another thought. What's done is done.

Strong tattooed arms embrace me from behind. Simply by smell, I can tell who it is. I love his scent it triggers a tingling sensation in my stomach.

"Hey," he murmurs in a sleepy, hoarse voice. I close my eyes and smile as I lean against him.

"Hey." I smile broadly and blush a little when I recall what we did last night. Seth's fingertips slide under my t-shirt and over my stomach, leaving behind goose bumps. So far, only one other person was able to trigger it, however, it is best not to think about *him*. I won't do that to myself since it might tear me apart.

"Let's jump into the shower," Seth says, not exactly bossily but he isn't asking either. I gladly follow him as he takes my hand and pulls me into the shower stall. He does not make me feel like he's dragging me straight into the darkness. Unlike *him*.

***

The two of us are too exhausted to go to classes and decide to play hooky. Instead, we grab to-go coffees and take Venus for a walk through Central Park. It's a warm day, warm enough to wear my denim shorts and a white top that I tucked in my waistband. Seth, on the other hand, wears baggy shorts and a tight-fitting shirt that shows off his tattoos — as well as attracts women's gazes, as always. I'm not affected by it since I know he loves me. Half a year ago, I accidentally bumped his car in the college parking lot. That was how we got to know each other. I gave him my number but he never called to ask for compensation, merely if I would go out with him for a coffee. At the time, I had no intention of going out for coffee or getting involved with someone, potentially setting myself up for more heartache, but Seth was so personable and sexy, I couldn't say no. Actually, I was only interested in a one-night stand, but he was persistent. Nowadays, I can admit that we complement each other really well. Not only looks but also in bed. And not in a way it was with *him*. I no longer plunge myself into addiction. I no longer care for that pain. I no longer have to punish myself because I've forgiven myself. Attending a self-help group regularly for one year and sharing my experiences with others – with strangers – has shown me that I was not alone. And that what my father did to me was not my fault and that I deserve the right to a normal life and good treatment. I've spent many sleepless nights, crying and sweating while trying to come to terms with everything. Riley was by my side while I suffered for more than a year, though now – three years later – I am carefree like never before. I even made new friends, some in group, some at college. I even reestablished contact with my former neighbor and best friend, Bridget.

I date the hottest guy on campus and I read so much that half my money goes to books that have nothing to do with college, but with deep love and bloody horror.

Keaton calls me regularly to make sure I'm all right. He even sends a monthly allowance that I don't even want. But he feels responsible for me like a father and I let him share everything in my life like a father. Now and then, I even talk to Olivia over the phone, but we always avoid making *him* the subject. Granted, I'm curious about how he's doing but I don't ask. I also forbade myself from stalking him over the Internet. It would break my heart to see him laugh without me. Still.

Yes, I love him. Part of me will always love him, but it is no longer all-consuming. I keep feelings for him on the backburner and under control.

"What's on your mind?" Seth asks as he puts an arm around my shoulders. I like feeling the weight of his muscled arm around me. Venus is off the leash and having fun chasing butterflies.

"To be honest, I was thinking about my ex," I say. I won't lie, there is no reason. Being honest with myself also means being honest with others, especially when it comes to Seth. Naturally, I've kept a few secrets to myself, but then who doesn't do that, right?

"And?" He raises an eyebrow. "Why?"

I nudge his side with a shoulder. "Don't be jealous! It was three years ago."

"Are you talking about the one whose name it is forbidden to mention?"

"Yes. Besides, it ended rather ugly and I have no reason to think of him in a positive way, okay? He broke my heart."

"You want me to kill him?" he asks dryly. I stop, take his hands, and look up at him.

"I'll let you know, right now, I'm undecided." I stand on my tiptoes and kiss him.

I used to be unable to counter or give funny answers because I had no self-confidence. Now I love seeing life through new eyes.

It is nice.

And nobody can take it away from me.

Seth takes my chin between his fingers and kisses me passionately as I'm about to withdraw. He slides his hand to the back of my neck and leans his forehead against mine and asks, "Why am I so smitten with you?"

I pull my head back because there's only one person with whom I've shared this particular intimacy.

"Well, maybe because I'm so hot!"

He laughs, slaps my buttock, and we continue on our way, holding hands.

It's almost perfect.

***

Seth is still studying for his next exam, which is coming up, and I stretch naked in his bed and smoke a cigarette in the loft. The sheet is pulled up over my chest and I stare down at his back. Down at his bare back, spine, and tattooed skin. His shoulders are broad and he has lowered his head to be able to read the text on his laptop better, and as if he senses that I'm staring at him, he turns his head towards me and says, "Don't look at me like that or I'll come up, baby."

I grin cheekily. "Maybe I want you to, *baby*?" I say, seductively sticking out one bare leg from underneath the covers.

"Are you trying to get a rise out of me?"

I bite my lip, wondering if I might have fallen for someone like Mason – though a much subtler form – but quickly reject the idea. Seth would never do anything like *he* did.

"I'll be with you in 30 minutes, so stay put and stop seducing me for now, you nymph," he says seriously. I laugh and turn around to grab the cup in which we throw our cigarette butts. Yes, I have been smoking recently. All right, for three years, but only because I couldn't get over Mason and the pain was eating away at me so much that I needed something to remember him by. The smell of cigarettes was probably the most familiar thing about him. I think about how he put his lips around the filter and the cherry flared up as he took a drag. And he always blew smoke in my face even though I hated it. But I didn't even bat an eye or tell him to stop. I would do so today. Today, I would do so many things differently.

Shit, I just broke my three-minute rule. I made a special rule at some point. In order to get over him better, I allow myself to think about him three minutes a day. And that was at least five. As a distraction, I reach for my cell phone with my eyes rolling and open Instagram. I have a new comment. Probably Bridget again, talking some shit.

But I'm wrong, it's not from Bridget.

Under the last photo I posted, the first photo of Seth and me, titled *Summer in New York*, is *Winter in Chicago*. It's by M. K. Rush.

I freeze, clutching the phone in one hand as my heart starts beating frantically and I feel the pulse pounding in my neck, even in my temples. Until I can no longer breathe. Before I can stop myself, I click his photo and I am immediately redirected to his profile, which I have avoided for so long.

And there they are.

All the pictures.

At once, I notice I've completely forgotten how hot and beautiful he is.

Nowadays, he is even hotter than before — and that means something.

He seems even broader and more masculine. I had no idea that was possible. It's obvious he still doesn't care for t-shirts as his tattoos, which there are even more of, cover him. I swallow.

He must be working with Keaton at the FBI because, in two pictures, he's wearing an FBI jacket and sunglasses.

"Oh, shit," I whisper and scroll with my eyes so wide open they hurt. In his profile picture, he's sitting on the floor with a cigarette dangling from the corner of his mouth. Then there is a picture of him working out, doing pull-ups, showing his muscles flexed. Holy shit! The picture has received over a thousand likes. If I were still together with him, I'd probably insist he take it down or at least have freaked out. There are also pictures of Missy. One shows her wearing his sunglasses and FBI cap. She looks so cute it makes my heart ache.

I absentmindedly stroke Venus, who lies on the bed next to me, and grab her fur a bit rougher than is good for her. Or me.

He also posted pictures of *parties*.

And of tables loaded with the most expensive champagne and whiskeys. Underneath is a caption: *Today, we treat ourselves.*

The further I scroll, the more fucked up the pictures.

It seems it wasn't until about six months ago that he pulled himself together.

Before that, the photos make me furious.

One is of his hand on a *woman's thigh* — inside a car.

Another of his backside at the pool in swim trunks...with a blonde in a bikini sitting directly in front of him at the edge with her feet dangling in the water.

A poker table with cards. Sunset over Chicago. And how he's leaning against his Mustang. A photo of him and a chick in the hot tub.

A picture of him in his chair, stoned out of his mind, with smoke swirling around him. That's the Mason I know.

I continue to scroll.

A picture of him and Missy sitting on the couch at some party.

Then a snapshot where he's laughing — I mean actual carefree laughing. Was that *her* doing?

A picture taken on the porch of the beachside cottage from the side. Hair frizzy, arms resting on the railing, looking out to sea. It is three years old. Oh, God, I'm sure *she* took it. I wonder if she came back afterward and they finished the vacation at the beach house together.

I have to put the phone away because there is a lump in my chest that has been gradually contracting until now, until I can no longer breathe.

"Fuck!" I swear softly as I plop back, close my eyes, and place an arm over them. Why did I have to do that? Why did I have to look at all the pictures?

It's like I'm a recovering alcoholic and I walked right into a liquor store. I hear the phone hum next to me and flinch. I receive a message from an unknown number and I know before I open it that it's from him. *How are you, Emilia?*

My heart skips a few beats as I stare at his words. It feels like I can hear his voice saying my name when I see his profile picture on *WhatsApp*. It shows Missy wearing sunglasses.

Where did he get my number? And why did it take him until now to contact me? Did he sense I was thinking of him?

It is mind-boggling.

Once again.

I refrain from answering, block him, toss my phone aside, and crawl under the covers with Venus.

Fuck!

20. You Blocked Me, Emilia

Mason

You blocked me, Emilia.

I don't like that.

Are you sure you don't want to hear what I have to say, baby?

Annoyed, I sigh and lean back. Dad is forcing me to work *overtime*. He's also in his office making sure I follow through, Emilia. I mean, *why*?

Today, I just couldn't keep it together, I finally had to write to you. And what do you do, you little self-righteous thing, you block me, Emilia. I really don't like that.

What are we going to do with you now?

I mean, as soon as I saw the picture of you and your new wannabe Mason, I realized I had to have you back. I do, no matter what my parents say. Three years I've restrained myself, yet every time I come in a pussy, I think of you. Now *I want you.* Genuinely. Live. Screaming. Under me.

I don't want that Seth kissing your lips or looking into your eyes, Emilia. I'm going crazy as I refresh your profile every ten seconds, Emilia. Why did you block me? But on Instagram, you didn't, perhaps you wanted me to see what was going on in your life so that I'd explode from jealousy. That means I still have a chance because you're not over me, I mean why else would you want to make me jealous.

Still, why did you block me?

You could have written to me normally or are you still angry about *Cherry*? Fuck Cherry. She tried to hook up with me again and I told her to take a hike. It's her fault you're gone. She's a cold-hearted bitch who seduced me. She knew I would not be immune to her. She also knew you would be there with me. Still, she didn't care as I thrust into her.

You just blocked me and four minutes later, you uploaded a new photo, Emilia.

Oh, I don't like it one bit.

You're naked in bed with that pissant. I know it even though the blanket is pulled over your chest as you snuggle up to his equally naked chest. He rolls his eyes and you beam at the camera so that your perfect little teeth can be seen. With both arms, he holds you as if he owns you, as if you are his *property*. But you're not, Emilia. Haven't I told you that you'll be mine as long as I say so? Even though I've kept my mouth shut for the last three years, you've always been mine. And now it's time for you to realize that too.

I thought we understood each other.

And I thought we understood each other.

I said *you* could not end it, baby.

You give me no choice but to run a check on you through a program at work. It doesn't take long before it displays 452 hits. I narrow my search to New York. I'm shown that 21 Emilia Sullivans live in the city, one of them is you.

I've decided, Emilia, I'm coming to New York – soon – and I'll come prepared.

***

Emilia

The night is bright, the sea swooshes in the background, and strangely enough, seagulls fly over our heads even though it is late. Riley and I are walking on the beach. The sand is soft under my bare feet.

"Baby, you have to run. Run!" Riley says to me.

Confused, I stare at him. "Why?"

"Because he will devour you, Emilia, haven't you learned that yet?" I hear moaning behind me and immediately know who it is.

Cherry.

I turn around and there you are.

You and Cherry.

Your pants are down, her nails are digging into your arms, and you've buried your head in her neck.

You groan her name as you look at me, Mason.

As you smile and I break…

"Heeey!" I hear next to me. "Been fucking too much again?"

Bridget asks and I cringe. "You really look like shit today, Emilia, honestly. And you have drool running down your chin!"

Crap!

I quickly wipe my mouth and shake my head to snap back to the here and now. Fuck, I dozed off with my head on my fist in the middle of the lecture. I also had my mouth open. I hope I wasn't snoring.

Seth says I snore. I don't believe him, if so, Bridget would have rubbed my nose in it long ago.

"Fuck, I'm so exhausted," I whisper. She tugs on one of her golden curls that immediately bounce back up again.

"I'd always be exhausted with such a hot stud in my bed," she whispers and breaks out giggling. Bridget is always in a good mood, real sunshine. She's always been like that, ever since childhood. She was the one who always made me forget the bad days and who always put a smile on my face, no matter how bad I felt, or how much my body hurt. For this reason alone, she was the first person I visited when I came back to New York.

She has blue eyes, blonde curls, and angelic features. I think Riley and she would make a good match. I've been trying to get those two together for a year now; it's just that Riley won't play along. I believe because of me, he's still single. However, I'm sure he'll eventually come around.

I straighten my white chiffon top because a strap slipped off my shoulder and I rub my unmade face. It's been a while since I've looked as haggard as I do today. For the first time in two years, I didn't sleep at night. The darkness wants to reenter my life and I must drive it away somehow. But it's not that easy. I haven't had that dream in ages and although it has been so long, everything still contracts in my stomach. The pictures are still as clear as if it was yesterday. I have to see Dr. Daniels again because I feel the loss in my chest too clearly. It is too present again, which frightens me. For the first time in a long time, I am afraid, as soon as he appeared on my phone.

Tonight I'm meeting Seth and his parents for dinner at one of New York's hipster restaurants. I have to play the good daughter-in-law. I'm still familiar with that. Fortunately, Seth doesn't have a brother, but a sister, so there's no chance of a repeat.

Seth comes from a wealthy family – that too I am familiar with. My therapist, Dr. Daniels – who, by the way, is a DILF, Dad I'd like to fuck, but only marginally – believes I have a father complex. That would explain why I like him even though he's 43. I also had a little fling with him — before Seth. According to him, I create situations that I know and that are familiar to me because I feel safe in them. In essence, new people, same old story. I actually thought Seth would provide me with a new start – a new life – but the more I think of Mason Rush, the more I see the parallels. He has both Riley and Mason's traits, which makes it even more typical.

Shit, Emilia, I hear Mason's voice in my head and I want to slam my forehead against the table. It's starting again, I hear his voice and feel like I'm going crazy.

Baby, he says in that wicked motherfucker way. *If you don't stop thinking about guys who could be your father, I'll tie you to my bed and make you stay all day, Emilia.*

"Shit!" I whisper and Bridget gives me a funny look. I cannot relapse; I've been making so much progress. I rub my forehead in resignation.

Great!

I think so too, Mason says and grins.

***

The next morning, I'm tired — still. We sat in the restaurant with Seth's parents until 11:30 p.m. talking about palm oil and rainforest deforestation. Seth must have been as bored as I was because he fumbled between my legs under the table.

Shit, the guy is a bit sick.

And, baby, do you realize something? The Mason in my head says while loosely holding a cigarette between his fingers as he lolls about on a huge bed with black silk sheets. *You'll always search for what you had with me, but it will never be as good as it was with me, Emilia...*

"Hey, baby!" Seth's voice startles me out of my reverie.

"Yes?"

"I asked you if you want caramel in your latte."

I'm going to caramelize you, motherfucker, my inner Mason growls. I shake my head in an attempt to drive him away. My God!

Seth is as tired as I am since I kept him awake all night by taking my frustration out on him. Physically.

It's what I do now.

I fuck like Mason — and the men love it.

I know Mason would love it the most, but then, he won't ever again get to enjoy my pussy.

Even you don't believe that, Emilia. If I want your pussy, I'll take it, Emilia, the silk sheet Mason says and blows smoke into my brain.

I sigh heavily and hiss, "Get out of my head!"

"What?" Seth asks sleepily. "Yeah, put caramel in my latte, please!" I shake my head. "God, I'm exhausted."

Seth strolls over to me. I'm still lying on the couch, trying to wake up. He sets my latte down, grabs my face with one hand so my cheeks are slightly pressed together and says, "It's good to know I can also fuck your brains out, baby!" I shiver a little.

No, Emilia, we don't resemble each other, your new man and me! imaginary Mason says and raises his eyebrows.

Seth kisses me briefly before he leaves to make himself a coffee and I plop back into my pillow, exhaling and thinking, *Shit, Mason!*

21. Therapy With Dr. Daniels, Mason

Emilia

Seth and I part ways at 2:00 p.m. He has a lecture to attend to this afternoon, and I'm taking a taxi to Dr. Daniels. Granted, Keaton bought me a car, but I don't use it often as the New York traffic scares me and I'm afraid of causing more damage, especially since the accident with Seth.

I store the car in a rented garage close to the dorm, but I am hardly ever there. I always stay at Seth's place. I don't care for the *unisex bathrooms* at the dormitory, they are disgusting.

I call Keaton during my ride to Dr. Daniels. He picks up after the first ring. "Emilia?" he says. I love hearing that voice. It reminds me of Mason and at the same time, it creates a familiar feeling in my chest.

"Hey," I reply softly and cautiously.

"What's going on, Emilia?" he asks. During our calls, he almost sounds like he's talking to Mason. That probably means I've become part of the family.

"Am I bothering you at work right now?" I reply and hear a door closing.

"You never bother me."

"Okay."

"The fucking toad should be doing something," he hisses to himself. I try to ignore it because I know exactly who he's talking about. When I imagine that Mason might only be a few steps away from his father right now, everything contracts inside of me.

"So...I'm on my way to Dr. Daniels," I say hesitantly.

"Emilia..." Keaton hates beating around the bush. "What's going on?" He sounds a little tired.

"Are you all right?" I ask in return.

He sounds anything but okay as he utters, "I'm okay…how about you, Emilia?" He deflects. "Why are you seeing that motherfucker, Dr. Daniels, again?" I turn bright red. "You know I'm aware that..."

"Yes, I know!" I cut him off. God, I feel like I'm talking to my real father. My heart actually starts to pound.

"Please, make sure to keep your legs crossed in his presence, Emilia!"

"Yeah, yeah, I'm not calling for your advice!" I answer angrily and receive a pissed off look from the Pakistani driver.

"Sorry," I mutter quickly. "I'm definitely going to see, Dr. Daniels, I am seeing Dr. Daniels because the journals are no longer enough. He's back in my head and he has written to me."

"That bastard!" he thunders. "I expressly forbade him from doing that, Emilia."

"You know what he thinks of restriction! Now everything is back and I'm confused. I need someone..."

"The next shithead, naturally."

"I didn't call you to get an ear full...uh...Keaton."

I sense him smiling. "Why don't you come visit us for a few days? He won't be here, I'll make sure of that. You could do girl stuff with Olivia and get away for a bit. You can even bring your new shithead. But I don't want to see any lovey-dovey crap. I don't like that, Emilia."

"Oh, shit..." I murmur. "Okay, why not, but please make sure he actually stays away. You know what will happen if we see each other again."

"Oh, I can imagine, and trust me, I'm in no mood for that!"

"Hey, there's something else."

"Which is?" he asks.

"So...uh...since I'm going to bring my new boyfriend..." I turn bright red again.

"What is it, Emilia?" Keaton asks.

"Maybe you could pretend to be my parents? I mean...he once asked me about my parents and I immediately thought of you. So, I told him you live in *Chicago* and he believed me. I guess I messed up, stupid."

Keaton actually laughs, which he usually only reserves for Olivia. I love it. "I believe we can accommodate you!"

"Oh...by the way, I'll also be bringing my dog."

"Anything you want, Emilia, we have plenty of space, Missy is with...him anyway."

"Okay," I say sheepishly.

"Okay, so we'll see you in a week? I'll tell Olivia."

"I'll call again before we leave."

I hang up and cannot help but smile a little. I love Keaton John Rush.

***

Dr. Daniels is a little pissed off as he looks at me. Which man in my life isn't pissed off when he looks at me?

I haven't been in touch for four months and now I just barge in, making him reschedule other patients.

"Hi," I say sheepishly. He is still pissed off. "I'm sorry, but I met Seth and he asked me to be his girlfriend after two months and for some reason, I said yes, and maybe that's why I missed all my other therapy sessions because I didn't know how to deal with you, Dr. Daniels."

Oh, Emilia, my imaginary Mason sighs and nibbles on grapes.

Though Dr. Daniels shakes his head, he smirks a little. He always talks as if he's stoned and he's not stoned at all, he's just extremely relaxed.

"Do you know what your problem is, Emilia Sullivan? Ever since you realized your potential and what a great woman you are, you've been seeking validation everywhere."

"And?" I say hesitantly, scratching the back of my head.

"That's not how it works. Other people have feelings too." He eyes me meaningfully over the edge of his modern glasses. Now he looks like the DILF – the daddy-who-wants-to-spank-my-ass – and I slide around uneasily because he looks at me so piercingly from his gray-blue eyes.

Fuck, I really have a problem.

A problem getting over Mason.

I'm confronted with trees with too many sweet fruits, all of which I want.

That is, except for cherries — those I hate. I'm a complete mess again since he contacted me.

"I have a boyfriend now, as you know."

"H'm."

"And he's really great."

"H'm."

"I mean, he makes me lattes with caramel and I'm really...so grateful to you that I've found my new self, but I think Mason is back."

Now he no longer looks bored. "Say again?"

"Well…he texted me, so I blocked him. But then I looked at his pictures and I felt a funny feeling in my stomach. Now, he's in my head, lying on black silk sheets, nibbling on grapes, and talking to me again. Besides, yesterday I had that dream again." *I told you a thousand times to forget about that dream, Emilia!* My pissed off Mason says.

I open my eyes. "See, he's back!"

"And, what is he saying?"

"That I shouldn't dream that dream again, that he forbids it."

Dr. Daniels eyes me for a moment. His gaze makes me nervous and I fidget.

"Well...maybe you've crossed some boundaries and are using him to get your life back in order since he was the only one who put you in your place." *Oh, yes, baby, that I did.* My imaginary Mason tosses a grape into his mouth.

"I don't want to hear him anymore. I don't want to see him anymore either!"

"You cannot ignore your problems, Emilia. Not even with sex. It just messes with your mind."

"Maybe I just have sex because sex is fun," I reply.

"Are you certain?"

I glance out the window and make a face.

"What do you feel when you sleep with a man, Emilia?"

"We've been through this already, I've even *shown* you!"

"We shouldn't talk about that, otherwise, I won't be able to treat you any longer." I restlessly rub my collarbone and chest because I still feel his stubble scraping my skin. He follows my every move and naturally notices exactly how nervous I get.

"I always feel so...desirable, like a queen. As if I have the power, at least over it because I can't control my feelings... I know."

"And how do you feel after sex?" he asks softly.

Oh, Emilia, don't do that now! And it's as if that's why I always do it. Because he's always there. Because he always glares at me so angrily and I miss him so fucking much. Holy shit.

God, Mason, get out of my head! I growl to myself.

"It depends... After having sex with Seth, I feel good. After sex with other people, I feel like shit. That's why I want it. Because I always felt like shit with him. Because he *fucked* me, not the other way around. Because he *used* me. Because he took out all his aggression on me. Because he didn't care how it made me feel and because he *punished* me. Sometimes I still need that." I wave my hand dismissively. "Even if I've forgiven myself — about everything that happened."

You're such a little bitch, Emilia, he growls in my head. I smile complacently and reply, *Do something about it*.

Dr. Daniels knows exactly what I want from him. He's the closest thing to Mason even though Seth looks more like him. He is large and well built. His hair is black and his green eyes are framed by laugh lines, his lips are beautiful and sensuously curved. He is a real man, a dominant man, a man who knows my psyche. It can be rather sexy.

I sigh. Of course I know there is still Seth. I feel bad for thinking that about Dr. Daniels.

You search for situations you are familiar with because you can control them and feel safe. New things can be frightening, the words from one of our sessions pop into my mind and I know it's true because I'm doing it again. I do what I did with Mason and Riley. Cheat. Feel the rush. And even though my life and personality have changed so much and I feel free, Mason still holds my heart and soul in chains. I have more self-confidence, I see the world more positively, I am happy and feel good about myself. But, there is a hole inside me that I try to fill. I always had one-night stands before Seth because I didn't know what to do with my newfound awareness of what a great woman I was and because I had to feel it. I had to feel I was desirable and alive. Again, Dr. Daniels is right. It was hard for me to commit to Seth, so it took him two months to, as he says, *capture me*. Even now, I am restless again, in turmoil. That's probably why I started thinking about and conjuring up Mason again. But why the hell did he write when I was thinking about him? Do we still have a connection even though I broke off all contact? That is, apart from his parents? Which I will not end, you'd have to kill me first.

Dr. Daniels also says I want to punish all men for what my father did to me. He thinks that's how I deal with it. And anything that helps is legit, isn't it? My conscience was lost a long time ago.

I sigh. "Seth's great," I say.

He raises an eyebrow. "You said that already, Miss Sullivan." I like it when he calls me that, it makes me feel wicked.

"The trouble with Seth is..." I continue and lean conspiratorially toward Dr. Daniels, giving him a good look down my top. His eyes unwaveringly fix on mine. "...he looks a bit like Mason, don't you think?"

"Um..." he stutters, raising his eyebrows and shaking his head. "I don't know anything about Seth."

"Do you want to see a picture?" I ask and he makes a sweeping gesture.

"Please, if you must."

I quickly pull out my phone and show him the last picture we took. The one I uploaded. Seth holds me firmly in his arms and I smile into the camera, as we lie naked under a thin blanket so that my contours can be seen.

"Uh-huh."

"So, what do you think?"

He tensely licks his lips. His eyes still have that slightly pissed off but totally indifferent look. "Possessive. Arrogant.

A child. Looks a lot like your previous partner, whom you've shown me pictures of."

"Yes!" I shout. "That's what I said. How am I ever supposed to forget him? That's probably why he is back in my head. I mean, we have an intense history together. He was...so incredibly possessive. I should never have been together with you here." *You shouldn't now either, bitch,* Mason says in my head. "And if he knew," I continue and let my fingertips dance across the low table until they touch his knee,

"the way you've treated me, he would kill us both, Dr. Daniels." I bite my lip and pull my hand back.

His face appears *slightly* grim, his nostrils a little flared, and his teeth clenched. A muscle twitches in his cheek, like Keaton when he is about to lose control.

"No matter what I do, no matter how often, no matter with whom, or how hard!" I roll my eyes theatrically to the ceiling. "I can't get rid of that feeling."

He stares at me in disbelief and his fingers tighten around the clipboard in his hand.

"Maybe I'm a sex addict," I utter, turning my legs the other way, giving him a brief glance under my skirt.

"Fucking hell," he growls, tossing his clipboard aside as he gets up and walks around the table.

He leans on one knee next to me, grabs my hair, and says directly at my mouth, "Let's see if I can get him out of you, Emilia Sullivan."

22. You Are Standing Before Me, Mason

Emilia

I'm actually going to Chicago with Seth and Venus. We're taking his car because he has a Jeep and Venus has more room in the back than in mine. I'm nervous and my fingers are shaky. I haven't felt like this in a long time. Only Mason manages to bring out that insecurity in me.

It's been a week and a half since I fucked Dr. Daniels. I didn't tell Seth, obviously. I like him and he's good for me, so I'll just leave it at a one-time thing with Dr. Daniels. Next time, I won't get so carried away no matter how sexy he looks and no matter how much I believe I need sex. And no matter how much I want to drive the Mason in my head crazy. He called me names during my entire performance with Dr. Daniels. It was a little hot. I could almost feel his hand on my throat as

I took William Daniels' hand and held it around my neck. He's the only one I submit to anymore. Sometimes, I just need to be submissive.

"Baby, why are you so nervous?" Seth asks and I give him a sideways glance. He just cut his dark hair and it's not long enough now for me to run my fingers through. His blue eyes are focused forward and he is unshaven. I like that. And I like thinking like Mason. It's only now that I realize how much fun his life must have been with that I-don't-care-fuck-you-all-or-I-fuck-you-attitude. When I think back about how insecure and awkward I was and how little I managed to tell him what I liked and didn't like. Or dragged him back to bed, trying to make him understand that he was a bastard when he cheated on me. Or I could never open my mouth. I can only shake my head at myself. But it's okay. It's in the past. At the time, I thought what I was doing was right. Dr. Daniels says I should live in the here and now.

"Oh, I don't know," I say with a sigh and shrug my shoulders. "It's complicated." Which is not the right word. The whole thing is a shitty idea. It's idiotic. That's what it seems to be. Saying Keaton and Olivia are my parents is one thing, but what's worse is the panic I feel thinking about Mason showing up and fucking everything up. Unfortunately, I can't explain that to Seth. I've already gotten myself in way too deep for that.

"I like complicated," he says. "That's why I like you. So, what's up?"

"My ex lives there," I mumble quickly. "Being in the city, I'm afraid I might run into him."

He looks at me like I'm a bit stupid. "Emilia, I don't think that's going to happen. There are a lot of people living there."

"It's a suburb," I say, shrugging my shoulders again. "There aren't that many people living there. It's like a village!"

"Are you truly worried about your ex right now, baby?"

Oops! I take his hand and interlock his tattooed fingers with mine. "I don't know why. I don't feel anything for him anymore. It's just that he hurt me severely and I haven't seen him since."

"You never told me what he did." Seth opens his window and lights a cigarette.

"He cheated on me, which is classic. And I caught him red-handed. That's it." That's not everything, but I'll leave it at that. Things burned deep into my heart are nobody's business. No one, really.

"Oh, baby." He smiles slowly. "Anyone who cheats on you must be a complete idiot. Honestly." I don't think he would think that if he knew me back then. I was so much the victim type back then. I mean, I practically begged to be treated like shit.

Instead, I say, "Thank you."

"I can't wait to see where you came from. Your mom must be really hot."

I'm forced to smile. "You're going to love my family," I respond tensely and Mason says in my head, eyebrows up, *Shit, Emilia, you are so fucked.*

***

My heart no longer works. I need a pacemaker when we stop in front of the house. Memories overwhelm me like an avalanche. I haven't been here forever. I put it off for too long and when Seth cuts the engine, I can't move. I just stare at the porch and the empty porch swing. How many hours, how many days was I here? Alone or with Mason. The weeping willow still dips into the garden. I remember how many times I sat under it watching him through his basement window, back before things really started to happen between us. After that first time in the cemetery. Sometimes he'd just lie there, stoned out of his mind. I always imagined that he was thinking about me too. I take a deep breath.

"Shall we get out?" Seth asks. Venus fidgets impatiently in the back. She must have noticed that we have arrived and now she really wants to get out.

"Yeah, sure," I say, clearing my throat because my voice sounds meek. Not like the new me.

"Are you all right?" Seth asks.

I take another deep breath and lift my chin. God, amazing how a place can affect you. "Yes, let's go in!"

I grab Venus and Seth takes our bags. I limited Keaton's offer to a weekend because I can't handle the fear that Mason might show up for long. Keaton said he would make sure it didn't happen, but Mason is probably still unpredictable and a ticking time bomb.

My white shepherd sniffs like crazy in the front yard because she smells Missy. She is the exact opposite. Friendly to everyone, a real cuddle dog.

The door opens before we climb the porch stairs and Olivia Rush runs towards me screaming. The last time I saw her was a year ago when she visited Riley. When she and Keaton come to New York, the two of them or Riley always lets me know. Then we all meet and do family stuff. Always without Mason. And I'm always disappointed. And I always hate myself for it.

Olivia hugs me. She smells familiar. Sometimes, I think she's a vampire because she simply doesn't age. Sure, she has a few wrinkles on her face, but you don't see a single pore in her skin, no gray hair, and she has a sensational figure. If I were Keaton, I would not be able to keep my hands off her. She would die. *Fucked dead* would be on the tombstone.

She's a bit taller than me and her golden blonde hair goes straight to her shoulders, and when she pushes me a bit away, she shakes her head in amazement.

"How can you grow more beautiful every year?" she asks softly and kisses me on the cheek.

I kiss her back and grin before stepping aside. "Thanks, Mom. This is my friend Seth." Her eyes sparkle a little when I call her *Mom* and I sense she's about to cry. I smile warmly at her. She turns to Seth. "Wow, now I know where your beauty comes from," he says.

Kiss ass, Mason says in my head. *He shouldn't talk about my mother like that, Emilia.* I'm slowly getting used to the shit in my head. I even start to like him. This is not good. *Maybe I should talk to Dr. Daniels over the phone,* I think to myself.

"Oh, what a charmer!" Olivia laughs, obviously flattered. And then a shadow falls across Seth as Keaton Rush steps onto the porch. He looks over the group, sighs at Venus, and comes down to us.

"Emilia," he says and I grin.

"Hi, Dad!" I call and smile. He thinks it's quite funny, I can see it in his eyes — I, on the other hand, think it's a bit strange. He takes me in his arms so tightly, I'm moved to tears because Keaton Rush doesn't actually do that.

Then he turns sluggishly to Seth. "So, you're Sam?" he asks and I glare at him.

"Seth," I correct him. "Dad, I told you that."

Keaton enjoys the game or he is truly worried about me because he is checking him out thoroughly. Actually, he should worry about Seth, I think, a little embarrassed when William Daniels and his miracle fingers wander through my head. And how mine danced over his knee...

"You must be hungry!" Olivia says and I flinch.

"Oh, yes!" I say to clear my mind. "Famished!"

***

We are sitting at the dining table and I must say it was delicious. The potatoes were well done and tasty. I can't believe I'm sitting at this table again. Back in the summer and again with another man. Again, I wear a dress, this time black, with spaghetti straps and a V-neck, gathered at the waist, and flowing down to my knees. I know *he* likes my legs and some part of me believes he will come. Yes, I realize how stupid it is. I wear my hair down and straight. It is not as long as it used to be, only to my shoulders. And I wear subtle makeup, but my lips are painted a summery shade of red.

Keaton sits across from Seth and Olivia sits opposite me. I see Keaton doesn't like him. Probably because Seth is wearing a t-shirt that reveals his tattoos. Keaton doesn't like tattoos. They surely remind him of Mason.

So far, we have only talked about our studies, about Venus, who is sniffing around searching for Missy. Also, Keaton bought a new house that he wants to rent out. It only needs to be renovated. Seth is talking about his parents and how stuffy they are when I hear the roar of a car engine that I know only too well. Deep bass from aggressive rock fills the entire settlement.

Mason loves to make a grand entrance.

And I know I'm screwed.

My neck hairs rise and Olivia glances at Keaton in fear. Keaton, on the other hand, drops his head in annoyance and appears to be in pain, which would almost make me laugh if I didn't have a damn lump in my throat. The atmosphere in the room changes, grows tense and crackles. Everything is rebelling in my stomach and I have to force myself not to press a hand to my chest to somehow, soothe the erratic pounding of my heart.

I notice that my breathing is faster and my face is burning hot.

Keaton stands up clumsily, pushing his chair back as the engine turns off. Without a word, he marches out into the hall and slams the front door behind him.

Panicking, Olivia and I stare at each other and Seth asks, "Are you all right?"

"Yes!" Olivia says loudly. "Now it's time for dessert!" She removes my plate even though I haven't finished eating and takes everything to the kitchen. Seth places an arm around my shoulders and runs his nose over my temple as I sit there rigidly. He takes my hand and plays with my fingers, managing to distract me for a second.

At that moment, the front door slams again. Loud steps rumble into the room and my world shatters again.

Oh, my God!

I close my eyes, take a deep breath, smell him, and feel my blood rushing as my pulse pounds and I shiver because the coldness that he exudes instantly passes over me.

When I open my eyes again, *he* is standing in front of me. Mason.

And I am lost.

23. Sibling Love, Mason

Emilia

My heart is going to kill me. This is the moment, Mason, when you become *you* again. Because you're about to burst into my world again and take over everything that makes me who I am.

I can't believe what I see. You're wearing dark jeans with no holes and a white shirt, Mason. I've never seen you in a shirt before except at the funeral. And it looks so unbelievably good, the way it clings so tightly to your biceps. The sleeves are rolled up halfway and your tattoos stick out, just like Seth's. You're wearing an FBI vest, Mason. It almost qualifies as a uniform. Do you know men in uniform are sexy as hell? I'm sure you know that. Your hair is shorter and still so dark. I remember how many times I used to claw at it, how many times I used to stroke it when you were sleeping, and I remember how many times it tickled my cheek at night because we were intertwined. Whenever our consciousness switched off. I stare at you, your parents stare at us, and you stare at me. It seems like an eternity.

Your eyes are still the same eyes that I loved above all else. At the moment, brownish with a hint of green. Such hard eyes, Mason. Your chin and jaw seem almost a little more prominent, like you've lost weight in your face, but gained muscle mass. It's obvious you've been working out hard at night when you couldn't sleep. I know you can't sleep at night. I know how your naked back glistens when you do push-ups in your basement. I often sat naked in front of you with my legs spread and every time you sank down, you kissed me on my most intimate spot. Even now, I can feel your lips there, Mason, and you bound my hands because I wasn't allowed to help myself.

Suddenly, it feels 500 degrees hotter in the dining room.

Your high cheekbones look as if they were painted, Mason, and the way your dark beard dances across your clean tanned skin reminds me of how often I had held your face in my hands. So many times when you were desperate or out of control.

The dark rings under your eyes belong to you like your fiery temperament. I can see you are not well. I feel a bit of satisfaction.

"Mason!" Keaton thunders and we both flinch. "I told you a thousand times to wear your holster and not to carry your service weapon in your waistband!"

"And certainly not at the dinner table." Olivia points out.

Our eye contact is broken. My eyes shoot to your waistband – *oh, Mason* – where the gun is actually located.

Unobtrusively, I glance down a little further, I can't help it. Just because you're a shithead doesn't mean I find you ugly or repulsive. Just the opposite.

When I glance up again, you grin knowingly and slowly pull the gun out of your waistband. "Oh," you say. It's the first time in three fucking years I've heard your rough, now darker, hoarse voice, Mason, and it's pulling the rug out from under me. I swallow dryly, reach for my water, and gulp it down.

"You okay, baby?" Seth asks, eyeballing me with one raised eyebrow.

I nod quickly and you slam your gun on the table, making me wince. You put one hand on it and bend over so your right arm grazes me. I almost feel sick, Mason, when I smell your scent.

"Hi," you say confidently, stretching out your big hand to Seth. I can't stop staring at it as it floats between us. "I'm Mason. Emilia's..." You give me a quick snide glance before looking at Seth again. "*Brother*." The last word sounds like a swear word. Olivia presses her lips together, appearing a little disgusted.

Keaton shrugs in her direction and I swallow again. Hallelujah, a hundred degrees in the room — at least.

Seth seems confused and takes your hand. It's dick-swinging time, Mason. You squeeze and shake for what feels like 10 hours and your fingers are right under my nose. *God, please, make it stop.*

Why are you even here? Why did *I* come here?

When you let go, you fall into a chair on the other side of me at the huge round dining table so that you sit between me and your father. You put one arm around my back, Mason, and I know exactly why you are doing it. To claim your property again. I slide the chair toward Seth so that your arm falls off, which is why you're staring at me with your eyebrows raised. But I ignore you, Mason. You have no right to look at me like that.

"I didn't know you had a brother, babe," Seth says. Now he puts one arm around my back and I snuggle up to his side, one hand on his thigh, Mason.

"Oh, it's not really that important," I reply. Now you hear my voice for the first time in years and I see you clench the hand on the table next to your weapon.

"Get that damn thing off my dinner table," your mom says. Finally, she reaches out and gingerly picks it up and carries it out into the hall.

"So, Emilia," you say, staring at my hand on his thigh, his arm around my back, and his fingers stroking my bare skin.

I smile at you. "Yes, Mason?" and raise one eyebrow. You've never seen me do that before, I know. Your nostrils flare.

"How long are you staying?"

Olivia returns and I notice Keaton and her taking turns watching us. Keaton is ready to jump up if he has to, I can tell by the way he restrains himself.

"Only until Sunday."

"Uh-huh," you answer tensely. I love the way your brows lift, just like your chin. "And you?" Bored, you nod at Seth and slide your ass deeper into the chair. "So, you're my *sister's* boyfriend?"

I sigh. "We've been dating for six months. We met in college."

Seth laughs deeply and slides his ass in the chair like you. Seeing you two together rather scares me. You two are so much alike. "She hit my car in the parking lot and I didn't use her information for an insurance claim. I had to see her again. She was the most beautiful woman on campus." He's smiling mischievously. "And in all of New York."

You roll your eyes.

"What about you?" I ask cheerfully, digging my fingers into Seth's jeans. "Are you still with *Cherry*?" Olivia inhales sharply. She seems so tense, she even forgot to bring the dessert.

An anxious Keaton gives you a warning look. Seth holds me a little tighter as if he senses my anger and wants to hold me together. I reach for his fingers over my shoulder and interlock mine with his.

"I mean you were completely smitten with her. I thought you two were special. Forever."

You grow pale, Mason, the blood draining from your cheeks. I guess you didn't believe I'd mention her.

"Cherry." I hate the way that name sounds so special coming out of your mouth. "Cherry was only good for the summer, she bored me. She wanted the whole nine yards, so I sent her away. You know I don't want that, Emilia."

"Oh," I sigh. "So, you're still slumming, Mason?"

You shrug and throw one arm over the back of your chair. "Seems to run in the family, doesn't it?"

I hesitate and feel myself turning pale. Seth stiffens next to me and I swallow. How do you know, Mason, that I'm a slut? Were you stalking me? I stare at you, but you stay relaxed.

Not Seth.

"Did you really just say that to my girlfriend?" he asks in a dark and threatening voice that I've only heard in bed.

"I said that to *my sister*, that's a fact. Sam."

"Seth," I growl. "Are you stupid? Can't you remember a name?" Ohhh! Your eyes twinkle when I speak to you like that. Sibling love, Mason! You don't know me like this. You only know me as the intimidated girl who you locked in your basement. The girl who would do anything to keep you with her.

Well, I'm not anymore.

You completely disregarded my words. "So, are you making wedding plans yet?" You toss a cherry tomato from the salad on the table into your mouth. "Well, you do move quite quickly, don't you?"

I shrug. "Well, Mason." Your cheek muscle twitches, just like your father. How long has that been happening, Mason? You're becoming more and more like him. "Seth knows I was engaged and that I'm still in touch with my ex, that he helped me through a major crisis because of another man that I loved very much, and that we still see each other occasionally." I smile at Seth and he winks at me. "They even spoke on the phone when I wasn't there. They talked about me. But that's okay." I laugh.

Mason, I can see you're a ticking time bomb. Go crazy. Please. Expose yourself. I'm waiting for it.

You rest your chin on a fist and look at me, bored. "H'm," you say. I'm ready for the attack. One will follow. I know you,

Mason. “Well, I don’t know. I never understood what you saw in that fucker,” and my face reveals my astonishment. I didn’t see that coming.

“I don’t know either. I get up and start clearing the table because I can’t sit here looking at you one second longer. Your eyes follow my every move. I feel them as if you’re touching me.

Olivia helps until we move on to coffee.

“With caramel, right, baby?” I ask as I turn on the machine, turning to Seth, who is sitting in the living room talking to Keaton.

“Yep!” he yells. I turn around, stand on my toes, open the cabinet above me, and reach for the syrup. Wonderful, I feel your hard, hot, and extremely good smelling body behind me, pressing itself presumptuously close to me. You’re like a force of nature, Mason. Then you push my hair behind my ear, giving me goose bumps, before you bend your head slightly and whisper, “That you made me your brother, Emilia, opens completely new doors for me. I like it.” You reach for the syrup and set it in front of me. “By the way, you look hot.” You press your crotch against my ass for a second and let me feel how hot I make you. When you finally leave, I lean against the counter with both hands and gasp. Three minutes later, I’m still standing like this, your scent in my nose, as Seth’s body presses itself against me. I feel it immediately, I don’t have to turn around for that.

“Are you okay, baby?” he asks hoarsely. I turn my head to him.

“I feel a little sick,” I say. “And dizzy.”

He turns me around so that my tailbone presses against the counter and I can look into his face. "I could fuck it out of you," he whispers near my lips. "But your parents are here."

I laugh and breathe. Breathe you out of my system and pull Seth in. "Later, with pleasure, mister."

He grabs my chin and pulls me into a kiss. "You're hot when you make me coffee," he whispers. "You could do that more often naked."

I roll my eyes, kiss him, and grab the syrup. "My parents are here, Seth. Do you want to spoil me in front of them?"

He smiles and his ice-blue eyes sparkle playfully. "It's worth a try."

"How long is that coffee going to take?" you interrupt, growling, and I flinch.

Seth wraps his arm around me anyway. "It's almost ready," he says coolly and with that, he kisses me.

How about you, Mason? I think you're a little angry. Have you been listening to us? It can be fucking painful to see or hear something you don't want to see or hear, right?

24. Now You Are Mine, Emilia

Mason

Emilia, you have no idea the feeling I get when I track your phone, which I've been doing for the past few days. That's why I now know – you can't get anything out of Dad – where you live, where you get your coffee, where you like to eat, where your guy lives, and your therapist, Emilia. I have access to your phone now, *Emilia*, and I've seen what you do with Dr. Daniels. You're fucking him, Emilia. You've turned into such a bad girl. I don't even know what to do with you. It's not only Dr. Daniels, Emilia. You have half of New York stored in your phone and you send sick pictures to your Seeeeeth, *Emilia*. Just this morning, you corresponded with Dr. Daniels about how that last hour taught you so much and that you'd have to repeat it soon. And you sent him a picture. Of your tits. *You bitch.*

Okay, I admit, I got a little hard and just as mad when I saw that picture. When I tracked you down half an hour ago, you were with my parents, Emilia, and nobody told me. In fact, Dad made it clear that he and Mom were going away this weekend and that I shouldn't even bother getting my ass home for Sunday dinner. Since I've been living in the apartment you once lived in, I've been coming to Mom and Dad's every weekend for dinner. Mom's always delighted, Dad not so much. I mean, he already sees me at work all day long.

Naturally, I raced over to my parents immediately, Emilia. What a lucky coincidence that you are in Chicago right now as I prepare to go to New York to get what is mine. You.

I was involved in a shootout with the Italian mob, Emilia. When the bullets started flying, I didn't know if I was going to get out alive. That is the same feeling coursing through me as I drive to see my parents — and you. Adrenaline rushes so violently through my body, I can hardly breathe. I open all the windows because I am breaking out in a cold sweat. All my senses sharpen, like I'm about to go into a big fight, maybe even the fight of my life, as I stop behind a piss white jeep and get out. At that moment, Dad storms through the door like an angry bull, growling at me, "What are you doing here?" Dad's always on defense when it comes to you, Emilia. Like he's your father and I'm some sick fuck stalking you.

"I know she's here, Dad. Just let me see her."

He grows to his full height in front of me like he's trying to block my passage. "She's with her boyfriend, Mason, and he thinks we're her parents."

I frown. "What?"

"Don't ask. You're her brother if you won't stay out here, you fucking toad."

What the fuck, Emilia? But okay, this could be fun. I'm game.

I shrug and raise my hands. "Okay. So I'll be her brother. I can be whatever she wants."

Dad snorts. "I don't think so. But you've been seen. So go in, but one wrong word, and I'll grab you by the collar and throw you out again, understand?"

I roll my eyes. "Chill out, Dad."

Dad is funny today, Emilia. "If I could chill out, I would have one problem less." He looks at me meaningfully. With that, he goes back in and I watch him, confused until I finally understand what he meant.

My dad is such an ass.

I inhale deeply and smell you as I enter the kitchen before I actually see you, Emilia. There you sit, *holding* his hand. Your eyes are closed and he runs his nose over your cheek, Emilia. I will never get that image out of my head again. It's like a fucking déjà vu, except another guy is sitting at the table with you.

You seem different. And even more beautiful. I notice when you open your eyes and look at me, the expression in your ocean blue eyes is so much stronger and more confident than before. Your long black eyelashes are made up and even longer than before. Your skin is soft and tanned, your cheeks red, not as pale as before. Not so shy and much more feminine. Your cheekbones stand out and you painted your lips red, Emilia. I am lost when they smile at me. I just want to kiss them, hard and long.

Fuck, Emilia.

***

We're sitting in the living room. Dad is in the armchair where he always sits. You and the motherfucker are on the couch and you lean against him for *support*. Are you afraid of me, Emilia? Mom's in the other chair. I lean sideways next to Dad and place my forearm on his hard shoulder with my legs crossed at the ankles. He looks at me with a raised eyebrow as if I was out of my mind, but I'm used to it, Emilia. It just bounces off me.

You cross your legs. They are sun-kissed and smooth. I know you're smooth all over. Just thinking about it makes me a bit hard again, so I shift my weight so that my cock, that traitor, is hidden behind the back of the couch. You'll be unpacking it soon enough, baby.

I don't like the way your little hand is in his and I don't like the way he possessively puts his arm around you while he keeps an eye on me. I'm only your brother, Emilia.

"Remember when I lived in the basement?" I ask. "And we spent those days just bumming around, Emilia? Remember when we played cowboys and Indians and I tied you up?"

Uncertain, you glance at my father, searching for help and I feel him hit my arm with his shoulder.

"Or back when Grandma died, at the funeral! And we sat under the tree and *mourned*." You close your eyes, beaten.

Dad stiffens noticeably and I know he's about to slap me. Inconspicuously.

I've never seen you like this, Emilia. Because when you open your eyes again, there's something evil. You were everything, but never wicked. "And remember, Mason, that summer vacation when I caught you with your little whore by the jetty? It was a little gross." Completely flat, you look at me, Emilia. No expression on your face. No reaction. You're upsetting me.

"Remember that time on the train tracks when you got drunk and wanted to die, Emilia?" I ask harshly and Mom raises her eyebrows.

"That shows how obtuse you are," you reply, completely arrogant. "I was at a train station where trains no longer run since I wanted to gaze at the stars. That's what you do when you're drunk."

"Well," Seth says next to you. He appraises me. "You have a turbulent past behind you."

"Oh, if you only knew," I reply.

"Mason," you can hear my dad's threatening voice, "Get your mother a glass of water!"

I hesitate and glance at Mom, who looks irritated from one to the other. "Yes, Mason, get me a glass of water. Or a whole bottle from the basement!"

"Sure!" I shout. "Anything else?"

"Since you are asking, I'll take another martini with three green olives, Mason. Thanks!" Now you turn to the motherfucker. "Do you want anything, baby?"

"I'll take a beer if you have one, *bro*." Why does he emphasize the word *bro* so condescendingly, Emilia? That is my creation. You've caught yourself Mason 2.0, you realize that? Does that make me Riley in this story?

I'm like a fucking maid, getting everyone's fucking drinks while swearing to myself. Fuck, Emilia. Nothing is going according to plan. I wonder where that shy little girl is who didn't dare tell me she hates having her ass beaten because it reminds her too much of her dad. Yes, Emilia, not only did I stalk you, I read your file. His too by the way. I know everything now. All those disturbance reports, all those times you were in the hospital. All those times he beat the crap out of your mom and she claimed she fell. And yeah, I may feel a little crappy about all the shit I did to you, but you never complained. It was almost like you wanted me to. I wouldn't have done it otherwise, Emilia.

I now know all about your friend Bridget. And I know all about Riley's new life. He doesn't have a girlfriend because he's still waiting for you, Emilia. Are we both doomed to wait for the rest of our lives for you?

I know which Italian restaurant you order your pizza from, as well as the toppings. I got that out of Dad's black notebook. Actually, I only went to the academy and joined the FBI so I could have access to everything I needed to get *you* back.

After inspecting everything in my old basement, I go back up. My furniture is still exactly the way I left it. Only Mom uses the kitchen to store her supplies. I didn't want them to clear everything out, Emilia. This used to be our fucking basement and believe it or not, I care about it, even if I can't live here anymore because you're everywhere.

I go to the kitchen and watch you play *Happy Family* from there, Emilia. I know you never had one, so you clung to mine. That's okay, but not with that motherfucker, Emilia. I don't like it. I honestly don't.

I'll make your martini and skewer the olives. For a second, I think about spitting or pissing in his beer, but I don't.

When you get up to go to the bathroom with your cell phone ringing in your hand, I glance out of the corner of my eye to see if anyone is watching me. Of course, why would now be any different, and Dad flashes me his infamous look. He shakes his head in warning, but I just grin and follow you. I still hear him swearing, but then I grab your arm as you are about to enter the bathroom and drag you in. It is the most beautiful sound in the world when I close the door behind you and lock it.

"Now you are mine, baby."

25. Say It, Emilia

Emilia

Dammit, Mason!

I'm about to answer my phone when you grab my arm. I feel it right away. Only you touch me like that. You drag me into the bathroom, press me against the door, and lock it before giving me a burning look.

"*Now* you are mine, baby."

With that, you grab the still ringing phone from my hand and glance at the display as you lean against the door with the other — right next to my head. Stupidly, I stare at your lips because they're so close after all these years.

Your gaze slides from my phone to me and I quickly look into your eyes. You raise one eyebrow. "So, DILF Daniels? Should I answer it, Emilia? What does that even mean? DILF?"

I narrow my eyes. "Don't you dare, Mason," I hiss and reach for my phone. You grab it and press it against the wood, grinning like the devil himself as you press the green button and answer the phone with a drawn-out, "Heeelllooo?"

Shit.

I can't hear what he's saying, but your head's tilted. "No, Emilia will never come to your therapy sessions again. Yeah, it's Mason. Yeah, that's the one. She's indisposed at the moment, sorry." Now you laugh. "I answered her phone because she's handcuffed under me right now and I'm licking her tits."

"No!" I shout in the background. "That's not true, Will! I'll call you later, hang up!"

You laughingly take the phone from your ear and hand it to me. Just as I'm about to accept it, you open your fingers and drop it on the floor.

The screen shatters.

"Fuck, Mason," but you grab my wrists and press them against the door.

"Did you just try to push me away, Emilia?"

The anger inside me is not merely seething, it's boiling over. Who the hell do you think you are? "Get off me, Mason!"

Slowly, you press your body against me, every inch of you hugging my body so I can feel your six-pack, which is now unprotected because you removed your vest earlier.

I glare angrily at you. Your eyes are half-open, your gaze resting on my lips, which I open a crack for a deep breath. Breathe, that's the cure for you, Mason.

Suddenly you push a knee between my legs. Your muscular thigh is now right where it throbs so hot and longing.

Shit, Mason. Shit, Mason. Fuck, Mason. Shit! Shit, Mason!

"I'm not even thinking about it," you whisper roughly and continue staring at my lips. "I won't tell him who I really am or what I've done with you, Emilia, for one kiss."

And there it is again, Mason, blackmail. You want power over me. For a moment, I feel like the girl I was back then. Scared, excited, insecure, and intimidated by you, but turned on at the same time like never before. Your aura envelops me and it's as if we are somewhere else. Your fingers squeeze my wrists so tightly my skin burns. I keep breathing.

In. Out. In. Out. And with every breath I take, I smell you until I have a headache because you muddle my brain.

I said goodbye to that little girl. She's at peace now. Mason, I have spent nights crying, suffering, and dealing with this. Do you think you can look at me and make me weak again? Is that what you think?

For a while, I'll leave your illusion. I swallow and bat my eyelids. You enjoy it. Because you love to see me like this.

Then I slowly stand on my toes. You leave me so much room to maneuver that I can glide my lips gently over your closed mouth. Your grip around my hands grows even tighter and your leg muscles tense up.

I run the tip of my tongue over your lip and you growl hoarsely that vibrates deep in my abdomen.

"Oh, Mason," I whisper. Your eyes are as hazy as mine. Your lips open slightly and the tip of your tongue touches mine. I nudge it briefly and just as you're about to pounce on me with everything, I lift my knee and ram it in your balls.

You let go of me, gasping. "Fuck, Emilia!" You're crouching. I look down at you, like you always did to me, like a little worm.

"I wanted to do that three years ago," I say as I exit the bathroom.

***

I'm sitting cross-legged on your old bed, Mason. You may not live here anymore, but you're everywhere. It's the middle of the night, a little after 2:00 our time. I didn't want to come down here, but I was lying upstairs in your guestroom with Seth in bed, not sleeping. Seeing you today and being here in your world brings back a time I never wanted to think about again.

Such dark times and such intense moments.

I admit it wasn't all bad between us. I noticed that when the anger subsided. Still, one question was never really answered: Why, Mason?

I'm glad it happened the way it did or I wouldn't have grown. But I don't understand why you did it to me. We were happy by our standards. At least, I was, but I don't believe you were.

The moment I entered this house today and you became you again in my mind, I knew wasn't as finished with you as I thought. I don't know if I can ever truly be finished with you, Mason Rush — you burrowed under my skin too deep. The memories alone are so vivid I can almost see us standing in front of this bed, dancing together. So banal yet so intoxicating, all-consuming, and almost surreal.

It cost me a lot to turn you down today because the line between the old and the new Emilia is narrowing with you. You're confusing me.

I fall onto my back – on this bed where we did so many things – and stretch out my arms. Through my headphones, our song echoes directly into my brain. If I concentrate, Mason, I still smell the faint scent of weed and feel you bending over me, letting your lips move over my jaw and neck to this song. I feel you pressing your hips against me and whispering in my ear how hot you think I am. How you stroke my hair while I lie on your chest and stare out the window into your garden. Just for the hell of it.

If I concentrate, I see all those strange faces in here and your dark eyes that follow me wherever I go. Under my fingertips, I still feel your skin as I stroke your chest and taste the salty flavor on my tongue as I lick across your throat. I feel your coarse fingers on my bottom, on my breasts, and on my neck. And I still hear you desperately shouting "I love you" after me. Goose bumps. I flip over on my stomach and fold my arms under my face, close my eyes, and listen to the music while my thoughts wander.

It was so much sex. Nothing else. We either fucked or remained silent. Everything I know about you, I know because I watch you 24 hours a day and because I pestered your mother with questions. I know you hate lasagna because once when you were seven, it was spoiled and you hung out all night in the bathroom. When you eat it, you eat it carefully and slowly. I know when you were 10, you fell out of the weeping willow and broke your arm. I know you participate in underground fights to feel something because, otherwise, you feel nothing but indifference. That must be tough, Mason. But you know what I didn't know, Mason? That you had a great love. I didn't know there was someone who could rip you right out of my hands just by looking at you. I wish you had told me that before. I wish you had told me *anything*. But you didn't. You never tried to find out anything about me either. You didn't care about my wants or what I like and dislike. I bet you didn't even know that I like to read and love photography. All that mattered to you was how I felt, the ways you could fuck me, and what I'd let you do to me. Seth already knows more about me now than you ever did. And I don't even love him.

If I did, I wouldn't cheat on him. And so indiscriminately. If I did, I wouldn't be down here right now thinking about you – in your basement, in your darkness – wishing it would devour me again.

As if you heard me, Mason, I sense your presence in the room. I know you're here, I don't have to turn around. My heart beats faster and my stomach tingles like crazy. I don't move. Suddenly, the mattress gives way as you sit on the edge. I have to pull myself together, to not purr like a cat when your fingertips touch my scalp. Because I know it's you, Mason. Nobody touches me like that and nobody feels that intense. I bite my lip as your fingers run through my hair. You love my hair even though it's not as long as it used to be even if you always said otherwise. With one hand, you stroke my upper back slowly over my shirt, so slowly, across my entire back to my tailbone. Goose bumps follow. Then suddenly, a sweet, familiar, thick cloud of smoke wafts around me because you blow it directly into my face, as always. I inhale deeply, which I would never have done before, and feel you bend over me, resting your arms to the left and right of my shoulders. You pull off my headphones and whisper the lyrics of our song into my ear with your husky voice.

"Bring your love, baby, I could bring my shame. Bring the drugs, baby, I could bring my pain. I got my heart right here. I got my scars right here."

Your breath grazes my neck and I shiver all over as you lay behind me and pull me by the hips. Your forehead is leaning against the back of my head and the joint is burning between your fingers. I take your hand and bring the joint to my lips. You stiffen briefly, but eventually, allow to me take a deep drag and when I exhale, I let my head fall onto your shoulder. As you watch how I exhale the smoke over my shoulder into *your* face for the first time, you growl with pleasure.

You wear *no* shirt, Mason, I *only* wear a shirt and panties. I lower my head again and you run the tip of your nose over my neck, sending goose bumps scurrying over my body again. Then I hear you inhale deeply.

I don't know what's happening here, Mason.

I honestly believed I was over you. But I'm falling for you all over again and I hate it. I take the joint from you and you allow me to smoke as you slide your hand up my thigh. Shit, Mason, what are we doing? But I can't stop you; I can't, this moment here is so magical. I'm back in another world, *your* world, and I love your world a little right now.

From there, your fingers slowly wander upward under my oversized t-shirt. Your fingertips move over the tender skin of my belly and I twitch a little. You have never touched me like this before. I'm melting. Your breath continues caressing my neck and as I hit the joint again, everything in my head blurs, as if wrapped in cotton. Your fingers continue upward, Mason, and I'm not stopping you. I've never stopped you before except that one horrible day and this afternoon. My skin contracts as your fingertips arrive under my breasts. You gently follow the contour before you grab it and run your thumb over my nipple. A deep groan escapes me. The joint is long gone and falls out of my hand.

I don't dare turn around and look at you, Mason, because then it becomes real. The song leaks out of my earphones next to us and envelops us like a blanket. Your hand slips out of my shirt. Gently, your fingertips stroke my arm before you grab my shoulder firmly and flip me onto my back. I quickly squeeze my eyes shut. I feel your thumb stroking my lips and then my chin and neck. When I throw my head back, it continues down my throat and over my collarbone where you feel my pulse.

I feel your burning gaze and your hardness against my thigh. You give to me without asking for anything. You take my hand – gently and carefully, not roughly – and place it on your warm smooth chest, right where your heart beats. And, Mason, it beats fast. I abruptly open my eyes and stare straight into your eyes. Your soft, soft eyes. A longing burns in them that I perceive in myself. Then you place one hand half on my cheek and half on my neck. It is so big, giving me such a feeling of security with just a single touch.

"I knew I'd find you here," you say softly. I nestle against you because I need to feel you, but take my eyes off you. It's too much. I lower my eyes and watch my hand on your chest. With my index finger, I delicately follow the new tattoos that have been added. You never told me what your Maori tattoos mean, but somehow I love the new ones.

"That's our story you're touching right now, Emilia." Your voice is so hoarse when you say that and my gaze shoots upward. There's nothing but honesty and desire in your eyes. Again, I stare at your chest where mystical symbols combine to form a whole. You take my hand and place it on some of the ink lines.

"This is when I first saw you." My heart stops and I glance up, then down again. You continue to run my hand over your chest, sideways to your upper ribs. "This is when we kissed for the first time." And then our hands go down. "This is where I felt you for the first time." I can't breathe, Mason, I can't believe it. "And this is..." You're going further down. "I've decided I'll never let you go again." There's more — beyond the base of your stomach muscles. "This is where I noticed how broken you were and this is where I took advantage of it." We slide over your side, further down. "Here, I knew I could never breathe again without you. And here, I lost everything I needed to breathe." Breathless, my gaze shoots up to your eyes, in which lies a tortured expression you've never looked at me with before. You lean on your elbow over me — your weight on me, your expression so penetrating. Your lips are moist and slightly open and you stare at my face for a while. Then you lower your lips to the line of my jaw and run them to the hollow under my ear.

I feel your breath there. "I'm sorry, baby. So sorry," you whisper. I close my eyes because they fill with tears. You continue kissing my neck, so soft, so tender, so apologetic; you apologize to my whole body with everything you are and everything that makes you who you are. My fingers tremble and I claw the blanket beneath me so that I don't lift them to pull you to me and never let you go.

I can't do that, Mason; I can never trust you again and I can never let you back into my perfect life.

You're staring in my eyes again. "You're never going to forgive me, are you?"

"You ripped my heart from my chest when you slept with her and I still haven't gotten it back... I'm as numb and empty as you are now," I whisper and stroke your silky hair. You close your eyes and let your head sink, absorbing my touch like a sponge until I drop my hand again.

"You broke me, Mason. And it's never going to be the same again." You look at me. Your eyes are so determined when you say, "It's not meant to be, Emilia. I know what I did to you. I know I kept you small because I knew one wrong move from me and you'd be gone. Because you're too good for me." Shit, those are exactly the words I wish I'd used. Hearing them now makes everything in me soften. I gaze into your eyes and when you bend down to me, I don't fight back. Instead, I lean towards you. *Just once*, I think to myself. *Just once, it can't hurt to feel your lips to remind me of what it was like*.

When our mouths meet, it's like a hurricane that churns up everything inside me. To feel your taste in my mouth, your tongue against mine, and to suck up your soft hoarse moans. I didn't know how much I was longing for it. I suppressed it with all my might and now that you are so close to me again, when I have a chance to get you back, I want to grab it with both hands and run at the same time. We kiss slowly and lazily, so sensuously that every single fiber of my being tingles and comes to life again. As if I've been in a deep slumber for the last three years, like a princess in a fairy tale, until you wake me up.

You, my weed-smelling, cursing, totally fucked-up prince of darkness.

I belong to you — and that's the curse I've suffered from the moment I first saw you.

You pull my lip between your teeth and the gentle bite you give me goes straight between my legs. Then you lean your forehead against mine. That's our thing, Mason, and it's also our thing that I run my fingers through your hair now and we calm our breath.

"Tell me you love me," you whisper. You sound so broken.

I won't say anything.

I can't.

That little part of my heart where I locked you away, Mason, just filled my whole being again and it's so dangerous.

"Tell me, Emilia!" You kiss my cheek. You've never done that before, Mason.

I remain silent.

You stroke my jaw with your lips.

"Say it."

I remain silent even as your mouth wanders across my throat and my racing pulse. "Say it."

I can't, I think.

You slide down me and pull up my shirt, staring into my eyes so piercingly. I know I'll never forget that look again. The way you kneel before me, your eyes so penetrating, demanding, full of emotion. "Say it, Emilia." You kiss my sensitive skin directly above my panties and my pelvis twitches. "Say it, Emilia," you whisper and stroke upward to my bellybutton with your nose. You kiss it and whisper to me, "Say it."

...and you continue to stroke upward, inhaling the scent of my skin deeply. Your eyes close briefly, allowing me to admire your lashes. They are so long and beautiful.

Three years of work, Mason.

It only took you an hour to ruin everything.

To make me forget everything but you.

Oh, my God.

"Say it!" I want to, but my broken heart forbids me to make a sound. You've reached the bottom of my chest now. Your breath runs hot upon my skin. You kiss the very spot where my heart beats. I can't help it and I grab your hair with one hand and run my fingernails over your scalp. Your expression invites me to say it, but my mouth remains silent.

"Admit it," you whisper, "that no man you have had so far could unleash in you what I have unleashed in you. "Admit that no one will ever take your breath away as I do, Emilia." You bite the swelling of my breast lightly and my breath stops. I let my eyes close as you glide your stubble over my sensitive skin straight to my nipple. "Say you're mine, Emilia," you whisper.

I bite my lip and raise my torso.

You put your ear to my chest right where my heart beats. I open my eyes and I run my hand through your hair and whisper, "I can't, Mason," and you say, "I know."

"You broke me, Mason." And then, lost in thought, you caress my arm.

"I know."

"And it will never be the same again."

"I know."

26. I Do Not Care Who You Were, Emilia

Emilia

My phone displays 5:03 a.m. upon waking from an extremely deep yet too short sleep. At once, I become aware of my surroundings and who is spooning me with his arm tightly wrapped around my stomach. I glance down at your hand pressing against me. I smell you and feel your body's warmth and your calm breathing against my neck. Gently, I grab your hand, bring it to my face, and kiss your palm before lifting it up and sliding out from under your arm. You frown. You don't like me slipping away so easily even when you are sleeping. As I watch you lying there so relaxed, I smile slightly. It is difficult to leave you even though I know we don't stand a chance. Last night was magical and unique. It must have been. Taking a deep breath, I get up and go upstairs, but my heart stays behind with you in bed.

Seth is still sound asleep when I slip back into our bed. There would have been enough time to take a shower, but there was no sex. Besides, I simply refuse to wash your smell off me. It is all I have left from last night. Venus jumps up on the bed, obviously happy I'm back, and almost wakes up Seth. I order her to lie down next to the bed and scratch her fuzzy head as I watch the day breaking out the window.

I've spent many times like this with Riley during our brief time before New York, where I experienced the emotions I do now.

I wonder what Dr. Daniels would say, probably nothing good. I know I won't be able to sleep even though I can barely keep my eyes open. I was only in your arms for two hours but I am still tired. As Seth snuggles up closer and hums contently, I finally close my eyes. I feel like I'm cheating as he presses against me and I give in, kiss him, and let him do all those things to me that I actually want someone else to do.

***

We're at the breakfast table, Mason. Your mother has outdone herself setting the table. She even made freshly squeezed orange juice, which I love her for. I no longer have such a difficult time addressing your parents as Mom and Dad. Somehow, it sounds natural, like it has always been that way.

The sun has long since risen and illuminates everything with its rays. I feel different than last night, like another person. Like my old self stayed in the basement and only the new Emilia made it upstairs. Seth is freshly showered and smells wonderful. He and Olivia are laughing about something. Keaton sits across from them and stares reproachfully at me with raised eyebrows, Mason. Now I know how you always feel. Nervously, I glance around the table but always return to his too knowing eyes. I should ask if he still has the cameras up, if so, I'm really fucked, Mason.

Shit, Mason.

Despite everything, I'm still hungry. But I'm also dead tired and yawn loudly as I pour maple syrup over my pancakes.

"You didn't have a restful night, baby?" Seth asks. Keaton tilts his head to the other side.

"I don't know, there's something about this house. I never get a good night's sleep here. It's always been that way, right, *Dad*?" I mutter irritably and Keaton raises an eyebrow.

"U-huh, what else could it be, Emilia?"

I turn bright red and take a sip of orange juice.

"Well, I slept soundly." Olivia's face is beaming. I've seen that glow before. Keaton turns to her and his other eyebrow shoots up. I find him pretty smug right now and roll my eyes.

It seems *my* parents actually had sex, Mason.

Yawning, Seth stretches and his shirt slides up to expose part of his abdomen. "I had a great night's sleep," he says just as the front door slams shut and I cringe. Olivia immediately looks at Keaton and asks, "Who's that?"

He sighs. "It must be the toad, he spent the night in the basement," and gives her a meaningful look. Her eyes widen and fly to me as I poke at my pancakes, avoiding eye contact.

You shuffle into the room and without a word, loudly pull back the chair next to me, and plop down into it. You are only wearing hip-hugging sweatpants, Mason, even though you know what your naked torso does to me. Especially now that I know what your tattoos stand for, *Mason*. Well, at least in part. You pour coffee into your cup and glance around the table.

"What?" you ask, confused as everyone but me stares at you.

"You haven't spent a night in the basement in ages, so why now? You have an apartment overlooking the rooftops of Chicago," Keaton says.

"Yesterday, I was in the neighborhood and didn't feel like driving all the way back."

"Where were you?"

"At Jenny's."

"Who's Jenny?"

"Dad, save the interrogation for work."

Keaton smiles diabolically. "I was merely trying to have a little chat with my son.

"Well, your son is not in the mood for chatting with *you*, Dad. Let me enjoy a cup of coffee first."

"God help us," Olivia whispers and goes to the refrigerator for a bottle of bubbly, as if booze will remedy the situation.

"Anyone a glass of champagne?" she asks.

"Yeah, good idea, Oh...uh, thanks, Mom!" I quickly correct myself. I skillfully ignore your anger glare as Olivia mixes champagne with my orange juice. We toast and deliberately empty our glasses. Keaton observes us with a dry expression. Seth frowns.

"Is everything okay, baby?" He asks me that quite often, Mason. Do I seem that uneasy?

"H'm," I utter with my lips pressed together and hold out my glass out to Olivia.

"Maybe you shouldn't drink so much this early in the morning," you say.

"Maybe you shouldn't talk so much this early in the morning!" Oh, oh, I can tell by your eyes what you'd like to do to me right now. Though you're faced with a dilemma, I'm no longer yours so you can't. *Boo-hoo!* Besides, I'm no longer afraid of you, Mason. Now, in daylight, everything is so much clearer. Last night, I had a moment of weakness, which has passed. I'm already a little tipsy, so today should turn out to be a fun day.

"Let's spend the day by the pool, okay, baby?" Seth asks. "Unless you want to go downtown or somewhere else."

I purposefully turn to him, my back to you, Mason. "The pool sounds great!" I sigh and give him a quick kiss.

I feel his smile against my lips and your piercing look on my back.

Oh, Mason, just wait and see the punishment I can dish out.

"We have to go to the market. Can you manage without us?" Olivia asks and Keaton warily eyes Mason.

"I don't know, baby, maybe we should stick around or perhaps, take *it* with us."

"Obviously, I can manage, old man. I'm 28, so go to your stupid old folks market!" you hiss and I grin faintly. Your dad does not look at all pleased.

***

A little later, I wear a black bandeau bikini top that squeezes my breasts together and matching bottoms that barely cover my ass cheeks. My outfit drives Seth crazy just like his abs do me as we sit comfortably on the soft poolside deck chairs.

I straddle Seth's cute little ass and massage his back with sun lotion.

"Oh, fuck, that feels good!" he murmurs with his head down in between his muscular arms as I firmly knead his skin. I like it when he moans, Mason.

"Your brother is a little full of himself, isn't he?" he asks.

"My brother?" I reply, completely confused before I remember who he means. "Oh, yeah, he's a dick. Can't say we keep in touch. We actually have had no contact whatsoever during the last three years I've lived in New York."

"Why haven't you been in touch?"

"He was fucking with a girl I really liked and I couldn't stand seeing her suffer, so I didn't want to see him."

I rise slightly as he turns around to lie on his back. Oh, abs alert... Seth props himself up on his elbows and gives me a questioning look. "Who was she?"

"What does it matter? You wouldn't know her anyway." To distract him, I stroke his chest with both hands as I slide forward until my lips meet his. "Don't we have better things to do?"

Seth remains totally unfazed. "I just realized how little I know about you."

"I introduced you to my parents. You are in the house I grew up in. Isn't that enough?"

"I don't see you in any pictures." Perplexed, he stares at me. "Your mother is gorgeous, but you don't look like her or your dad. Not one bit, quite unlike your brother. He is the spitting image of your dad. So, what's going on here, Emilia?" He sits up, puts his hands around my waist, and pulls me closer. "Whatever sick game you're playing, you can tell me. Believe me, I've seen some really sick shit in my life."

"I'm adopted," I squeal since nothing else comes to me. Then again, in a way, I am *adopted*. "They're not my real parents and he is not my real brother. The other boy you see in the pictures isn't either."

"Aha, that explains it. And you had a thing with that guy, right?" His expression is intense.

I swallow. "Is it that obvious?"

"He behaves like a Neanderthal defending his cave."

"Yeah…we had a thing," I come clean as it is hard to deny.

"For how long?"

"Too long."

"And, what did you two have?" he asks stiffly.

"Sex."

"And, how long did that go on?" he asks.

"For quite some time."

"Emilia, please, why can't you be honest with me?"

"I loved him," I say resignedly and lower my eyes. He lifts my chin and flashes his eyes angrily, Mason, just like you do.

"Next time, be straight with me from the start," Seth replies calmly.

"I don't like talking about it since it ended ugly and I was a different person back then."

"I don't care who you were, what matters to me is who you are now." I smile shakily. "You're *my* girl," he says and leans in for a kiss.

27. Do Not Wait For Me, Mason

Mason

Emilia, you're *my* girl. I heard every fucking word you said. You said you *loved* me, Emilia. That's past tense, but we are not finished, baby. We'll never be finished.

Now you're on the deck, sitting on Mason 2.0's lap, making out. I bet he has a boner of a lifetime.

Fuck, Emilia!

I'm about to end you two and beat the crap out of him, preferably with my gun. Too bad Dad confiscated it for the duration of my stay. He always overreacts. I would have merely stuck the barrel in his mouth or pressed it against his head. I think I have to resort to other means with you, Emilia, though I don't know anything but...violence and more violence.

Since last night, I want you even more. You weren't just sexy, you were everything to me. Everything a man could want. I only came to the basement because I sensed you down there. I mean, I know you, regardless that you think otherwise. And there you were, lying on my bed, illuminated by the moonlight. It was a sign, Emilia.

Emilia, I don't know how to react right now. Naturally, the FBI trained me to control my impulses, so I run the exercise through my head to restrain myself. Now I know how you must have felt when you saw me with Cherry, Emilia, and how it must have broken your heart. He lifts you up and carries you into the water as he continues to kiss you, Emilia. You have your legs wrapped around his hips and your fingers grasp his hair. In the water, he presses you against the pool wall and your head falls back as you moan, Emilia. The tip of your hair touches the water and... Shit, is he fucking you right now or what?

I clench one hand and press it against the window. I wish I'd told my father to lock me up, Emilia, I mean really, I'm about to freak out. His hands don't belong on your body and yours don't belong on him. You're moaning. I can hear you. The window is open, Emilia. Are you crazy? Now he pulls your bikini down and you smile wickedly at him. *Naughtily*, Emilia. Since when do you do that? I'm struggling to restrain myself as he bends forward and takes your nipple in his mouth.

I hate him, Emilia.

Oh, he will die, I decide soberly.

It was different with Riley because he's not like me. Not the way you needed him to be. *He*, however, is in every way Mason 2.0 or he would not be fucking you in the pool during the day with me around. And I'm sure he's aware I'm nearby.

That is also something *I* would do, Emilia. Now he lifts you up with one arm, and your face shows your tension as he lowers you onto him. He leans his forehead against your neck as you close your eyes and groan, probably because he's all the way inside you.

I can't breathe, Emilia, as you clearly move and the water keeps spilling over the edge of the pool.

Are you trying to provoke me, Emilia? It's working. I can honestly say that nowadays, I am no longer so easily upset, but right now, I'm incredibly worked up and, before I can stop myself, I step out the door. My hands clench as I approach the pool. You open your eyes and look at me over his shoulder. You act shocked and for a brief moment, I see that familiar panic in your eyes as you press your lips together. I freeze when you lift a finger and imperceptibly shake your head while eyeing me sternly.

The only thing I can do is stand there staring back. You used to be afraid of me in this state, but now you snap your fingers and I obey as if I were Missy and forget what I was doing. My pulse races and I flex my hands into fists. My breathing is labored yet it feels as if I am not getting get any air. You've wrapped an arm around his shoulders and your dark lust-filled gaze is fixed on me as if you're watching a snake that's about to strike at any moment. But I can't, Emilia, I can't hold back, not with you, and you know that.

So, I snap out of it and continue on my way when I see you push away from him, and I stop. Seth seems confused and gasps something like, "What the fuck, baby!" You ignore him, climb out of the pool, and run right past me into the house.

Seth turns to me confused and I growl, "Fuck her again anywhere near me and it'll be your last fuck!"

He gets out of the pool, every muscle of his flexing. "What do you want from me, you bastard?"

"You heard me right!" He's actually approaching me, Emilia. He must not know who he's dealing with. I briefly consider how you would react if I seriously hurt him and cannot come up with anything. When the pissant is only three steps from me, you step quickly between us. The world stops for a second because his arm is already in motion. I barely have enough time to push you out of the way of the uppercut that was meant for me.

Fuck!

Now he's dead!

I'm going for him.

"Mason!" you yell. "Stop it! Now!" Oh, Emilia, I don't think so. Why are you yelling back there anyway? Like I'd stop now! I've just begun. I get in three punches to his jaw before he hits my nose. It's already crooked so it doesn't matter, Emilia. I no longer feel the pain. We fall into the pool. I end up with the upper hand and push his ugly mug under the water.

"Mason!" you yell. "If you don't stop it this instant, I swear, I'll go home, and you'll never see me again. Never!" I refused to respond, it's not like I can. Instead, I push even harder because once I stop, I've lost anyway.

"Mason!" Your voice is louder and panicking. Suddenly, you jump in the water and pull on my arm.

"Let go of him!" I don't play along.

"*Mason, I love you*!" you yell and I abruptly relax my hands. I turn my head and look at you. Did you just say that?

Nevertheless, you move toward him without paying attention to me. He gasps when he breaks the surface. Your face is streaming with tears as you hold his cheeks. It seems I no longer exist. I snort wildly as I stare at you. Blood drips into the water and mixes with the clear blue liquid.

Fuck!

As you help him out of the water, you give me a hate-filled look.

***

Emilia

Seth and I are in the guestroom where I bandage his wound. By now, I'm pretty good at it, Mason, thanks to you. Seth is quiet, visibly tense, and extremely pissed off. I know he would love to take off for home right now if he wasn't so weak from almost being choked to death. After last night, I need to be close to Seth. I'm trying again to get you out of my system, Mason, but you're not making it easy.

The moment he said those words to me and showed me how much interest he has in who I am now, not caring who I was, I was blown away. It was a beautiful moment that I enjoyed without thinking — and that was stupid.

I should have known you'd be spying on us.

Foreseen your reaction.

I'm not you, Mason, I don't do it to hurt others, I do it to hurt or heal myself.

"Let me get you some more ice, baby!" I say to Seth. I am about to leave when he grabs my arm and stops me.

Looking at his beaten face hurts me. "What was that about, Emilia?" he asks softly, so calm and composed. "Is there still something going on between you two?"

I shake my head vigorously. "No!"

"Is he the ex you keep talking about? The one who betrayed you and whose name shouldn't be said out loud?" He sounds exhausted.

I nod once.

"Why did you tell him you love him?" he asks and I feel the blood draining from my cheeks. At the time, I thought he couldn't hear me since he was under water. Okay, I admit, the words involuntarily shot out of me. The only thing I intended to do was to distract you from killing him.

Shit!

"Because I knew it's what he wanted to hear. Because I knew he was about to kill you and I needed to distract him, Seth."

"Why would he want to hear that from you? Are you two finished or not?"

"We are finished, though he might believe otherwise."

"Emilia, if you cheat on me with him, I'll fuck the both of you. I'm not someone who puts up with that." *Shit*! I swallow because it was less than a week ago that I cheated on him with Will. Not to mention the thing with Mason in the basement — though that had nothing do to with sex. "Did you cheat on your ex with him?" The glare in his eyes scares me, Mason. I don't know whether to lie or be truthful, whether to placate him or clear my conscience.

I have to ask Will about that.

But Seth wants an answer now!

Shit!

"Your silence speaks volumes, Emilia." He abruptly pulls me close and spins me around so I'm lying on the bed with him on top of me.

"Last night, I noticed you were missing from the bed, if it happens again, I'll come looking for you. Did you fuck him?"

"No!" I cry out immediately. He stares into my eyes. I cannot breathe.

"What happened, Emilia? Something had to have happened?"

"There was no sex. We just talked about old times and I fell asleep." He studies me for a few seconds before his face relaxes.

"That won't happen again," he states harshly and rolls off me.

***

Tonight, I lie next to him, wide-awake, barely daring to breathe. Wow, Dr. Daniels was right. I always go for the same type of man. Still do. I thought by now I had that under control, was over it, but Seth really doesn't look like he's in the mood to be messed with. I'd love to talk to you, simply talk, but I'm too afraid to leave the room.

The neon-red digits of my clock read 2:00 when the door to my room opens quietly.

Oh, my God!

A quick glance next to me confirms that Seth is still breathing quietly. He puts his arm around me, Mason – firmly – and pulls me against his stomach as you enter the room.

I can't get away, Mason, I let you know with a look and a shake of my head.

You raise one eyebrow and nod toward the door.

I shake my head again.

You press your lips together and your nostrils flare. I know I must obey or you might render him unconscious in his sleep or whatever. So I turn to Seth and breathe right in his face because I know for a fact he doesn't like that. As I expected, a few seconds later, he rolls onto his other side, grumbling softly and clutching his pillow. I get up quickly. You regard me approvingly as I shove you out of the room and gently shut the door behind us.

"Fuck, Mason, what do you want?" I whisper.

"What's wrong with you, Emilia? I've been waiting for you. It's two o'clock."

"I don't recall promising to visit you in your basement every night, did I?" I whisper as I drag you away from the door toward the stairs.

"Why are you freaked out, Emilia?" You eye me questioningly and grab my arm so I can't escape you.

"Just leave me alone!" I try to break away and you grab my chin.

"What's the matter?"

"If he sees us...please, let go of me. I want to get back to bed, to him!"

"What would happen if he saw us together?"

"He'd fuck us both. So, just let me go."

"What?" You look at me dumbfounded.

"He said he would find out. Now, please, let go of me, Mason!"

"Did that bastard threaten you?" I sigh and run my free hand over my forehead and then through my hair.

"Not directly," I say faintly and flinch as your grip tightens. "Let go of me, Mason," I demand more forcefully. "You're hurting me!" You immediately take your hands off me as if you burned yourself. I'm surprised, in the old days, you would have never done that.

"I want you to leave that fucker. He's dangerous! I see it in his eyes."

"I see the same in your eyes. Are you for real? It takes a madman to recognize another madman."

"I love you, he doesn't. He merely regards you as a possession." I laugh harshly and try to suppress the emotions your words trigger. So far, you've told me twice — always during extreme situations. However, today, it spills from your lips so naturally, as if it is the most normal thing in the world and it makes my heart swell to about twice its size.

"You even said you love me, Emilia."

Shit, I think.

"Maybe I want to be possessed instead of loved." Maybe I also want to possess someone instead of love. Love is complicated and always comes with pain. I only said that to distract you, make you stop. You were like an attack dog and I had to distract you."

"You don't believe that, Emilia." You put your hands on my cheeks and push me against the cold wall. "You love me and I love you. That's the truth, no matter what I've done to you or vice versa — I won't allow anyone but me to possess you."

"I'd love to give in to you, Mason, but I can't. I always see the same images when I look into your eyes and every time we're together, you pull me down into the darkness. I don't want to give up on my life, Mason. You bring out traits in me that I don't want, that I've worked hard to get rid of. So, if you love me half as much as you claim, then let me go before you break me." You lean your forehead against mine and we close our eyes.

"I can't, Emilia. I've tried, I've tried for quite some time. But you are the first thing I think about each morning and you are the reason I cannot sleep properly at night. I just can't let you go; I'm too selfish, I need you." Your hands move from my cheeks to my neck, where your thumbs lift my chin so that I look at you.

"I consider you mine and that will never change. And I fight for what's mine, Emilia." You kiss me briefly, too briefly. "If he threatens you again, you call me immediately, understand?" you demand. All I can do is nod as I'm unable to breathe or anything else.

Abruptly, you turn and walk away.

Not following you is difficult. I know you're expecting me to; you probably will wait for the rest of the night.

But I won't come.

28. *Why Do I Love You, Emilia*

Mason

You fucked my world, Emilia, because you didn't come to my basement last night. Until six this morning, I lay there thinking about how close you were. I should've just stormed into that room and grabbed you, but maybe I should start respecting your will a bit. As far as you're concerned, Emilia, there's only one rule: Nobody fucks with my girl. Even when you're not with me, I want to know you're okay. And that crazy guy upstairs is as unpredictable as I am and because he doesn't love you, I don't trust him.

I would do anything to go back in time and erase all the times I hurt you, but he's going to hurt you more than I did and he's not going to apologize, he's not going to feel remorse, and he's not going to hold back one bit because he's a psychopath. I don't like that.

I like the fact he's so hardened even less, you don't even notice at first glance. Those are the most dangerous ones, Emilia. But I've seen the way my father looks at him and I know he knows it. My dad has a nose for that stuff, he merely needs to have a few words with someone and he already knows.

I still read Dad's old journal once in a while. He told me to give it back, but I didn't, and he never asked for it again.

Do you know my mom is the only one who can control the monster inside him, Emilia? The monster that he passed on to me.

Do you know that my dad would kill my mom if she wasn't his?

She's either with him or she's not with anyone.

Do you know why he's been so quiet over the years? Because my mom fought him every day until she tamed that monster.

Emilia, he locked her in a basement — and I hate him a little for that. But she still didn't leave him.

He broke her, then repaired her — and still she stayed with him.

There were so many chances to leave, but she never took advantage of any of them. Do you know my dad spent his entire time – when she didn't know him – investigating and spying on her? Yet, she went back to him when she found out — voluntarily!

He loves her so much that he punched me, his own son, in the face for accidentally hurting her. She is sacred to him and he has never stopped loving her, no matter what she did.

I think that's how I feel about you.

I think that's true love.

And I think I fucked it up.

I didn't go into it the way my father did because I can't control myself the way he can. After all, I'm much younger and angrier. It's like his monster inside me is twice as strong. And that's why, no matter how much he beats me, he never lets go of me. No matter how much shit I've done.

He knows how I feel.

He knows what I'm willing to do for the people I love. And that's what he's afraid of. And so am I.

I get up without a second of sleep. It's 9:30 in the morning and I hear footsteps overhead. I've forgotten what it's like. It used to be normal for me. I fell asleep to my father's steps when he went to work and woke up to my mother's steps when she came home in the afternoon. And all night long, I waited for your steps, baby.

I hear voices outside and the front door slams.

"Call me and visit more often, Emilia," my mom says. Even hearing your name fucks me up. I force myself to stay down here because I don't know if I can stand seeing you leave with another man. I might break down — as I did with Riley. I can feel Dad's tension all the way down here. He is waiting for me to appear. But I light a joint, sit by the window, just enough to be seen in the shadows, and wait.

"If anything happens, call me, anything at all, anytime, and call only me, no one else," my dad says. He loves you a bit, Emilia, and I love that. It's not easy to penetrate his heart, but once you do, you stay in it forever.

"I will," you answer my father. You sound so fucking broken and I hate that. It is not right that you are leaving.

Your place is here – with me and my family – and I involuntarily move.

Fuck!

I'm already on my way out.

I hear the car door slam, Emilia, and I know I'm late again because when I get to the top, you're driving off.

"Shit!" I hiss and run my fingers through my hair as I watch the white Jeep grow smaller and smaller. Your scent is still in the air.

Shit!

I hate to see you go every time, first with Riley, then at that fucking beach house, and now again. Is it ever going to stop? But I know this time I'm going to follow you.

A heavy hand lands on my bare shoulder and I know it's my father without turning around.

"Still?" he asks.

"Always," and I know, Emilia, that's what he *always* used to say to my mom.

We take a deep breath.

"I have to go to New York, Dad."

"Same girl, different guy, same city — you must really love her."

He sighs hard. "I'll push through vacation time for you."

I'm a little surprised because he's not arguing.

"I don't trust him either," and he turns around and goes in.

***

New York smells like fart.

And fumes and garbage.

Everyone rushes around, chasing things they don't really need. Everyone is stressed out. Nobody has time. Everyone thinks only about themselves. And no one there is really aware of what's happening around them. They are trapped in their own bubble. It's the perfect place for what I have in mind.

Because you can't see me for a while, baby.

I have to be careful.

I simply can't barge into your life and trample everything you care about or what makes you who you are. At least, at first.

I must *think*.

My first thought is that fate is fucking with us because right across the street from the house where your psycho Seth lives is a decrepit, tiny, old motel. After an endless flight, I check in and insist on a room with a view of Seth's window. What a happy coincidence. My father didn't even have to help me out with a stack of cash. I left Missy at my parents' and only took the bare essentials. I'm not planning to stay here long, just until I get you back.

I glance at the building, but nothing moves. My phone says you are there. Even if I broke the display, your phone works fine. You sent a message to *Dr. Daniels* two hours ago, Emilia. You want to meet with him.

Can we meet? it asks, but he's still keeping you waiting for an answer. He doesn't seem interested in seeing you.

I squeeze into the fucking mini-shower that alternates hot and cold water constantly. See what I do for you, Emilia.

This time I flew. I could not survive another 12 hours in a car, even without my dad.

When I come back into the room with the towel around my hips, I immediately glance at the window again. The door slams against the bed when I open it, just like the door in my office at the FBI bangs against the desk because it's so cramped. Does my dad do this on purpose?

It's hot. There's no air conditioning and the motel is on a street with heavy traffic all day, so the hot fumes come in through the window.

Everything's loud. And it smells like garbage. How do you stand it, Emilia? I just hope you stay put and don't decide to go to the dorm. Then all this will have been for nothing. Then I'd have to enroll in your college and study to protect you and I really don't want that. I've already gone to college, which I barely passed.

I can't see you even though that exhibitionist doesn't have any curtains or blinds and I can see right into the super-hipster apartment. My phone vibrates and displays a new message on your phone. Dr. Daniels: *You can come by at 4:00 pm, then I'm closed.*

Oh, Emilia, I'm so angry. I want to go straight to your William Daniels and smash his face in, but I can't. That would be reckless. And now I always have to think before I do anything. It's funny, lately, when I need to think, my father's voice is always in my head. It says something like: *Think about the consequences of your actions if you do this. You don't want to scare her, Mason. You've only one chance left, Mason. If you fuck it up, I'll rip your balls off myself, Mason.*

I like my balls on my body, Emilia.

You text back *okay*. What's the rush, Emilia?

Your pride is hurt because he kept you waiting so long. You don't think for one second that he might have a patient. Because you persuade yourself it's your fault. That it's always your fault if someone loses interest, doesn't find you hot, or treats you badly. Even if you've had therapy and you've had a lot, you just can't get rid of some things. You've become so confident and strong, Emilia, but I still see the fragile girl with the pain in her eyes that sat in front of me at the time. So innocent. That's the version of you that I love most of all. The version that would scare off everyone else because they wouldn't know how to deal with it.

I need to make a list of people to dispose of that are not good for you, Emilia. And I'm going to do it in strict adherence to my father's journal. He did the same thing. Without killing anyone, he eliminated everything that was not good for Mom and you have *things* in your life that are not good for you. But let's start small and work our way up.

First, Dr. Daniels...

I rummage in my suitcase for a pair of boxer shorts and put them on before throwing the towel over my shoulder and opening the window to smoke. I sit on the windowsill and pull deeply on my cigarette; I don't have any weed with me because of fucking airport security, but that's okay, I'll just get some later. Here in New York, there are dealers on every corner.

Seeing movement out of the corner of my eye, my head swivels toward *Seth's* window and there you are, baby. It was only yesterday you drove off and I flew off after you that night. It's 9:00 in the morning in New York, but it looks like you just got up, Emilia. You wear nothing but panties and a tight white top with no bra. Your hair is messy and you rub your eyes while holding your phone. Did you really wake up two hours ago to write to that loser and then fall asleep again? *Really*?

Nervously, you run around the apartment. Why are you so nervous, Emilia?

All of a sudden, you go to the window and push it up. You lean on the windowsill with both hands and breathe in and out frantically. I frown. I don't like how pale you are, Emilia.

Gesticulating wildly, Seth comes after you wearing only boxer shorts, *Emilia*. He is speaking to you and appears pissed off. Even from a distance, I see how tense he is, just like I am before I snap. I squeeze the cigarette so tightly between my thumb and forefinger it crumbles. I must be careful, Emilia. I'm about to storm over there, rip a beam from his ceiling, and wrap it around his head or hang him from it and use him as a punching bag. You're yelling at him, which is an unfamiliar sight. You never do that, baby. I don't know how I'd react if you ever did that to me, but I want to find out.

Face to face, you stare angrily at him. Even from here, I see how erratically you're breathing. You're not afraid of him. Are you afraid of anything anymore, Emilia? When you walk past him, he grabs you by the wrist and pulls you back. He holds it between you and you glare at each other for a while, but he won't let go. Instead, he hisses something at you, which makes you glance down. I don't like that, Emilia. *That* is the Emilia I know, but she's all mine. *I* have to rescue her, not some schmuck who doesn't appreciate her.

He pulls hard on your wrist, which is why your eyes shoot up again. As he continues hissing at you, you nod slowly. Then, he suddenly releases you so that you stumble two steps back. Fuck, Emilia! I can hardly restrain myself. I can't stop myself. Out of a population of over eight million people – *eight million* – why did you choose him? Why did you choose *me*?

He disappears and leaves you alone. You slide down the wall by the window, – I can still see you there – lean your head against it, and close your eyes.

Fuck, Emilia.

You cry.

I'm so pissed. When he leaves the house, I hear my father's voice telling me what will happen if I don't control myself now because I'd go after him and pound his face in some alley until the bone in his nose pierced his brain, but then they'd put me behind bars for leaving fingerprints. And it's all because of you, Emilia. I've always known it. But then it would have been for nothing and I would never get you back.

So I'm going to sit here and watch you cry. Fuck. I didn't know what pain was until I saw it on you and there is nothing I can do but watch from afar like I did with Riley. You don't even know it, but I'm still here, baby. I'm always here if you need me.

I reach for my phone and message you on *Instagram* because you didn't block me there.

Hey...

I watch as you glance at the flashing phone still in your hand. Sniffling, you pick it up and look at it. You raise your eyebrows in surprise, briefly close your eyes, and stiffen. You purse your lips as you write back.

What do you want, Mason? You sound tough even though you're about as messed up as the little broken girl who sat on the floor in my basement.

I want to know how you are, Emilia.

I'm really busy right now, Mason. I'm on the subway and things are crazy here, so spit it out. What do you want? I'm sure you're writing for a reason. There are no more nude pictures. You drop your head back and breathe through your mouth as your fingers clutch the phone.

What game are you playing, Emilia?

Have you always done that?

Baby, I have enough naked pictures of you on my phone. I want to know how you are, Emilia. Honest answer.

You're smiling a bit. I can see it.

Since when do you care how I'm doing? you write harshly back.

You go into the kitchen and turn on the coffee maker. While you're doing that, you barely take your eyes off the screen. You're *dying* for an answer from me.

If I had let myself be preoccupied with questions like these, the thought of how important you are to me would have become too real. Now, I ask one last time, Emilia, how are you doing or should I come to New York and beat your ass so you answer?

With a cup of coffee, you sit on the windowsill, baby. So you don't see me, I step aside, although that is unlikely given all the windows and people. You sigh and the snug top tightens around your braless curves. You stretch out your long tan legs on the windowsill like a cat lolling in the sun. You lean your head against the wall.

Do you realize everyone can see you as I see you right now? Do you like that? Are you like Mom used to be, Emilia? Have I fallen in love with my mother? It disgusts me to think that, but doesn't everyone somehow do that? Find their father and mother in their partners? Am I like your father, Emilia, or is he?

I'm fine, Mason, how are you? Are you really going to make small talk with me? I'm surrounded by approximately two million people who want to ride the subway.

Aha, I think as you take a sip of coffee and light a cigarette, Emilia. However, I'm *amused*, baby, as my mom likes to say.

I don't answer because you weren't honest. If you're not honest, you're not going to get any answers, Emilia.

You sit there staring at your phone like you're trying to hypnotize it. I hate that you're smoking because it's not good for you, but it's a bit hot the way you sit there smoking, waiting for me to answer.

You hold out for exactly one minute before writing back, but this time on *WhatsApp*, where you unblocked me again.

?, you text.

And I reply: *!*

I smile when I see you laugh. I love making you laugh. Why didn't I do it more often?

Okay... you type. *I feel like shit, it has been a really shitty morning. Now I'm sitting on my windowsill, drinking coffee and smoking a cigarette. I'm supposed to be at school, but*

I'm here staring at the ugly motel across the street and all the ugly garbage cans outside Seth's door.

Send me a picture of you, I write.

I just got up, Mason. I can clearly hear the grouchiness in your words.

That's why you should send it to me. You grin again. Are your cheeks turning red, Emilia?

You roll your eyes and sigh, but then you quickly straighten your hair, remove the makeup under your eyes with your finger, and pull your top further down, *Emilia*! You will certainly take ten photos and send me one. I love that you want to look beautiful for me.

This will be my new background, baby, I write and your smile is worth being so honest.

Since when do we even have conversations, Mason? you ask and I have to agree with you. We've never actually had a conversation in all this time.

Okay, we've never really talked much, you're right, but we've done a lot of other great things, Emilia.

You slide around on the windowsill, Emilia, and nibble on your fingernail. Do I make you nervous?

Remember when I fucked you on the running washing machine and you had to be extra quiet because Mom was in the room next door?

I'm going to play with you for a bit, baby, let me do that.

You close your eyes and let your head fall back Do you feel me inside you again, Emilia?

MASON! you write in outraged capital letters and send an embarrassed smiley face. I grin devilishly and type: *Or the time at the party when you wore that skimpy dress and I made you come three times in the back seat of my car.*

You are so bad.

Do you know that I love your ass, Emilia? ALWAYS.

You didn't tell me often that you loved anything about me. So, no, I didn't know.

I'm telling you now. I. Love. Your. Ass.

And your eyes.

And your lips when you put them between your teeth.

And the way you look at me when you think I am not looking.

And how you were always afraid to snuggle up to me because you knew I didn't like it. But I was always awake, Emilia. And I never said anything.

And I love the way your eyes sparkle when you want to talk back but don't dare.

And I love it when you open yourself up to show me how broken you are because I know you'll never show it to anyone else.

I love how you always bite your nails when you're hiding something from me.

I love that you can't lie and I love that I know you'd never betray me or let me down, no matter what's going on between us.

When you lived with us, with Riley, I always looked forward to coming home and seeing you first.

And I love that you blush when I say something that makes you uncomfortable, like where I want to fuck you right now.

And I love that on that horrible night when I lost you, I still saw love in your eyes.

And I love that one touch from you is enough to bring me back down.

And I love the way you smile when I walk into the room and you look away quickly so I don't see it.

And I love the way you stare at me when I'm half-naked. And even then you think I don't see it. I see everything you do, Emilia.

I love that no matter how many people were around us, I could always feel your presence. Your eyes always on my back, just as my eyes were always on you.

Shall I go on?

I hit send even though I could go on and on with this list indefinitely. You read it, sob, and put one hand over your mouth. You didn't expect that, did you? I know you're too overwhelmed to reply right now.

I'm so focused on you that I'm as freaked out as you are when Seth walks into the room and finds you crying by the window. He probably thinks it's because of him because he walks up to you and kisses you.

He puts both hands on your cheeks, Emilia. I don't like that.

And you're probably so afraid he might find out why you're really crying that you leave your cell phone and lead him to his mattress in the loft. Then you take your clothes off, but I turn around because I can't watch it again.

Fuck!

29. Take Your Panties Off, Emilia

Mason

It's six o'clock and you're with Dr. Daniels, Emilia.

My dad can be really cool sometimes. When I asked him to spy on Dr. William Daniels a bit, he actually gave me access to his laptop camera. Now I can see and hear everything you two talk about, Emilia. Isn't that amazing?

Dad never even asked why, he just said, "Two minutes."

I love that my father has no scruples. I guess I get that from him. No wonder I'm such a shit.

Anyway, now you're sitting on the couch fully clothed – thank God – across from that shithead who's staring at your tits the entire time, Emilia, but then they aren't exactly small. You love that he desires you. And I hate that he's not the fat disgusting fuck I imagined in my head. That fucker could be my father. He's my dad's age and he looks like him too.

Emilia. That's disgusting. Are you imagining fucking my father?

I'm listening. You tug on the handkerchief in your hands. It's a cliché, Emilia. You're nervous.

"What's wrong, Emilia?" Daniels asks. "What did you want to talk about?"

"We were there," you answer.

"I heard you. Did you sleep with him?"

"What?" you reply, confused.

"He answered your cell phone, so I am asking. Did he break it too?" He looks at your cracked display.

"No, I didn't sleep with him. Yes, he broke it."

"Does he still claim ownership of you?"

"Yes, that too."

"And? How do you feel about that?"

"How should I feel? Seth is beside himself with jealousy. Mason suddenly writes to me about how much he loves me, which he has only said or done once before and you're angry, Will. What's the matter?"

"Naturally he's beside himself with jealousy, Emilia. I can imagine how that went. Besides, you know why he suddenly started writing those things to you, don't you? He manipulates you, he's a psychopath, and he wants you because he saw that someone else has you. It's that simple. And yes, I am angry. You just come here and fuck me because you feel like it. Then you leave and some other guy answers your phone. How am I supposed to react to that, Emilia?"

Let me tell you how it really is, Emilia. This fucker wants you for himself and anything in his way bothers him. You have that effect on men, Emilia. That's why I wouldn't let you out of our basement. You know the type of person you are now and you've grown more confident. What do you think that does to men, Emilia?

"I'm sorry," you reply calmly and I roll my eyes. "It's not that simple with Mason. It goes deeper than superficial jealousy." Dr. Daniels is clenching his jaw, Emilia. "And as for Seth, I know I don't love him, he's Mason 2.0, but he has his good traits. He was there for me when I needed him and I betrayed him with you, Will." Bored, he stares at you, baby, with his chin resting on his fist. He knows you can't handle rejection and he's going to take advantage of that, Emilia. I can see that even over my phone.

"I don't know, Emilia, maybe we should just let it go. It has grown too complicated now that there's a third party involved. Maybe you should find a new therapist."

That's what I'm saying.

"What?" you ask, "But I've been coming to you for two years now. You know my whole story and I trust you!" You toss your hair on the other side, a sign you're growing restless. "You can't do that to me, Will."

"What else can I do? Be happy you come once a week and share you the rest of the week with two other guys?" Oh, man, Emilia, you have him wrapped around your little finger more than I thought or vice versa, I don't know. But I don't like it.

"I know why you chose that man, Emilia." Yeah? "But you'll have to figure it out for yourself." And I know why you chose *that* type because you have *daddy issues*. *Big daddy issues*.

"Will, don't be mad at me." That's your sexy voice. You play with your hair and run your hand over your collarbone. You are such a bitch. "You're the only one I have to tell all this to. What am I supposed to do if I can't come to you? I don't want a new therapist. It takes a long time to trust someone, Will." Emilia, I'm going to come over there right now and drag you out of his office by your hair, then, the problem won't exist anymore. "You can't abandon me when I am in such a dark place. As a person or a therapist, you don't do something like that." He sighs deeply, leans back, and slumps in his chair. Emilia, I know what he's doing. I do it too. Every man does it.

With an elbow on the armrest, he tilts his head and rests his temple on a fist. "Convince me, Emilia," he says, almost bored.

Emilia, you get up! Hopefully, to leave! But you stroll towards him and take your top off along the way. Again, you're not wearing a bra, Emilia. I'm going to spank your ass.

Do I do it now or do I turn it off?

I was really torn when you unbuttoned his shirt.

I can't let you do this, Emilia. Well, I have to do something because you're already sitting on his lap, his hands behind your back, and you're kissing. You already had sex with someone else this morning. Isn't that enough? I think I have to do what my dad did. I have to protect you from yourself. Every woman arrives at this stage, Emilia. I don't like this phase. So, I call you and when you don't pick up, I repeatedly call your number until you are annoyed and get off his lap and see that it's me.

"Fuck!" you whisper and your eyes drift from your phone to that fucker. You look like I woke you from a dream. "What are we doing, Will?" You reach for your top and put it back on. The bum, on the other hand, sits breathless in his chair, shirt half-unbuttoned, still staring at you with veiled eyes. "I can't do this. We have to stop doing this!" That's what I wanted to hear, baby.

"Why? What's wrong?" he asks and sits up.

"Just forget it, Will..." You appear completely unglued. "I should go." You reach for your purse without waiting for him to say anything.

I rattled you, Emilia. I like that.

***

"Hi!" I say and drop onto his sofa. He's closed now. You've been gone 15 minutes.

"Um, excuse me, but you need to make an appointment," he says, confused, staring at me skeptically. Have you shown him photos of me, Emilia, or videos? Maybe our video? Did you fuck him afterward?

"I won't take long!" I put the ankle of my right leg over my left thigh and stretch one arm out on the armrest. This is where you sat a moment ago, Emilia, showing him your tits as you bent over to pull a tissue out of the box. It's still wadded up on the table in front of me. I hold my badge under his nose and enjoy saying the next words.

"FBI, Mason Rush. You probably know me from pictures and stories. I am the manipulative psychopath." Dr. Daniels seems a little pale, Emilia, and he straightens up immediately.

"Mr. Rush, I can't divulge information from my sessions to the FBI or police."

"Now, now, I have my own information. For example, you enjoy interacting with your patients. *Sexually*."

"That is not a criminal offense."

"Of course." I toss a bag of cocaine on the table that I obtained from the New York Police Department's evidence room simply by using my badge. The name *Rush* is known even here. "But it is a federal offense to distribute cocaine to patients."

Now it seems like he's about to puke on the table, Emilia. I lean back and settle my arms on the armrests. "Naturally, I can choose not to arrest you for drug trafficking, but you have to keep your hands off Emilia Sullivan, that goes without saying. You won't look at her again, you won't touch her, and you certainly won't answer when she contacts you. Do you understand?" Finally, I drop my casual tone and change to don't-fuck-with-me tone. My dad would be proud of me. I didn't slam his face into the coffee table until it was pulp like I wanted to, Emilia.

He swallows.

"Understood," he replies roughly. I grin, rise, and point to the bag on his table. "I'll leave it here, you need it more than I do," and I leave his office.

Problem number one solved.

***

Hey, what are you doing? you suddenly text.

I'm lying in bed, Emilia. I finally got some weed and the ceiling fan is working. My life is not so bad. Dr. Daniels is gone and I've had a shower. Thank God it's not so hot anymore. I sit up and glance over at you. You're cooking and Venus, your white shepherd dog, stands behind you, hoping something falls to the floor, just like Missy does.

You're only wearing an over-sized shirt of his, Emilia. Your hair is pulled back, held loosely with a clip at the back of your neck, and you're probably cooking for *him*. Where is he, anyway? It's already 8:00 p.m. and he's definitely not in class anymore. Before I answer you, I call my dad.

"Hey, Dad..."

"Mason, what's wrong? Your mother made us dinner and it's special. What is it?"

"Oh, I don't want to interrupt your fuck dinner, Dad — your finally-Mason-is-gone-for-good dinner party. It's about Emilia."

"What about Emilia, Mason?"

"Can you look into her boyfriend? I think he's a little off."

"I already did. I'll send it to you tomorrow, you fucking toad." Oh, I'm a little baffled.

"Okay, remember to use birth control," I say.

"Of course, I've been thinking about using birth control since you were born. Bye!" Dad's always so funny.

Now I can answer just by calling you.

The cooking spoon falls out of your hand when you see my name on the broken screen, but answer anyway. Directly. That's how I like it, Emilia. We're starting to understand each other again — like never before.

"Hi ..." you say, panting slightly. You're so cute, baby.

"Are you okay?" I ask, watching you bite your lip as your dog licks the wooden spoon on the floor. Does my voice turn you on, Emilia?

"Yeah, everything is fine, what about you?"

"Are you making small talk with me, Emilia?" You close your eyes because you're embarrassed. "What's wrong with you?" I ask again. It amuses me a little, Emilia.

"Nothing, I just thought I'd ask what you were doing. Just because. Can't I do that anymore?" You pick up the wooden spoon and you're so nervous, you place it back in the pot and utter, "Shit!" before pulling it out again, splashing tomato sauce all over the kitchen. I have to be careful not to laugh out loud. Have you always been this funny or did you just never let me see it?

"Of course you can, but the last time we saw each other, it sounded a little like goodbye, Emilia. Do you miss me?"

"What? No!"

"No?" You sit on the kitchen floor without noticing that Venus has her front paws on the counter, licking the pot, Emilia. Perhaps, you don't care because I'm all that matters to you.

"Yes," you whisper.

"Do you want me to come, baby?" *I'm closer than you think.* How would you react if I were there in two minutes?

But you say, "No," and with your eyes closed, lean your head against the kitchen cabinets.

"I miss you too," I admit. A few years ago, that would have been unthinkable for me. It takes you by surprise when I say things like that to you.

"Why are you suddenly like this, Mason?"

"Suddenly? It took me three years to get my head out of my ass, Emilia."

"I wish you would have done it three years ago."

"Three years ago, I was a horny fucker." You remain silent, pull your knees to your chest, and wrap your arms around them. "I know what you're thinking."

"You don't know how it was when I saw that." I too must close my eyes because, like her, I see the same image in front of me: The way you looked at me. God, I never want to be looked at by you like that again.

"You'd think I'd want revenge for what you did to Riley in front of me, but I don't. What I did was much worse, Emilia, because I thought I had *feelings* for her because of some childhood illusion and because I did it not only once while you were sleeping, but often..." You swallow and squeeze your eyes tighter shut. I hear your breathing is fast and erratic. "I was so afraid to love you, Emilia, I searched for an easier way, and with Cherry, it was easier. She is a simple person and you are a deep, complex, and complicated person, but that is what I find so attractive about you. I just didn't see it. I pulled you down. I didn't even let you go to college. I wanted to own you, I was afraid someone would take you away from me. Maybe it was easier for me to break your heart so I wouldn't have to deal with all the shit that was going on in my heart. I don't know. It wasn't her. It was the illusion of her and my fear of you. I'm sorry." You breathe deeply and I realize it's going to take time for the words to sink in.

"I trusted you. You were always so jealous, Mason, you wouldn't even let me *talk* to Riley. What you did pulled the rug out from under me. If only you had confessed to me before I caught you or figured it out on my own. *It* was too much. I still remember exactly where her hands were, where *your* hands and her legs were, and what you sounded like, Mason, and where you kissed her. I simply can't forget that no matter how many therapy sessions I attend. No matter how much I try to put the past behind me."

"I don't remember anything about that anymore. I only see the way you looked at me."

You clear your throat because you're afraid your voice might falter. I know there's a lump in your throat. I have one myself.

"What do you want from me now, Mason? What's the point? It happened."

I merely spoke without thinking, Emilia, because it feels fucking right. "I miss you and I want you back. I want you to break up with that fucker because he's not good for you. This life here is not good for you. Come back home to me."

You laugh without joy. "And then what, Mason? We sit in your basement and vegetate?"

"Baby, I work, you work. We're not the same as we were three years ago."

This time, I hear the smile in your voice clearly and I see it on your lips. "Life with Mason Rush, babies and all?"

I chuckle softly and notice you shiver. "Whatever the fuck you want."

"Did you *really* just say that?" you ask, amused, and I smile.

"If I tell you I'll do anything for you, it's not just a figure of speech. I mean it, Emilia."

You sigh. “I can’t, Mason. I’ve built a life for myself here that works for me and I know if you enter this life, you’ll only bring havoc and chaos. We both draw each other too deep into the darkness and I’m afraid I won’t find my way out next time.”

“Fuck, Emilia!” I shout into the phone because what you said hurts.

“Are you angry, Mason?” I pull on my hair with one hand, trying to calm down, trying to think about the consequences. You’d hang up and that’d be that.

“No, I’m not angry,” I say through clenched teeth. But you only laugh because you are not standing in front of me and therefore, have nothing to fear.

“Because you’re not getting what you want?”

“Who says so? Maybe I just have to wait a little longer.”

“If there’s one thing you’re *not* it’s patient.”

“I’ve waited for three years. I can wait a little longer.”

“You’ve waited three years for me? Your voice is teasing and an eyebrow arches. Emilia, are you trying to provoke me?

“Of course I’ve waited three years for that ass.” You blush, Emilia. “I wish you weren’t so far away from me right now so I could talk you into a quickie.”

“I don’t think you’d have to talk me into anything!” slips out and you put your hand over your mouth with your eyes wide open. I guess you didn’t expect to say that.

“Really? When you were here this weekend and if I had tried a little harder, would I have had a chance?”

“You always have a chance with me, Mason, that’s my problem with you.” Fuck, I’m going to go and take that chance. It demands a lot from me not to because the consequences would be that I'd be busted and you wouldn't trust me ever again.

"Shit, Emilia..." I whisper hoarsely because you make me hard.

"What, Mason?" you reply innocently. Oh, my God, you are such a bitch!

"I want to fuck you right now," I say *forcefully*.

Your laugh is strained and you change positions on the floor every second. Your breathing increases. "Well, it doesn't work that way. There are miles between us and I have a boyfriend, Mason."

"Don't remind me of *that*," I snarl.

"But it's a fact."

"Fact: You're *my* girl and you are going to take your panties off…now!" You hold your breath.

"What? No, I'm not. How do you even know I'm wearing panties, Mason?"

I raise my eyebrows. "Oh, Emilia, what is wrong with you? I've never seen you like this." You look around, Emilia, and consider playing along.

"*You* made me this way. I hear your voice in my head, always. It says the nastiest things and tells me what to do during sex."

"Emilia," I growl.

"What?" you ask cheekily. "What do you want me to do, Mason? I have no inhibitions."

"Remove. Your. Panties." You do it, Emilia. You take off your panties and toss them onto the dining room table. You little bitch.

"Where are you right now?" I ask. My breathing is already intensifying. Holy shit.

"On the kitchen floor."

"Sit on the kitchen counter." You giggle but obey. Oh, baby, I can see you so well now. I better not think about all those other fuckers that also can.

"What are you wearing?"

"A t-shirt, no bra." I love how dirty your voice sounds.

"Take it off!"

You do it, just like that.

You're such a little bitch with an undeniably, incredibly hot body.

Fuck, you're like a hundred paces away, sitting naked on the kitchen counter!

"Where do you think I would touch you now?"

"Here," you say immediately and you reach for your neck.

"Baby, I can't see you." You giggle and say, "On my neck...and you'd put your thumb on my lip and stroke it. That's our thing." Shit, yeah, Emilia, just like that.

"And then what would I do?"

"You would kiss my body...here." You stroke your chest and then over your side. I wonder if you have any idea that I'm watching because what you're doing right now is the hottest thing you've ever done, Emilia.

"I can't see you, Emilia." You giggle again. You're so excited. "Where do you want to feel me? Now don't say *there*."

"My breasts!"

"I could flick your breasts if you want," I offer casually and I hear you draw your breath in sharply.

"Yes, you could," you whisper and I have to reach into my trousers and grab my cock at the tone of your voice. You. Turn. Me. On.

"What would *you* do, Emilia?" As the new you, you bitch!

"I'd sit on top of you because I couldn't stop, Mason."

"Fuck!" I swear and grip tighter as you penetrate yourself with two fingers.

"And then I would..." You moan, "Moan because you would fill me so deeply. You are so big, I miss that."

"Me too, you have no idea how much!"

"Are you touching yourself, Mason?"

"Are *you* touching yourself, Emilia?"

"Yes."

"Yes."

We both laugh and moan at the same time.

You are moaning in my ear, Emilia. I'm listening and fuck, I'm about to come, although, I'm frustrated because I can't put it in your pussy and have to jerk off in my hand.

"Fuck, Mason," you whisper.

"I want to fuck you in the ass, Emilia."

"And I want you to, Mason."

"*Fuck*!" I gasp and tense up.

"*Fuck*!" You're also gasping, but not for the reason I want. "I think Seth is coming. I have to go."

"What?" I glance out the window and actually, you can barely get into the shirt and panties as he comes in. Apparently, Venus warned you by running to the door and jumping up and down.

Fucking.

Shit.

30. I Must Take Care Of That For You, Baby

Mason

I'm on my way to your school, Emilia, and while in the back seat of the taxi, I scroll through the information Dad sent me. About your boyfriend.

He's not a happy man. From drug-related charges to assault to sex in public, everything is there. He did three months in jail for almost beating a guy to death.

Did you know he was in jail, Emilia?

Do you know anything about him at all?

Dad cleared my record back then, thank God, or I wouldn't have stood a chance with the FBI, but we really are one and the same, your boyfriend and I. I don't like it, Emilia.

A guy like that is not good enough for you.

I'm not good for you.

Dr. Daniels is not good enough for you.

But *I* can at least *try* to be good enough for you. I mean, what was that thing about admitting your mistakes and making the first move and all that?

I arrive at the university and tip the cabby before getting out. Everything's green, like something out of a picture book. People with backpacks, tablets, and nerd glasses, who think they are better than anyone else, are everywhere. I hate students, Emilia. They think they're doctors simply because they're studying medicine in their first semester and right away, unpack the first aid kit when someone faints after a bar fight. I've seen it all before.

I want to see what you do all day. I want to see you smile when I write to you while you're sitting in class. And I want to see what the relationship is like between you two. Leaning against a tree, I light a cigarette and put a hand in my pocket. With the other, I check where you are. You're getting closer, Emilia. The red dot comes straight at me and I step behind the tree as you pass by. With him! He has an arm around your shoulder – tightly – he wants to show everyone that you belong to him. He has to because you look fucking hot. The jean shorts reveal the outline of your ass. I love your ass! I want to see my handprints sticking out of the bottom. You're wearing a black Rolling Stones t-shirt. Your hair is loose and wavy, hanging over one shoulder. You're so hot, Emilia, and you're hardly wearing any makeup except for a luscious red lipstick. Your eyes hide behind sunglasses, which upsets me, Emilia. I want to see what is going on in them — always. Your cell phone sticks dangerously out of the back pocket of your shorts, about to fall out at any moment. But you don't care. It's already broken, thanks to me. Your fingers are intertwined with his. Do you ever imagine they're mine?

I let you pass by, Emilia, because I'm not here to tear you apart yet. That will happen soon enough. I must be patient and consider the fucking consequences.

I'm on another mission today, Emilia. I'm waiting for a short, busty, curly blonde. No, not because I want to pick her up, but because she's your girlfriend and I need to *check her out*. I remember when you only had one friend that I knew about. That was Chloe? Chloe? Claire? Clarissa? Something with C. Anyway, I know you two stopped seeing each other because of me, but it was for the best, Emilia. She was not good enough for you. And now I have to find out if this Bridget is. You're a bad judge of character, Emilia. I have to fix that for you, baby. I have to take care of you.

Bridget is a disaster — just like my mom. Her shirt hangs half out of her jeans and her hair is a mess. Her unprotected laptop is pressed against her chest as she searches for something in her bag with her other hand. I see the disaster even before I set it off. She curses and tries to cope, but she can't manage and before I can react, the laptop slips out of her arm and she barely catches it.

"Shit!" she hisses. At that moment, I step out of the shadows and stand in her way.

Since she is still distracted, she runs straight into me. What a coincidence.

She stares at my chest, which is covered by a dark green shirt. Her eyes widen a bit as she slowly lets her gaze wander further up. I sigh. It always takes so long before women can finally address me because they first have to stare for an eternity. I hate that. I want to tell her that my eyes are *up here*. I mean, if I was staring at her chest the whole time, I'd be a pervert. I mean, seriously. I hate women's libbers.

Now she's arrived at my chin.

"Hi!" I say and she winces. Finally, she makes eye contact.

She blinks and looks like the deer you used to be. "Hi?"

"Coffee?"

Bridget's brown eyes are getting as big as saucers, Emilia. She quickly shoves her shirt into her pants and tucks her wild curls behind her ears. She's pretty and insecure. But she's not you, so she doesn't really interest me.

"Coffee?" she asks breathlessly.

"Arabic hot beverage. Usually consumed in the morning. Awakens the spirit. Want some?"

"Sure." She squeaks more than she speaks. Naturally, she has a lecture, but she forgets about it. A guy like me has never asked her out for coffee before. She's too introverted, too plain, too natural. We men are idiots, we're more into *Playboy* bunnies.

There's a well-stocked Starbucks right next to the campus and I'm going to settle down with her in a cozy corner. She stares like a fish, Emilia, and I have to force myself to be nice.

We get two coffees that cost three times more than what you can get on any street corner that don't taste half as good. Filter coffee. Not even worth 50 cents.

I lean back and put one arm over the backrest. She's staring at my biceps and my tattoos, Emilia, probably imagining what it'd be like if I pressed her up against the wall and fucked her because I'm the type that does that.

"So? Where are you from?" I ask.

"New York!"

"What are you studying?"

"Photography."

"Do you have any friends?" I have no patience for beating around the bush, Emilia.

"Um..." She seems confused. "Yes?"

So she doesn't suspect anything, I also ask, "Do you have a boyfriend?" and she blushes.

"Not exactly." Oh...little, sweet Bridget has a lover, does she?

"Not exactly?"

"Well, there is someone, but it's a bit back and forth and I don't know if he really wants me... Why am I telling you this? I don't even know your name."

I'm so glad I read my Dad's journal. It taught me so much. I would love to casually put on sunglasses.

"My name is John."

"John?" she asks, eyeing me critically. "You do not look like a John."

"What do I look like, baby?"

"H'm... like a Kyle or Alec or Cole or something hard."

Oh, Emilia, she gives me so many openings, but I'm not going to bite because I'm not looking for sex. Not with her or anyone but you. Back there at eleven o'clock, is a tiny brunette who has been staring at me the entire time and at nine o'clock, I discover a petite Asian woman who keeps glancing at me, apart from the waitress who has painted a little heart on my cup, Emilia.

"What's your name?"

She's thinking, sipping her drink. "My name is Bridget, but it's not Bridget Jones. It's Ashford."

"And, Bridget Ashford? Ever had a one-night stand?"

She frowns and thinks I'm looking to take her home with me. "Um... She blushes and plays insecurely with her fingers while I constantly push the ashtray, which you are not allowed to use in here anyway, on the table from left to right.

"Just curious," I explain. "Because I want to know who I'm having coffee with."

"Is drinking coffee so intimate for you?" she asks, amused. I like her, Emilia. "I had one once, but it's not for me. I think you have to know and love each other or at least be intimate with each other, to... well, to be able to do it," she continues.

She would be a good match for Riley, Emilia, I can see that right away.

"I like it," I say. "How do you feel about drugs?"

She raises an eyebrow. "You want to sell me something? Are you a dealer or a cop?"

I smile mysteriously. "Neither."

"I see, it's still about the coffee."

"Right."

"No drugs, except at parties, when they pass a joint around."

"Good attitude, Bridget Ashford."

I lean forward and rest my chin on a fist. "So, what kind of friends do you have?" I know my eyes hypnotize her. This is the look I use to keep most hookers from squealing that I was *abusing my power* again.

"Actually, not many." She thinks about it and appears a little surprised. "Well, when it comes to real friendships, I only have one. Emilia Sullivan is her name." Then she shakes her head. "Why am I telling you this?" I flash a little grin because I heard your name, baby. This is really embarrassing. I keep thinking about yesterday when you were sitting on the counter doing all those things and I get hard. I can't have that right now.

"And why only her?"

She slides her lower lip forward and shrugs. "Because Emmy is the only one I can really tell everything to without her judging me. I've known her since I was a little kid. She was my neighbor and we went through some shit together. My mom was like her mom and her mom was shit, just like her dad. I'm glad he is dead. And I don't know where her mother is. Oh, man, I'm talking too much again, sorry. It happens all the time."

I wave dismissively. "I'm interested in what you have to say about anyone. You have a lovely voice, Bridget." She shivers when I say her name and shakes her head slightly to come to her senses.

"Well, I don't know about that. However, Emmy moved because she met someone." She blushes. What does that mean, Emilia? "That's why we lost touch. She came back three years ago and contacted me right away. She had a bad breakup – with *Riley* – and she wasn't doing too well." I'd love to tell her that it was because of *me* that you weren't well, not because of him, but I'll keep quiet. After all, camouflage is everything. I don't know what you told her, baby.

"And I was there for her without asking too much. Because that's our thing, no matter how long we have been apart from each other. Once we're back together, it's like we were never apart." I know, Emilia, you have that effect on everyone. Even me. "Well, now she's with Seth. He is a guy in our class and she's trying to hook me up with her ex, but I'm not comfortable with it and I don't think he is either. I think he is still mourning her. Anyway, all we ever talked about is Emilia, it's like we stopped dating at some point. I don't hear from him often, but it still feels like there is something. Shit, I told you my whole life. You do this thing with your eyes. How do you do that?"

I shrug. "What do you mean?"

"Forget about it." She laughs. "In any case, it wouldn't be right to go with you. No matter how attractive you are and you are, John, but as I said, I don't do that and there is this other guy..."

Oh, Emilia, I learned so much more than I wanted to know. So, Riley still has a crush on you? And Bridget likes him. It's a soap opera.

Her phone rings with your name displayed. I can see it clearly because it's on the table between us.

"Oh, sorry," you mumble. "I have to take her call, she's a terror!"

I make a sweeping gesture and she picks up, her eyes resting on me. "Hey!" she answers. Unfortunately, I can't hear what you are saying.

"Yes, what a coincidence! I was just talking about you! ... No, oh, I'll tell you later," she whispers. "Yes, I'm on my way. I'll be there in 10 minutes. Yes, I have that spare phone for you, Emmy. No, I haven't forgotten you. Okay. Really? Yeah, I'm at Starbucks. I'll wait for you. See you soon.

Fuck, Emilia, you always fuck up my plans. What the fuck are you doing? I don't need you to come here and see me with her. Emilia!

"Sorry," she says, putting her phone away. I'm under the gun. "Unfortunately, I have to end this. My friend wants to talk to me about something important and..."

"No problem!" I exclaim in between and get up. "See you! Nice meeting you." She is totally stunned, but I leave without paying attention to her.

As I depart Starbucks, I see you rushing into the café, your eyes wide and stressed. You seem paranoid, Emilia, but not about me.

That was close.

31. At Home, Mason

Emilia

Mason, what are you up to? Yesterday we had *phone sex*! Mason! What am I to make of that? What am I to make of everything you wrote? Telling me everything you love about me has ripped the rug out from under my feet. You stated you'd do anything for me. It's like there's a new you, but I don't believe it. Not at all. What if Dr. Daniels is right and you simply want me because you can't have me?

Oh, Mason, since I went back, it seems my world is upside down. Seth and I've been arguing nonstop. He's become increasingly more controlling, possessive, and paranoid. Today, he stared at me throughout the lecture. And not in a sexy way like you used to do. It was quite the opposite.

I believe Dr. Daniels is history. After my last session, I have forbidden myself from seeing him or sleeping with him again. The only reason I did it is because I miss you, which is not right. And seeing your call during my session was like an epiphany. Suddenly, it seemed I was cheating on you, not Seth.

I should talk to someone about this. I had to reassure Seth a thousand times that I was merely meeting Bridget at Starbucks before he finally let me go. Whatever lectures we have left to attend I'll skip since I'm not quite myself. I claimed that Bridget was feeling ill and lonely. Eventually, he believed me. Hallelujah. Then again, Mason, you were just as bad when you took me home from New York. However, nowadays, I no longer put up with that shit. Seth is convinced I cheated on him with you. It's ironic I find myself in that position again. Will it ever end? Will what we have between us ever change? Although, now that you said and wrote all those things to me, nothing is like it was anyway. No matter how hard I try, it will never be like it was.

Currently, Bridget and I are sitting at Starbucks drinking Frappuccino. Bridget is red in the face and seems a bit distracted. Perhaps the empty cup in front of me with John and a little heart scribbled on it has something to do with it.

I skeptically eye Bridget. "Who is John with a heart?"

She sighs dreamily. "The most beautiful man I've ever seen, Emmy."

Shit, she's a goner. What's gotten into her?

"Okay, so you skipped school to have coffee with John."

"He said having coffee is intimate. Oh and the look he gave me..." She stares conspiratorially at me wide-eyed as if I need clarification.

I'm beginning to question her sanity.

"Honestly, Emmy. If it wasn't for that cup there, I'd think I imagined it."

"Imagined what?" I ask irritably, wondering where the nearest psychiatric hospital is.

"I was walking across the campus ground to my class when I saw this sex god in a tight green shirt with arms full of tattoos. Oh, my God! His eyes and that three-day-old stubble."

"Okay," I say cautiously. "Then what happened?" I've long since forgotten why I came here. It seems Bridget met an extremely hot specimen that completely derailed her, like how you always make me feel, Mason.

"He asked if I wanted to join him for a coffee. I couldn't say no! And then he asked me a bunch of things!"

I raise my eyebrows and sip my drink before asking, "About what?"

"Everything. If I have a boyfriend, if I do drugs, how I feel about one-night stands, and then for some reason, you became the topic."

"I was the topic?" I ask, irritated like never before in my life. "Why?"

"He inquired about my friends. I only have one and that is you. So I told him about you and Riley. And that he and I have an on-off relationship that…I don't know." She raises her shoulders. "Anyway, he just left! I don't even have his number or a way to contact him. Perhaps because I told him I wasn't going to sleep with him. Oh and his eyes. You know, I couldn't tell if they were brown, green, or blue!" My stomach knots up and I feel sick. I believe I misheard, Mason, though come to think of it, you're not the only good-looking man with tattoos and mesmerizing eyes.

Oh, dear.

"What color hair did he have?" I ask casually.

"Black as night."

"And the tattoos on his arms, did you get a good look at them?"

"I saw those tattoos in a documentary on Hawaii that I watched a while back."

I inhale deeply and slowly exhale, unable to believe it was you, Mason. What could you be doing here?

"They are called Maori," I say tonelessly and continue my breathing exercise.

"Are you okay?" Bridget asks anxiously.

I nod hastily. "My stomach is a bit queasy, that's all. Go on."

"I noticed something between his thumb and forefinger, though I didn't ask him about it. It looked intimate." I already know what she'll say next, Mason, and I have no idea how I'm going to handle it. "A small cross with the date 02-14 under it. I couldn't make out the year. I think it was the date of someone's death.

Fuck!

I close my eyes as everything around me starts to spin. I try to keep up my breathing exercise to suppress my nausea, but it isn't easy. It feels like I'm going to faint at any moment.

I open my eyes again and look directly at the cup. Were your lips on that cup not too long ago, Mason? The tattoos and indefinable eyes cannot be a coincidence. Especially considering John is your father's middle name.

"Bridget, I believe I should go. I'll call you later," I mutter.

She shakes her head. "My God, why is everyone dashing off today like they were stung by a scorpion?"

"I'm sorry, sweetie, I just feel sick. I believe I've had too much sugar." Did you react the same way when you heard I was coming, Mason?

She sighs and rolls her eyes. "Okay, but don't forget my spare cell phone." She pulls it out of her pocket and slides it over to me. Since the display on mine is broken, she lends me her old one.

I pocket it, thank her, and make a run for it.

As soon as I'm outside in the smoggy air, I support myself with one hand against the wall next to me and breathe deeply. I cannot believe what I heard. What are you doing here, Mason? If Seth finds out, there's going to be trouble. So, where are you, Mason? Were you here *yesterday* too? When we were...you know?

Before I think about it any longer, I search for your number in my phone. I stored you under *Missy* in case Seth snoops through my directory and I delete our chats on a daily basis. All chats.

You immediately pick up. I move away from the Starbucks to the nearest sunny spot I can find between the concrete high-rises and sit down.

"What's up, baby?" you ask. Hearing your voice still makes my heart go pitter-patter, Mason. It has gotten darker and rougher over the years from all the smoking and recalling your moans from yesterday is giving me goose bumps.

"Are you here in New York, Mason Rush?" I hiss immediately. A few passersby give me distraught looks. However, I'm a native New Yorker and can now assert myself, so I hiss, "What?" at them, sending them on their way.

"What makes you say that, Emilia?" you reply. I hear heavy traffic in the background. Yeah, Chicago has that too, however, what are the odds I hear sirens over the phone and in my vicinity.

"I just talked to Bridget, Mason. You know, that little blonde whose head you've just turned to mush, John?"

"Emilia," you say sighing, "I think you're delusional, baby. But if you want me around so badly, it can be arranged."

"I bet you could," I growl. "Did you hit on Bridget, Mason? Were you trying to get back at me by luring her into your bed like you did Claire? All that because I'm with Seth?"

You sighed in surrender and actually remain calm. I don't understand. Considering I'm onto you, you should be pissed off or at least because I mentioned Seth or both.

"Meet me at the *Cherry Blossom* in an hour and we'll talk."

I don't think I heard you correctly. "Are you kidding me? You want me to go *where*?"

"Oh, just get over it, Emmy! Just be there. It's the motel across the street from you. I'm in room 701," and you hang up.

***

I lied to Seth about spending the morning with Bridget because she's such a mess and I'm now standing in front of room 701. I feel my pulse in my neck and my hands are sweaty. I don't know if I should run away or scream. Why is it that you merely have to snap your fingers for me to do exactly what you want? I believed you were out of my system after all these years. Mason, it wasn't even a week ago that I was at your parents and, already, my whole life is turned upside down. Just what I was afraid of.

I'm afraid to knock. I raise my hand only to drop it again and again. I have no idea what awaits me on the other side of that door or what I will do because I don't trust myself. But I know one thing; as soon as I set foot in that room, my life will irrevocably change.

I attempt a few more knocks but I'm still lacking courage. I know you're waiting for me, Mason, and that you will smell incredibly good. I also know I will be overwhelmed with old emotions that will shake up my world until I'm pulled into your darkness again.

As I raise my hand for the seventh time, you make it easy for me by ripping the door open. It seems two minutes pass where we just stare at each other. Your indefinable eyes pierce mine so expressively that the rug is immediately pulled out from under my feet. Your hair falls across your forehead and you're shirtless.

For a moment, you stand there with your arm braced against the doorjamb and hold the door open with the other. Lazily, you eye my body until your eyes meet mine.

You are here. I can't believe you are *actually* here. Before I can say anything, you grab my arm like you used to do and pull me into the small room, whose blinds you have lowered so that only a few rays of light shine through the cracks. The room smells of you and weed and a thousand butterflies explode in my stomach.

You take my breath away, Mason. You make me high without me even taking a breath. You overwhelm me. This is *it.* All-consuming, real love that I will never find again because nobody is you and because I locked my heart in your basement back then.

You push the door shut and press me against it. You put one hand next to my head while you lift my chin with the other. I press my palms flat against the wood and I tilt my head back against the door. We are so close, I feel your naked upper body against mine, your breath on my cheek, and your scent shooting straight to my soul.

Fuck. I am so lost when I'm with you.

I look into your eyes as you gaze into mine. It seems as if hours go by as we stand there staring at each other like in the old days. We communicate without talking. We experience emotions without exchanging words. I love this, Mason. I've never had this with anyone else. Suddenly, I don't care anymore about why you're here, about what you did, or about what *I* did. Nor why you or I shouldn't be here.

All I know is that I love you with everything that I am, my entire being.

I inhale deeply and as I exhale, I lower my shoulders and my resistance, my anger, and my disappointment disappears. Everything leaves me. Only you and I remain in this moment.

God.

You are everything to me.

Your hand gently caresses my cheek and then my hair so that I feel your fingertips on my scalp. Then you lean your forehead against mine and we close our eyes.

"Shit, baby," you whisper. I nod in understanding. After all, I can feel your emotions. My longing for you is tearing me apart despite being so close. I raise my hands and place them on your chest. I feel your heart beating through your skin. It is racing as fast as mine. My knees grow weak as my breath mixes with yours. I love these moments. I love what you do to me. You gasp softly as I stroke your skin, up to your broad shoulders and upper arms and my fingernails scratch lightly over the places I have just gently touched.

Wordlessly, you move toward my lips. I lean in and pull you even closer into my arms because I can't get enough of you and never will, no matter how close you are.

Your lips on mine set off a veritable fireworks display within me and although I felt them only a few days ago, it is as if I am dying of thirst and you are giving me water. I sigh because I can't express my emotions other than when our tongues meet and I can taste you. Your hand on my head clenches my hair into a fist and pushes me closer to your head. As close as is possible.

I simply want to feel you, your skin, your lips, your touch. I've missed you so much. I think I'm going to be sick from all the emotions I'm feeling. I simply cannot express how you make me feel.

"Mason," I whisper hoarsely against your mouth and you nod. Yeah, you know what I want. I want to feel you. I need to, as do you.

You wrap an arm around my back and push me up the door. My legs automatically wrap around your hips as your hands grab and support me by my ass. I love your hands grabbing my ass. I love your hands all over my body. You carry me so confidently. I know you would never let me fall.

That was always the case, Mason. Our naked bodies could always communicate better than our words. I think that was the reason we talked so little. Then again, it's not like we have to know everything about each other. We know what counts most, besides, we are people who express themselves with emotions rather than with words. I've never thought of it from that perspective — until now.

And fuck, I love you.

You set me down on the bed that's right next to us. I watch you linger at the foot of the bed, eyeing me. The soft light shining through the slits in the blinds allows me to see your eyes, part of your arms, your chest, and your flat, slightly muscular stomach. I merely lie here, breathless, and it seems as if it's the first time I am seeing the *real* you. And you see me.

You tilt your head and take in everything I have to offer. I reach out to you. For too long I couldn't do that: give in to the desire to just touch you, feel you, and be with you. Oftentimes, I entertained the idea of asking your parents for your number and I frequently searched for flights just so I could see you for a brief moment. I have often wondered what it would be like to feel you again – your weight on me – and to know that I am safe and at home. But what I'm feeling now, Mason, being alone with you, goes beyond anything I imagined.

You remove your jeans, which land on the floor with a dull thud before you bend over me and unbutton my shorts. We continue staring at each other as I lift my ass so you can pull them and my panties from my hips. Your palms brush up each leg, starting at the ankle. Everywhere you touch me you leave a burning sensation.

Fuck. I just love you.

I love the way you are looking at me right now, Mason. Like I'm a goddess, like I'm the one who makes your world. That's what I'd love to believe for now.

You kneel between my legs, grab the hem of my shirt, and I sit up as you pull it over my head.

You exhale and it sounds like you've been holding your breath for some time. That too I'd love to believe is true at the moment. After you unclasped my bra with one hand, you toss it on the floor. Now I'm completely naked, but I don't mind since I'm not feeling vulnerable or put on the spot. I feel safe here with you, in your arms, in your little room, in your darkness.

You slowly lean your head against my skin and I feel your breath on my collarbone. I love the way you always linger in the crook and listen to my pulse like you're making sure my heart is still beating.

I moan slightly as you kiss my breast as I hold on to your strong arms. Suddenly, I wish I could hold on to you forever. Goose bumps spread across my body as you slide over my belly and your hot breath leaves a wet trail behind.

Your fingers search for mine. I take your hand and interlock our fingers. God, it feels so good to hold your hand

and feel your skin on mine as your big hand encloses mine. It's like they were made for each other.

Fuck.

I spread my legs wider as you move between them and stroke my most sensitive part with your tongue.

Shit.

I lift my pelvis and you push it back down with one hand, making me smile. I've missed this so much.

You continue to leisurely circle your tongue around my pleasure spot and I have to bite my lip to keep from climaxing right away. I've been longing for you so much I can barely restrain myself, Mason. No matter who I was with, no one could hold a candle to you. I don't think there's anyone else who could rock my world the way you do.

I arch my back as you slide two fingers inside. The sun's rays shining through the slits in the blinds caress my skin and illuminate your eyes. You're looking straight up into mine while the hand that was linked with mine rests on my lower belly and holds me in place. *Fuck.*

I dig my fingers into your thick hair and scream your name as I finally climax.

Though I fight for breath, I haven't had enough of you yet. A lifetime won't be enough. You kiss your way back up to me while sliding your arms under my back. With one quick move, you flip me so that I end up sitting on top of you. I feel you between my legs despite your boxer shorts as I support my hands on either side of your head. My hair falls around us like a protective shield, so you lift your hand and tuck it behind my ear before you run your thumb over my lip. I close my eyes as you start to speak for the first time since I entered.

"Look at me." Your hand slides down my neck and you just hold me.

I open my eyes to directly meet your burning gaze.

A smile plays on my lips. "Shit, Mason Rush," I whisper and your hands move to my back and push me down. My chest touches yours, my stomach touches yours, but our lips are still an inch apart.

"Tell me you love me," you whisper hoarsely.

"I love you," I reply.

And then it's like the last barrier inside you breaks. It's like I blurred the boundary. It's like nothing is separating us anymore, nothing stopping you.

"Fuck," you whisper and reach down between us to pull down your shorts. Oh, my God, as I feel you right now, a thousand tiny flashes explode through my body in anticipation of what I'm about to feel.

Again, you spin us around. It seems you can't make up your mind, as if you want it all at once now that you can finally have it.

Finally, you pin me under you. I simply love that. My legs automatically wrap around your perfect hips as your hand runs from my rib cage up to my collarbone and over to my neck. Your fingers are rough. I can feel every inch of my sensitive skin and stretch out to you longingly. But you are not rough, not even for a second. Gently, as if I would flee, you slide your hand into my hair and clutch it while pushing completely into me. For a brief moment, we remain in this position.

You lower your forehead to my shoulder and I throw my head back. I cannot breathe, Mason. You don't seem to be breathing either.

I had forgotten how you feel. Really, it escaped me. I forgot about everything you trigger inside me. I forgot how fucking addicted I am to you.

I wrap my hand around your neck and pull you tightly against me as if I am afraid of losing you. With the other, I claw at your muscular back.

As you start to move, you support yourself with one hand on the headboard above me. Your muscles flex and your jaw clenches so that your cheeks twitch.

Again and again, I moan every time you thrust deep inside me. You're breathing through your nose. I see you holding back and put my hands on your cheeks, which is why your eyes fly open.

"Let it out," I say hoarsely and you stare at me questioningly. You seem torn, like on the verge of losing control. "Mason," I add, "I need you the way you are. I need you as you are. Please."

Now there seems to be no stopping you for you thrust so hard I have to scream and the headboard slams against the wall.

Shit! Shit!

I feel like I'm about to be ripped apart, but that won't happen. You are through restraining yourself and hoarsely moan my name.

"Fuck, baby, I missed you so much." All I can do is nod uncontrollably as I claw at your pillow and lift my pelvis, meeting every thrust. "You feel so good, baby." We are growing rougher, louder, and letting ourselves go. You slide one arm under my ass and raise it with your fingers digging into my sweaty flesh as I throw my head back and forth, as you devour me.

Again and again, the headboard slams against the wall. As I contract around you and you thrust one final time, pulsating inside me, one side of the bed gives way with a crack and we abruptly find ourselves on the ground. But you don't seem to care. You hold me tightly and continue pushing into me as we both climax.

A little later, we lie on the broken bed, breathing heavily, happy in the knowledge we're together again, at last, and...burst out in resounding laughter.

Finally, we're home again.

32. Listen To Your Heart, Emilia

Mason

The bed has collapsed, Emilia, which is entirely your fault. You told me to let myself go. Now you're lying in the rubble with me, breathing erratically, but I'm holding you in my arms, as it should be. I smoke a joint with an arm wrapped around your shoulders. Your head rests on my sweaty chest and one of your long legs is intertwined with mine. I feel your heartbeat next to me. Thick smoke engulfs us and shimmers in the sunlight that squeezes through the blind's slats into the room.

You said you love me, Emilia, and this time you meant it. I hear your rapid breathing, feel it against my skin, and for the first time in three years, I don't feel empty, I feel whole again.

Your nose caresses my skin as your fingertips follow the tattoos that tell our story. I glance down at you and you up at me. You are no longer afraid, Emilia. You are no longer unsure. You no longer hide from me. I love that. It's like I truly see you for the first time after you have broken out of your shell.

You smile at me. I hold the joint to your lips simply because I want to see them wrap around the filter and expel the smoke because I never want to stop you from doing something that you decide for yourself. You pull on it, your lipstick long gone and the rest of your makeup smeared, but you are still so fucking beautiful.

You blow the smoke in my face, Emilia, and grin cheekily at me. I pinch your ass because I will never stop touching your ass whenever I have the chance. Your giggle is the most beautiful thing I've ever heard. You have never been so relaxed and detached in my arms.

In the next moment, however, I see something else appear in your magical turquoise eyes. You slowly pull your brows together so that a V forms between them, then you hold the blanket in front of your chest and prop yourself up on one arm.

What now?

"I'm actually still mad at you," you say, as if you only just now thought of it and are totally outraged.

I have to grin, baby. You are so cute when you hiss at me. I pull the blanket from your body. You shouldn't hide from me. "Oh yeah?"

"Yes, Mason. Are you here in New York stalking me? Have you met with *Bridget*?"

"And Dr. Daniels," I lazily inform you and take another drag from the joint.

Your mouth opens and you stare at me in shock for a few seconds, then you shake your head and yank the joint out of my fingers for a drag. "Why?" you ask.

"Because you are mine, Emilia, and because I told you I wanted you back. And by any means was and is right for me."

"Mason!" you exclaim. "Were you watching me?" You point your finger at the window and stare at me sternly.

"You mean yesterday when you were sitting on the counter pleasuring yourself?" I love shocking you, baby, and how you blush.

"Yes?"

I sigh and take the joint back for another drag. "First, the guy you're with is an ass and I was worried about you. Second, you slept with a married man who could be your father, Emilia." When I think about it, I get angry again, but I try to control myself for you. Because you would leave and I can't go through that again. That's why I take your hand and kiss each knuckle one by one. "Everything I did was only because I love you, Emilia. I merely wanted to know that you were okay. And I saw that was not that the case, no matter what you told my parents. I also see it as my duty to protect you even if you want me in your life or not."

You're torn between being angry and giving in. "I'm going to explain something to you now, baby. I only learned it myself. You can be angry because you think I did something that didn't conform to the social norm. Or simply ignore that nonsense and listen to your heart. I listen to my heart, Emilia, that's why I'm here."

You swallow and place your hand on my chest where my heart beats. "And I always thought you didn't have one."

"I didn't want to show it to you nor did I want to admit it myself. Because if you have a heart, it can be hurt, and you're the only person in my life who has the power to do so."

You exhale long and hard. Then you smile, lean forward, and kiss me. It's a lazy, long kiss. We're both stoned and so happy. I feel the smile on my mouth and don't know where it came from.

When you try to swing onto me, you almost fall to the floor. I hold you by the arm and you stare at me wide-eyed. "Oh, my God," you say and laugh. "I'm fucking wasted, Mason!"

"I know. You're sexy when you're high."

You're sitting on me, Emilia – naked – a bit too high, unfortunately. I pinch your ass and you squeal.

"Move, Emilia." Your cheeks immediately turn bright red. "I know you have the bitch in you. Just let it out, baby." I reach for my cell phone lying on the floor next to us, turn on our song, and close my eyes.

You drop your head back, circling it from left to right, letting the music fill you as you run your hand over the side of your neck and start rotating your hips.

"Oh, fuck, baby," I whisper. I cross one arm behind my head and place the other loosely on your thigh when you smile at me, Emilia. You know exactly what you're doing to me, you can feel it against your butt. As your hand slides down your neck, between your breasts, over your stomach, and between your legs, I moan. I grasp your thighs with my fingers and you massage your clitoris. Your pelvis jerks directly above me, Emilia. You torture me, you punish me. But I accept the punishment, even if I have to grit my teeth a bit.

"Now, Mason Rush, I'll show you what it's like when *I fuck you.*" With that, you reach behind you and stroke my cock a few times. Fuck, Emilia, you're so wet. Slowly you crawl down between my legs, holding my gaze in the process. Your hair falls over your shoulders and caresses my lower body. When your lips close around me, it's like fucking paradise in this dark fucked up room. I have to close my eyes for a moment, baby, otherwise, I will come immediately. Only you can do that to me.

Your ass is in the air and I imagine what it would be like if I could have it now.

"I've been without your ass for far too long," I murmur hoarsely. We moan at the same time, which is why I grow even harder and my hips twitch upward. You close your eyes because you imagine what I would do if I were behind you. I run one hand through your hair. I always lied, Emilia, I love your hair. I can't hold back now. As I grab your hair, I fuck your mouth. You give me a few strokes, damn, you're so good at blowing, baby. I'm so close.

"If you don't want me to come in your mouth, turn around," I say, but you don't, Emilia. Instead, you look me in the eye and make your tongue twirl. I am lost and come deep in your throat. It's the best fucking orgasm I've ever had.

* * *

We're sweaty after round three and if you're in pain, baby, you don't show it. I love that about you. You are so brave

In the meantime, the other side of the bed has collapsed so that only the mattress separates us from the floor. We both lie on our backs and share a cigarette. You are still breathing heavily from the last round and I admit you also wore me out. It must be after four in the afternoon. Outside, everyone lives on, cars race past, and people rush from point A to B, but time has stopped here, like in our basement. Yes, it has been *our* basement for a long time, but when you fled from me during our vacation, I moved into the apartment because I couldn't stand it any longer.

Your cell phone, which is lying on the floor next to us, vibrates again and again and beams light up to the ceiling. We know who it is without looking. Seth keeps calling trying to reach you. I don't want to let you go and you don't want to go, otherwise, you would have left a long time ago.

I'm stroking your spine as you turn to grab the phone.

You inhale deeply and straighten up. "I have to go, Mason."

My first impulse is to tell you that you won't be going anywhere unless I want you to. But if this is going to work between us, I have to learn to trust that you will come back to me.

You look at me as I lie on the floor as if you expect me to flip out now, hold you tight, and order you to stay.

But I just say, "Okay."

Your eyes widen. "What?"

I try to stay calm and stroke your hair. "If you have to go, go, but come back to me."

“Shit,” you whisper, then lean forward and press your lips firmly against mine. It is a promise that you give me without a word.

But when you get up, Emilia, the familiar horrible feeling comes back to me. The fear that I will lose you if you step out into the light and leave our darkness.

You step into your panties and shorts and put on your t-shirt. Damn, there aren’t enough prints on your ass yet, Emilia. I’m really trying to hold back. You go to the bathroom again. I hear water running and count to ten. Then you come back into the room. I count to twenty. If I hold you here now, you will want to flee again, and I cannot allow that. But when you go to the door without looking back and put your hand on the knob, I involuntarily move.

I push against your body from behind and you freeze when you feel me.

“Wait,” I whisper in your hair and open your pants.

With a tug, I pull them over your butt. Without resisting, you drop your bag, your hands resting on the door in front of you. Fuck, baby, I’ve never seen anything hotter than your ass stretching out to me.

I hit it and penetrate you. Once more, I have to feel you, once more, know that everything is good. With one hand, I reach around your chest, grab your neck, my fingertips on your jaw and I push hard and fast into you, making you whimpering.

You love what we’re doing, Emilia. And although you’ve had five orgasms today, after three minutes, you explode hard around me. I love that you keep coming for me, baby.

With my forehead on the back of your head, I drive deep into you one last time and let go.

"You have until two o'clock, Emilia. Otherwise, I'll come get you." With that, I step back and disappear into the bathroom. I can't watch you go, Emilia.

Never again.

33. I'd Rather Die, Mason

Emilia

I never encountered something as difficult as entering this apartment. My fingers tremble as I reach into my purse to pull out the key Seth gave me to his apartment. You were just in me, Mason, and yet I feel like I'm cheating on you, not him. I can still feel your fingertips on me as well as hear your moans and you telling me I have until two o'clock. It's shortly before half-past four now, which leaves me nine and a half hours, which, in my opinion, is too long. I want the time to go by as fast as possible so I'm back with you.

I've made up my mind. I don't know if I ever had a choice. My heart wants you, Mason. *I* want you and I can no longer ignore it. No matter what has happened between us. You let me go. And I know how hard it was for you. I never expected it because I know you differently. It shows me how much effort you put into getting me back. I too want to get back together with you, but this I have to face alone.

I take a deep breath, unlock and open the door, and enter the apartment. Venus runs joyfully toward me and I pat her head as I set my purse on the floor. When I turn around, I'm confronted with a pair of bare feet. I slowly raise my gaze. I don't experience the pleasantness I did earlier with you. Granted, my heart is racing now too, but for completely different reasons. My gaze continues up over a pair of dark jeans, bare, tattooed torso, and... Yes, Mason, you're right, he is Mason 2.0.

It takes all my courage to look at Seth's face and I immediately regret it. His eyes are ice cold. His gaze slowly takes in my body, the one you just pressed against the door. He is gritting his teeth, his cheek muscles twitch. He appears pissed off, but then I cannot blame him.

"You look freshly fucked," he says coldly. I'd like to suggest that he step back because I can feel your eyes on me, Mason. I realize this is going to get ugly and I don't want you to do anything rash.

However, it wouldn't be prudent to suggest something to Seth now.

"Where have you been?" he asks when I remain silent. Intuition tells me that I should choose my words carefully.

"Why do you ask?" I sound hoarse, as if I've talked, screamed, and laughed too much the previous hour. Besides, I'm sure it still shows that I had a few tokes.

"I called Bridget, that's why," is his only reply and my heart skips a few beats. He circles me slowly and I feel his piercing eyes. "Imagine," he says dryly, "she said couldn't talk since she was in the middle of a lecture, but I did find out she had no idea of your whereabouts, Emilia."

He faces me again and I glance up. I feel so small, I just hate it. No matter how much I've changed, situations like this trigger old behaviors regardless of whether I want to or not. However, right now, I have no choice but put up with it. I just hope you stay where you are, Mason. I know I'm asking a lot of you.

"Do you have anything to say for yourself?" Seth asks harshly. Only now do I realize I've been silent the entire time.

I clear my throat and run a hand through my hair. "I..." I want to tell the truth, Mason, I want to tell him that I love you and that the relationship I have with him won't work in the long run. However, considering how pissed off he looks, I'm afraid he might lose it.

So I come up with a white lie. "I was on my way to see Bridget when I remembered she was in class. So I sat in Central Park and chatted with my father. Call him if you like." I feel my heartbeat in my neck. Fuck, Mason, what am I doing here?

"You were supposed to have coffee with Bridget at Starbucks, but instead, you chatted with your father the entire time?" he asks with one eyebrow raised. "So, you didn't hear other calls coming in even though you were on the phone with him?" Shit, Mason.

"I deliberately didn't pick up."

"Emilia, shut up," he snaps and I flinch. Venus stands next to me and growls at him. She's not like Missy, she might bite if provoked enough. I pet her reassuringly as Seth's gaze shoots to her, though he doesn't retreat. At the moment, he seems unpredictable and I'm afraid he might harm her, which is why I position myself in front of her.

"I'm sorry, what would you like to hear, Seth?" I ask, sounding more confident than I feel.

"As I said, I'd like to know why you look freshly fucked. And why you smell like sex? Explanation? No? Dumbass."

Shit, Mason!

I swallow. "Could it be you're a little paranoid? I mean, I know what your ex did to you, but I'm not her."

"No," he says, shaking his head. "You're worse, Emilia."

"Really now, Seth?" I ask, and despite being scared shitless, I try to flash my eyes angrily. "I'm getting fed-up with your jealousy! I once had a guy who tried to control me, so, no thanks, not a second time."

Out of nowhere, and quite quickly, he grabs my arm and pulls me close so hard, I slam against his chest. "Who are you trying to kid?" he growls. "You're such a little bitch, Emilia. You still smell of him. Couldn't you have taken a shower afterward, you bitch?" I flinch as I try to hold his gaze. "I can tell, so don't lie to me!"

"Let go of me!" I hiss. "Now."

I point my index finger at the ground, signaling Venus to stay put. Though she growls louder, she does as ordered.

Oh, Mason, I can imagine how frustrating you must feel, not being able to interfere, just like I am frustrated knowing you're sitting in your hotel room watching us.

"Or what?" he asks as he glares at me. "Will you sic your dog on me?" He laughs dryly. "I knew from the start you were a whore, Emilia. Ever since you told me about the poor slob you cheated on. You were engaged but fucking another man. And it went on for months. Aren't you ashamed?"

"Yes, I am, but mainly I am ashamed of getting involved with a fucker like you, Seth! I saw something in you that never existed to begin with." Mason, I'm growing angrier than is good for me. Your voice in my head has been a calming influence, just not when it comes to impulse control, then more like the contrary. My blood is boiling and I want to hit him, but I know I'm not strong enough, not enough to do him harm.

"It's no wonder I repeatedly cheated on you!" I hear myself scream, unable to stop even though his increasingly angry expression tells me I should. "Look at you, you control freak! What woman would…" is as far as I get for he slaps me, Mason.

Shit.

And quite hard.

I'm knocked off my feet. Venus immediately attacks and bites his arm before he realizes it.

Fuck!

"Venus! No!" I shout and she immediately comes to me and licks my face. Shit, I have to get us out of here or he'll kill us both.

"Shit!" he yells, holding his bleeding arm as he spins around to me. "I'm going to kill you!" he shouts. "*You bitch, I'm going to kill you*!"

I jump up, open the door with Venus right by my side and as I'm about to dash out, I slam directly into your chest. Fuck!

"Mason!" I say emphatically. My cheek is throbbing and I can see that the monster is already free and there is nothing

I can do about it. I mean, Mason, it is more intense than ever before. It glows in your eyes, your body vibrates with rage, your veins pulse, and your muscles twitch. You stare over me, stretch out an arm, and push me — insanity on your face.

"Stay here," you growl as you enter and close the door.

I'm left behind, wondering if the moment I always feared is about to come to pass, namely, where you become a murderer because of me.

***

"Fuck!" I swear as I stand helplessly in the hallway and pound against the door with the flat of my hand. "*Mason! Open the door*!" I roar, only to be ignored. Instead, I hear cursing and furniture toppling. I pull at my hair in desperation because I don't know what to do. Shit, you might be killing him as far as I know.

Call the police? When my dog just bit someone and we just smoked 20 pounds of pot while you still work for the FBI. That probably wouldn't go over too well.

Call Keaton? But then, he cannot do anything from that distance. I only have one choice. The only one who might be able to do something, who is nearby, and who always picks up when I call is Riley.

Nervous, I pull out the phone of my back pocket. My fingers tremble so much, I have a difficult time unlocking it. I hear something else inside break. Fuck!

Riley answers after the fourth ring, which felt like an eternity.

"Yep?" he asks casually.

"Riley, I need you right away. I'll text you the address, you have to help me. It's Mason."

He sighs deeply. "What's going on?"

"It's an emergency. I think he's about to kill someone. Riley, please, just come over and bring a weapon! Please, hurry!"

"I'll be right there."

I hang up and immediately text him the address, shove the phone back in my pocket, and resume banging on the door.

"Mason!" Inside, I hear more banging, but no one responds. In desperation, I ram my shoulder against the door and kick at it hoping it'll open, but nothing happens. There are still sounds of a battle and I wonder how much longer you two can fight before you finally kill each other. Panic engulfs me as tears start running down my cheeks.

I hope you won't do anything we'll both regret. Abruptly, the door opens and I stumble into Seth's arms.

"*No*!" you roar as he pulls me to him — and you pull your gun.

Fuck!

Venus barks. A blood-drenched Seth bends my arm behind my back and I gasp.

"Let go of her!" you unsteadily demand. Your hair is disheveled, your lips are split, and one eye has a shiner, although, overall, you're okay. Nevertheless, looking into your eyes, Mason, scares me. Actually, your expression frightens me, just as the shiny weapon in your hand does.

Who would give a gun to someone like you?

"Mason!" I say. "Put the gun down!"

Seth runs his nose through my hair. "Yeah, you better listen to your little bitch!" and he breaks my arm. The pain is so sudden and intense, my knees weaken and I scream. Venus is about to charge Seth again when I command in trembling voice, "No."

"You bastard!" I hear the gun cock and my eyes shoot up. Glowing fire seems to course through my whole body starting at my arm and overpowers me so that I can't think straight. The most important thing now is to stop you from pulling the trigger and to get you under control; otherwise, it's all over.

"Mason, if you love me, lower your gun," I gasp even though the pain makes breathing, let alone speaking difficult. "Trust me, baby, listen to me and I will go home with you, but if you use your gun, we will never have a home. That is exactly what he wants."

Seth grins, takes my hair, and pulls my head back. "Oh, and here I was under the impression you didn't know what I want. But you know perfectly well what men want, don't you, you little bitch? You hypnotize them with your magic pussy and wrap them around your little finger." He kneels next to me and glances up at you while still holding my hair in his fist and pulling my head back. "Come on, tell him everything you've done with me. Tell the man you love so much."

Shit, who knew Seth had such psychotic tendencies.

"I can't talk..." I gasp. "I'm in pain, Seth. Mason, lower your gun!" Panic makes my voice seem louder and firmer. Your gaze shoots from him to me and your nostrils flare. I see the decision in your eyes just before you pull the trigger. I cry out. A bullet bores into the wall inches from where Seth's head is and he lets go of me. The shot echoes in my ears so that they whistle.

"Touch her again and the next bullet will hit your forehead dead center." Your voice is so calm, so infinitely calm, it makes you sound even more dangerous than if you were yelling.

Seth pulls me up onto my feet right in front of me, like a shield. I feel his body pressing against my back as his arms wrap around my stomach. My nose is bleeding and I have a coppery taste in my mouth.

What does Seth want from me? Why doesn't he stop?

"You're so fragile, Emilia..." he says, "I could just put my hands around your beautiful neck and squeeze." He wraps a hand around my neck.

"Mason, lower your gun!" I bark.

"Yes, Mason, lower your gun before I strangle her." Your right cheek twitches as Seth squeezes my throat. I cling to his forearm. "Let go of me, Seth!" I gasp and my knees grow weak again. Crap! Suddenly, you raise your gun again, aim it straight at his head, and march angrily toward us. "No, Mason!" I gasp. "I'd rather die than see you go to prison. Please, baby, stand still!" Unexpectedly, I feel Seth's hands loosen from around my neck and he slides down my back, hitting the floor with a dull thud. I am not sure if you shot him as I merely took my eyes off you for a second, but then, you appear just as surprised as I am.

As you look past me, I turn around. There's Riley, breathing heavily with a baseball bat, saying, "You two cannot be left alone, can you?"

34. You Are Still My Brother, Mason

Emilia

I'm in the bathroom wiping my body with a washcloth. It's in the apartment Riley and I had rented to start over in before everything went south. My arm is in a cast, which at least is pink, and the pills I'm taking aren't doing anything for the pain. You and Riley are in the living room sharing a bottle of sherry. Venus is lying at your feet, exhausted from all the commotion. You spoke briefly over the phone with your father, who will *take care* of Seth, who I'm done with for good. Who knew Seth would go nuts like that. Obviously, I knew the breakup wouldn't be pretty — what breakup is? But like that? I was always worried you would eventually kill someone because of me, but when it counted, you kept yourself in control, Mason. You didn't shoot him even though you wanted to. I saw it in your eyes. So now you are on the right track, *we* are on the right track. That's all that matters.

Awkwardly, I put on a t-shirt and walk barefoot to you two.

"Riley, if you're not okay with this, we can stay at Mason's hotel or my dorm room." I recall the broken bed and wonder where exactly we would sleep. Then I think of my tiny dorm room and the shared showers and I frown.

You two are still sitting there. I can't tell if you two hate or love each other. You always maintain a certain distance between each other, but now, at least, you look at each other instead of being at each other's throats.

Riley turns his head in my direction. "Oh, don't be daft, I have a guest room, as you know. So relax, take a load off, and get a good night sleep, tomorrow we'll see what's what." I remain standing next to you, undecided. I have no idea how to behave in Riley's presence for everything is still so fresh and new. Thankfully, you wrap an arm around my legs and kiss my hip.

"How are you feeling, baby?" The way you peer up at me...oh, I'd do anything for that look. I run a hand gently through your hair.

"And, how are *you* feeling?" I ask hoarsely. Speaking hurts since Seth squeezed my throat hard. You pull me next to you onto the couch and I gaze at the fireplace with the artificial fire crackling so beautifully. Actually, I don't want to, but, for some reason, my body snuggles up to you the second you wrap one arm around my shoulder. As soon as your scent hits my nose, I know everything is going to be okay. The pain subsides almost immediately and I fall asleep peacefully for the first time in three years.

Mason

You lie with your head on my lap, Emilia. I hate to see that plaster on you and I hate what that fucker did, so I drink another glass of sherry to forget about that for a few hours. My brother brings a blanket and throws it over you. It is already dark outside. We spent four hours at the hospital with the nurse glaring at me as if I had given you these injuries. Thank God Riley, Mr. Clean, was there, otherwise, she probably wouldn't have let you leave with me. Now he's sitting across from me staring. Psycho. My body is still full of adrenaline. I still haven't come down, Emilia. When I think about that fucker's face, my hand twitches with its banged knuckles and I want to beat him again. I never want to be in a situation where I can't help you again, baby. Yeah, I wanted to shoot, but the look in your eyes stopped me. I wanted to beat him unconscious but not hurt you at the same time, so I couldn't get to him because of you. God, I never want to see you so helpless again. You always choose the wrong men, Emilia.

"Maybe you'd be better for her," I say slowly to Riley, but he knows exactly what I mean.

"Probably." He takes a sip. "Actually, certain. But you know what she's like when she gets something in her head. She wants you. I saw her looking at you. She loves and adores you. Reason no longer matters." I like hearing the words, Emilia. I adore you too.

"I love her too," I say.

"I know."

"How? You said all the time I was just fucking around and taking advantage of her. What changed your mind now?"

"Mason, for years, your path has lead you back to her. No matter how much shit you did, she forgave you, and now you've found each other again. I also see how you look at her. And it is because of your love for her that you didn't go totally crazy today and shoot the bum."

"God, I hate it when you're right."

"That was always your biggest problem with me. You couldn't stand the fact that I was not malicious and did my job, that my biggest goal was to make Mom laugh by doing everything she wanted. If you worried her, I wanted to show her that not everything was shitty...and tried to take the burden off her shoulders."

I snort. "Do you actually know what it was like to live in your shadow? You, the bright light of the family, the child prodigy. Straight A student, piano lessons, student representative, best in class, a beautiful woman, nice apartment, good job, and me... the fuck-up in the basement. Do you know what it was like to compete with you all these years?"

"Oh God, Mason, do you have a clue? You think you had to compete with me? All the attention has been on you ever since you were born. I was only so focused on you because you were the problem child and I wanted a piece of the pie. Once you were there, it was all about you, and it still is. Can't you tell? How often do I call Dad because I have a problem and how often do you call? How often does Mom cry over me and how often does she cry over you? How often do you need something and how often do I need something?"

"What are you telling me, man? That I can't stand on my own two feet?"

"I'm simply saying that it's always about you, Mason, and maybe you should try looking at it from my perspective. And yes, dammit, you should really stand on your own two feet. Dad also needs some rest. And Emilia needs a man who is stable in life and can support her."

I raise an eyebrow. "I don't live at home anymore."

"Yes, but… you're still at home there. You work with him, you eat with him, and you take his car if you want to go away. You call him when you have problems and you expect, deep down, he will always do everything for you and that is why you have a free ride. But that's not how it works. Imagine if you had shot the guy today, Dad wouldn't have been able to help you."

"I didn't do it."

"It's a start." We both take a sip.

Then he says, "I didn't want to hate you at all, I merely wanted to get along peacefully with you."

"Until I took the girl away from you."

"The woman I love, not just any girl." We both look at you as you sleep so peacefully, one hand on my thigh, your head on my lap, and I stroke your hair. I imagine myself in his place, watching you sleep on someone else's lap. And I probably understand it for the first time.

"She chose the dark, not the light, and it was her decision. But I'm sorry for you. I don't want to imagine how it feels." When I look at him, he seems a little surprised. He has never heard such words from me. But I want to finish the old shit — for you.

"You should finally let her go and find someone new, Riley. Because there is one out there who can give you what you need and what you deserve."

"It's not easy to let her go. You know that."

"Oh yes, I know." We remain silent for a moment and stare at you. I know I never want to lose you again, baby, and I never want to be able to let you go again.

I inhale deeply and look at Riley. He is watching me, Emilia, but for the first time, there isn't a bitter expression in his eyes. "I'm going to sleep, I'm exhausted." I carefully push myself out from under you and lift you into my arms.

But I turn to Riley again. "Hey, thanks for before," I say as I walk by him.

He swirls his sherry in the glass and laughs. "You are still my little brother."

We both grin and I carry you upstairs, knowing everything will be fine.

Epilog

Mason

I sit on an armchair in your tiny dorm room and wonder why every goddamn bastard knows your name here. When we drove from my brother's to your dorm this afternoon – to your dormitory – I almost freaked out for the first time since Seth. I couldn't walk down the hallway with you without some son of a bitch saying, "Hey, Emmy!" What's this Emmy business, Emilia? And, you blushed. Why did you keep blushing, Emilia? What have you been doing here over the years?

I don't think I want to know, but I must.

That's why I let the smoke escape from my lips and stare at you through the haze. You're still lying naked and sweaty in your much too small bed, but I don't care how tiny the bed is, baby. I always manage to fuck you somehow. No matter how little space we have.

You lie on your back and reach for my joint, but I consider not giving it to you just because I can and you don't deserve it, Emmy.

"Why does every cock on this campus know you, Emilia?" I ask and take another hit. You turn on your side, a hand under your cheek, and look at me calmly.

"Are you jealous, Mason? Did you really think I only had Seth during the last few months and no one else?"

"DILF Daniels! What does that mean anyway?" I growl. I high-jacked your cell phone and read your messages, but you always deleted the really important ones. Everything except the numbers of a thousand tails. Your cell phone looks like mine used to look like. With names like Blowjob-Kyle, Doggy-Daniel, DILF-Daniels, and so on. I do not like it at all.

Now you laugh — cheekily! "Daddy I'd like to fuck!" I almost fall over in shock. You really don't have an instinct for self-preservation anymore because, giggling, you climb onto my lap completely naked and take the joint from me. You take a hit, lean forward, and *blow the smoke directly into my mouth*.

"Calm down, Mason," you whisper directly next to my lips and throw an arm around my shoulder while holding the joint in your other hand.

Calming down is easier said than done. I raise an eyebrow when you take another hit. "So you worked your way across campus, Emilia? Really?"

"Yeah."

Oh shit, Emilia!

"What should I do with you?" I ask, placing a hand on your thigh.

"Whatever you want, Mason."

"Have you forgotten that saying that to me is dangerous, baby?"

"No, I haven't." You move your hips provocatively. I am only wearing shorts and suppress a moan.

"I still don't trust you, Emilia," I say softly and take the joint from you and place it in the ashtray.

"I also don't trust you!" I gently lift your chin and run my thumb over your lip.

"We truly are going to kill each other," I say quietly.

"I know."

"It won't be easy, Emilia."

"I know."

"And now I'm certain I won't let you escape."

"I know."

The End

Preview – STAY, BABY, STAY

You are mine, Emilia.
Now and forever.
Stay!

To the most loyal friends in the world
Mia, Hercules, Jack, and Juni.
Our inspiration for Missy, Rosie, and Venus.

PROLOG

You are torn between the light and the dark.
But you need the dark. You need the abyss.
You need me.
Don't play the lion if you're only a little kitten. One move from me and I'll crush you like an ant.
You are mine, Emilia.
Now and forever.
Stay!

I Don't Like That, Emilia

Mason

I keep telling myself, just one more week, Emilia. Then I'll either lock you in my basement or in my apartment. I have to keep my mouth shut for that long, but it's not easy. I hate the way you are.

You're not my sweet little Emilia anymore.

You are the party bitch who knows everyone, who greets everyone, who hugs everyone, who is given a mug of beer by everyone. You're giving out fucking kisses and at least eight guys have grabbed your ass. Your dress is so damn tight you can see every curve of your body. I told you not to put it on, but you did anyway. And that's not all, I had to come here with you because I can't let you go out alone in a dress like that. They're students. They're sick in the head, Emilia.

I hate American Pie parties, I liked the parties in my basement — and then, not really.

We are in a small, fucked up pub and I cling to my beer so that I don't wrap my hands around some neck and strangle them. I'm so glad Dad called Riley and forced him to take the gun away or someone would be dead and I would be in jail while you were still bouncing around in that damn scrap of cloth.

I lean against the bar and watch you, Emilia. How you shine, how you laugh and throw your hair back. What are you trying to prove to me? That you now have such a great life, that you are so popular and independent you don't need me?

Are you provoking me, Emilia?

Just wait until we are back in Chicago.

I'm only letting you go as far as I think is right so as not to scare you off. Because I'm going to take you home with me. Besides, I want to know how you'll react if, for once, I ignore what you're doing. Dad used to do this to Mom all the time — I read it in his journal. She wanted to tease him, but Dad just ignored her. So, she had to get out of the situation on her own even if it was anything but pleasant.

The music is so loud you can only be heard by shouting. You see Bridget enter and I smile because it's going to be funny when she discovers me. She doesn't know about us yet, Emilia.

"Emmy!" she cries out and I roll my eyes.

"Hey!" you reply.

Oh, God, Emilia, you've become one of *those* girls. The *hey* girls. The girls who scream along to every song as if it were their absolute favorite song and who clap and embarrassingly jump on the spot. Emilia, I love you, but I don't like what you've become. Even if your self-confidence suits you, you're an attention whore and I don't like that. You love that I watch you do it. But, baby, the only attention you should be craving is *mine,* not those morons around you.

Bridget has now fought her way to you and you hug as if you haven't seen each other in 50 years. Right away, she asks about Seth. I see how your gaze wanders to me and I know that hers is about to follow. I start smiling.

Bridget opens her eyes wide when she sees me — and I wave.

You narrow your eyes and I figure this is my chance to give back a little of what you have been doing right now. So I push off the bar and stroll casually towards you with one hand in my pocket.

"John?" Bridget asks wide-eyed. You can't answer because you're too busy glaring at me. Especially when I stand next to her.

"Hi, Bridget, my real name is Mason."

"Huh?!" she replies and I don't get the chance to continue talking because you wrap your arms around my stomach like a boa constrictor.

"Yes, this is Mason and we're together now." You're drunk, baby. I like that.

"Huh? What about Seth? What's going on, Emilia?" When I hear his name, I inhale deeply. You don't let go of me, but grip me a little tighter because you feel how tense I've suddenly become. Because you're afraid I'm going to freak out.

"Long story, Bridget." You give her a secret sign, Emilia, to keep her quiet. It's so sweet my anger wanes a bit. Slightly.

"I don't get it, how do you two know each other?" Then realization flashes in her eyes. "Mason Rush?" She looks at you wide-eyed, then grabs your arm – I see a pattern, Emilia, how you pick friends and lovers, you like people who control you – and drags you off somewhere.

I'll let you two withdraw and I'll go outside this stinking hipster joint for a cigarette. I also need fresh air, even if the air in New York is anything but fresh. I can't stand confined spaces, let alone crowded ones. Sweat, alcohol, sex, it's all in the air and I hate that you're in there without me. But, you are strong and tough, you will surely manage five minutes without me.

Emilia, I held a gun to your ex's face and he hit you just a few weeks ago, but you act like it never happened. You're running around happy and presenting me as your new friend. Emilia, do you realize how sick that is? Is this your new approach? Instead of hurting, you repress it? Instead of appearing fragile, you sweep it under the rug?

Aren't you worried about Seth? *I know*, but you haven't even asked. Aren't you worried about how Riley is handling all this and how he feels about us being together now? Like you usually do? Do you ever ask yourself if it will work out for us, as different as we are, even though I will never leave you alone?

It seems you have no problems, no worries, that everything's fantastic. The only reason I'm still here with you is because you have to sort out all the paperwork to finish school in Chicago. You have to get back on your feet, baby. You're not you. And I don't like it.

You slept with half the campus, Emilia. You dated a woman beater and thought he was awesome. You suppress the fact that you have parents, and instead, pretend my parents are yours. Do you realize what's happening in your head?

Why Dr. Daniels? Why did you sleep with a man who's too old for you? Didn't he ever tell you what I was thinking?

Why did you cheat on Seth?

Is it all about the thrill?

Will you do it to me? Like you did to Riley? Like you did with Seth and actually, with Dr. Daniels, if you want to be accurate?

Maybe the problem isn't me, but you.

Emilia, you're sick.

But I can never get away from you and you can never get away from me. I'll see to that. My phone rings. The number is blocked, but I don't care, I always answer my phone. Maybe it's that bum Seth, although I don't think he can talk now that my dad's done with him. Did you know my dad was around, Emilia, taking care of the grunt work? He is so good at sneaking up on someone that he could stand behind them without them noticing, even though he is merely one step away.

"Yeah?" I answer nonchalantly and flick the rest of my cigarette into the street. Some drunk fuckers walk arm in arm past me. God, I'm not in the mood for this shit. I want to go home and fuck you and expel the little hurt girl out of you again.

"Mason?" I freeze when I recognize the female voice. "Hi." My eyes fly to the door as I mumble, "Shit!"

"What do you want, Cherry?" I ask roughly. I can really do without her right now.

"Am I interrupting? Sounds like you're out and about."

“What's the matter, Cherry? It’s 2:00 a.m., why are you calling?”

She pauses. “I just wanted to ask...oh, never mind.”

“Don’t play the innocent little deer. I know you can articulate what you want. So, what do you want, Cherry?”

“In two weeks, it’s summer break. I want to know if you’re coming.”

“And you needed to ask me that at two in the morning?” I light another cigarette. Emilia, I know I shouldn’t talk to her, but I need to know what she wants at 2:00 a.m. “No, I’m definitely not coming! I’m back with Emilia, okay?!”

“Oh!” she utters. She is quiet for a moment before asking, “Hey, I want to know why you are angry with me?”

“You know why!” I exclaim.

“You stuck your dick in me; I didn’t force you to get a hard-on and fuck me, Mason, while your girlfriend was upstairs sleeping. It was your choice. You cheated. I only loved you and tried to win you over.”

“You’re calling me now while I’m in New York at 2:00 in the morning to tell me that?”

“No, but I can’t stand that you are so mad at me. I’m not to blame for what happened. Yeah, I had sex with you. Obviously, it affects me too. But in the end, *you* crossed the line, not me.” *Shit*, I think.

“Who’s that?” you ask from behind me. And I know I’m fucked.

Fuck, Emilia.

I just hang up and for a tiny second, my fucking heart slides into my fucking stomach. Fuck! I feel like I cheated on you again, but I didn’t do anything.

You stare at me skeptically and raise an eyebrow.

I don't like that bitch look.

"Who was that, Mason?" you ask again. Your voice sounds unusually hard.

"You better tell me who *you* are because I don't recognize this bitch in her little short dress. She's a pain in the ass!"

"Excuse me?" you ask hesitantly.

"Oh, you understood me correctly. I don't have to repeat myself, Emilia!" You snort and cross your arms over your chest.

"I knew you weren't strong enough to handle the new me. You only like the little, submissive, opinionless Emilia. But as soon as I have character, people who love me, a life that isn't only you, it doesn't suit you."

You want to turn and run away, Emilia, but that's not how it works. So, I grab you by the elbow and yank you to me.

I look into your eyes. "Have you forgotten everything we've been through the last few weeks and that you've been running around acting like a diva? Did you even think for a second about the fact that you fucked some old guy or what happened to your little Seth? Have you thought about what you will do with your little princess ego when we get to Chicago? You're not strong, Emilia, you're weak now. You're the weakest I've ever seen because you pretend to be strong and hide your feelings from everyone," I growl. With a fascination in your eyes that I've rarely seen, you suddenly place your hand on my cheek and ask, "When did you become so deep, Mason Rush?"

"Since I admitted to myself that I love you, now come!"

You Are My Damaged Whore, Emilia

Mason

Your dorm room is as small as my office, Emilia. There is an ancient bed, a closet, and a desk. The room is stuffed. Kissing and groping, we stumble into your room as I rip open your dress at the back. Oh, fuck, I will never stop loving you. No way. Not even when you're eighty.

I'm still mad. About so many things, Emilia. Now I can't hold back anymore because I have been controlling myself so much lately. But there are a few things I need to clarify. Now!

The list is endless. But finally, I have you back and I can use you. I slap your ass hard. You love it, don't ever say otherwise. I notice deep inside, you are not connected to anything. Baby, you're still so fragile. Don't play the lion if you're only a little kitten. We've been over this, one move from me and I'll crush you like an ant.

"Bend over the table," I growl in your ear. Still in your high heels, you grin provocatively at me over your shoulder and follow my orders at a snail's pace. Baby, it doesn't work that way. It's obvious you haven't been with me for three years. Besides, I have been wearing kid gloves for the last few weeks, but that's about to change. I grab you tightly by the neck, push you the three steps to the table, and slam you against it with my upper body. You gasp. The moonlight falls across your skin and the yellow glow of the street lamps mixes with the silver shimmer. There are still drunk students running around the hall as I bend over you. "Don't move!" I command and I rip your barely existing panties off your body with one yank. I know it hurts, baby, but I know you can take it.

With a rag, I tie one of your ankles to the table leg — so tightly you hiss. With one quick move, I pull the black shirt over my head and tie your other ankle. You're so exposed, I like it, baby. That's why I'm going to smack your ass again. I can't help it.

"How are you feeling, baby?" I ask. Without touching you, I stand behind you. My shadow falls over you because I'm standing right in front of the window.

"Fine," you reply lightly.

I smack your ass again.

"I asked how you are feeling, Emilia!"

"Fuck, Mason, I told you I feel good," you hiss at me over your shoulder. I slowly open my belt so that you hear the jingling and pull it out of the loops. Your pupils widen.

"Mason," you say warningly.

"Shut up, Emilia!" I wrap the belt around my hand a few times, take a deep breath, and whip it across your ass so hard you scream.

"I asked how you are feeling. If you lie to me again about your true feelings, there will be five more lashes — one after another, without a break. So, honest answer!"

"I feel like shit!" you yell. "Satisfied?"

With my head tilted, I approach you and gently stroke your center. You're always so wet for me, baby.

You moan and drop your forehead against the tabletop as I move my fingers up and down without penetrating you. "There is a reward for every honest answer, Emilia. What shall you never do again?"

You're just moaning, so I'm going to pinch your clit hard until you gasp.

"Lie?"

"Wrong!" I smack your ass.

"Fuck, Mason!" I slap your ass again.

"You used to be a fast learner, baby. So, what shall you never do again?"

"Hide my feelings from you!"

With a *Good girl!* I open my pants and thrust my boner of a lifetime all the way inside you. You moan and I wrap your hair around my fist and pull your head back so that you stand almost upright in front of me.

"And the next time I tell you not to wear that dress, don't wear it!" I pull out of you.

"Fuck!" you whisper.

"What won't you do anymore, Emilia?"

"Put on dresses you don't like," you stammer and I sink back into you. Exactly three times, I push into you, enjoying the sounds you make, and your contractions around me. Then I pull out again — right to the tip.

"The next time we are in a room with several people, you will stand next to me and laugh with me and talk to me. You won't look at another dick. Do you understand?!"

"Mason, you're exaggerating!" You glare at me over your shoulder.

"What was that?" I ask, still holding your hair. I don't move.

"I said you were exaggerating!" you state clearly. "Mason, you're not my father." Oh, Emilia, is it possible you want me angry?

I pull out completely and push into your back entrance that has been dampened by your moisture. Because I know you can take it. I also know you even love and miss me acting like a cold bastard. The last few times haven't been rough between us, Emilia. I was extremely restrained, but you got cocky. It's your own fault.

"Fuck, Mason!" you yell. I love that everyone in the hall can hear what I'm doing with you. I want them to know that you're off-limits, that you belong only to me.

I stay motionless inside you once I'm all the way inside and ask again, "How do you feel now, Emilia?"

When you defiantly say "Perfect!" I abruptly move with a jerk and you scream.

"Shit, man! I feel like shit, okay! Please!" I know, Emilia, I shouldn't move for a while, but you're teasing me.

"Fine, Emilia, what won't you do the next time we go out together?"

"Look at other dicks and stand with you. Oh, my God, please get out of my ass, Mason!" I withdraw immediately and calmly stroll with my behemoth boner into the tiny fucking kitchen.

"Mason, where are you?" you yell breathlessly because you can't see me anymore. I love it, Emilia. Without answering you, I wash up and grab a bottle of water and another cigarette. Then I stroll back and sit down across from you at the table where I slam down the water with a loud bang. Your head flies up, you didn't expect to find me here. I rest my chin on a fist and stare at your beautiful, sweaty, desperate face, the lust in your eyes, and the slight tremor of your lower lip. I love it when you're this close to coming, Emilia, and I won't let you.

"So, let's summarize what we have learned today, Emilia," I say in a teacher's voice and light a cigarette. You narrow your eyes.

"Mason, you can't treat me like this anymore!"

"Oh, you don't want this? Shall I untie you, Emilia?" I ask, honestly interested.

"Just fuck me," you snap. "I want to come and so do you."

"Oh, I'm patient, baby." I lean back and take a hit from my cigarette. "Are you going to tell me what we learned today or not?"

"No, I'm not!" I bend over and pinch your nipple hard, holding it tight until you whimper. "What was that?"

"Ouch, Mason!" I squeeze harder. "Fuck, okay, I'll tell you, but first let go!"

"Tell me like this," I say lazily.

"I can't lie to you about my feelings anymore...please, Mason, ouch!"

"That's not everything, Emilia."

"I can't wear anything you think is too short or too tight!" Your breathing becomes labored and I loosen my grip a little.

"And."

"I can't focus on other dicks when you're with me."

"And other times!" I squeeze harder.

"Fuck, Mason! Yes, always you! Now let go!"

"Good girl!" and I remove my hand, step behind you again with the cigarette between my lips, and push deep inside you until you scream. And not in pain this time.

You do that weird thing with your pussy muscles and I back off. We're not coming yet, baby.

"You will not talk back to me again."

"Please!" you order arrogantly again. God, Emilia, what am I going to do with you?

With a jerk, I withdraw again.

"It doesn't suit you to be such a bitch," I say, picking up the belt from the floor. You hear it and fidget. "What was that, Emilia?" I smack your already flushed butt, but not as hard, not as intense as the first time. Then I bend over to face you.

"I shall not talk back to you," you say tensely and roll your eyes.

"And never roll your eyes again!" I slap your ass again. "You can be hot and you can be confident, but with me, you're my little broken whore again, aren't you, Emilia, or, you have to stay away from me, but I can't and I won't let you!" I push myself back inside you. "Is that what you want, Emilia? Should I stay away from you?"

"No!" you scream and I fuck you so hard, my pelvic bones bang against your ass. I know this is going to hurt tomorrow,

Emilia, but that's good. Then I stop and kiss your shoulder. "And what do you want from me?"

You're soaked in sweat, your hair is sticky, and you're breathless when you turn to me and gasp, "What?"

"You have one wish, Emilia." For what feels like an eternity, I don't move, just like you, and I grow a bit apprehensive imagining what you are going to ask of me now. You turn as far as you can and look me in the eye. With every passing second, I realize I shouldn't have said it. When you take a breath to speak, I want to cover my ears. "Who was on the phone earlier?" you ask.

Fuck! My heart races. Emilia, you won't understand if I explain it to you now, so I thrust my hips forward. Your eyes close and your forehead sinks to the tabletop.

In a minute, baby, we both have to come.

I dig my hands into your shoulders and lean on you as I take you hard, but I know you love it when you feel my weight on your body. It is getting hotter and hotter, our bodies are becoming wetter and wetter, and our breath is increasingly faster and faster. Pretty soon, you'll hear nothing but our moans. I feel you contract around me and you throw your head backward, but I push you back down by the neck. My gaze wanders across your form, how you are at my mercy. I love this, Emilia.

It won't be long before I explode too and come deep inside you.

Marry Me, Emilia

Mason

I untie you and set you on the table in front of me, Emilia. You are still breathless, shaky, and covered in sweat — so exhausted you slowly fall forward and I push you back with one hand.

"Stay seated!" I demand. You open your eyes and nod. Quickly, I put on my shorts and grab an ointment from your tiny bathroom. You are still on the table when I return. That's good, baby. I pull up a chair and sit in front of you. I brush your hair back and gently rub the ointment on your sore nipple. You hiss and I feel your eyes on me. I know you're still waiting for an answer from me. I won't be able to take that away from you either. Other than that, I am a man of my word. So, I say calmly, without looking up, totally focused on your breasts, "It was Cherry." You stiffen immediately, but I skillfully ignore it and treat your other nipple even though there is nothing there. I feel your relentless little fingers digging into my collarbone. You're trying to push me back a bit. I don't like that, Emilia.

Sighing, I lift my eyes and gaze into yours — they burn with rage. Your breathing accelerates, your face takes on an unhealthy red color, your lips press together, and your nostrils flare.

You stare at me, Emilia, and I stare back.

I could ease the tension a little by explaining exactly how it was, but for some reason, I want to know what you're going to do now. Then I see your hand rise as if in slow motion, your trembling fingers becoming rigid before you reach out and slam them full force against my cheek.

Baby, there was so much anger in that.

My head even jerks to the side.

And I'm proud of you.

I deserve it after all I've put you through. I clench my jaw and look at you again.

You jump off the table, march to your closet, and pull out some long over-sized sweater that you put on. I love it, baby, when you wear such loose clothes and you're all sweaty because I was inside you a minute ago. Finally, you can dress yourself again because the stupid cast is gone, so I can fuck you again the way we like it.

"*You son of a bitch*!" you yell and when I try to get up, you hiss, "No! Stay where you are. Don't you move, Mason!" With a furrowed forehead, I remain seated. My cheek stings a bit, baby, but play the devil and let it show.

"May I explain?" I try to stay calm. It's enough when one freaks out.

"No!" you scream. "You listen to me, Mason! I put up with everything from you! Every type of humiliation, torture, and being kicked out of your bedroom when you were done with me like a little whore. I put up with being treated like dirt, like scum, who belongs on the street for years. I was slapped in the face by you and I still didn't leave your side. I let you call me names. You kicked me out of your basement when you were mad at me. You beat me every chance you got and then you cheated on me, Mason, while I slept a few feet away. You son of a bitch! How dare you talk to that bitch on the phone?" You march up to me and before I know it, you slap me again. Same spot, baby. Hard. I'll take that too.

"How dare you come into my life after all these years, remind me again that I love you, and then beat me because you don't like my character even though I am doing everything possible to keep myself above water. Mason, this is how I *survive*. You hurt me so deeply and I hate you..." Tears fill your eyes. Fuck. You want to slap me again, but two slaps are enough. This time, I catch your wrist, hold it tight, and slowly rise. You swallow. With your wrist, I push you back against the wall and your moist eyes widen. "You are such a self-righteous bitch, Emilia Sullivan. You came to me, to the graveyard, and I told you to stay away from me, Emilia. You should have run. What did you do?" You stare at me with clenched teeth. "If you hadn't gotten involved with me, I could not have blackmailed you, Emilia. I wouldn't have stood a chance if you had truly loved Riley. *You* know that and *I* know that. You practically begged me to hurt you, Emilia. Everything. I. Did. You. Wanted. Except the punch. But I believe you did that deliberately because I warned you three times that day. You know I could not restrain myself, yet you continued with sick defiance in your eyes. It was like you wanted me to lose control so you could convince yourself I was a monster. Whenever I sent you away, you returned to my bed."

"And every time I voluntarily left, you brought me back again."

"Shut up. You fucked my brother in my bed and you knew I was there."

"And you fucked Claire in *my* bed and came on my blanket because you wanted me to see it!" I press you harder against the wall. "You fucked your shitty guy in my pool and you can't tell me you didn't know I was somewhere in the house watching you because I always want to know what you are doing. Your mind is fucked-up, Emilia!" I growl.

You want to push me away. "Don't forget your Cherry problem!" But I won't let you and press you tightly against the wall.

"She called me, her number was blocked. I didn't know it was her. She wanted to know if I was coming to the beach house this summer." Your eyes are so empty, I don't like it. "I said no. I said I was back together with you."

"Why didn't you hang up when you realized it was her?"

"It was 2:00 a.m., Emilia, and Cherry called me, which meant it could have been Aunt Amber or Mom. I don't know, anyway, I just wanted to know why she was calling and then I hung up. I want nothing more from her!" I grab your cheeks tightly and make you look at me. "I love you, not Cherry."

"There's only one way I can believe you, Mason," you say in a voice choked with tears and your eyes sparkle again.

"As long as you don't slap me, what do you want?"

"Tell me everything!" I take a step back and run a hand through my hair.

"I won't do that to you!"

"Okay, Mason. Then go!" Fuck! "I'm tired of you not telling me anything, always leaving me in the dark so that I have to figure it out on my own!" I won't go. That's not even an option, Emilia.

I don't say anything and you point to the chair. "Sit." You've never looked stronger, baby. Now you are no longer a little kitten but a real lioness as you stand before me. Now you're my equal, so I'll sit down.

Emilia, I think this is the first time I've taken you seriously. Except for that one time when you left me.

You stand in front of me with your arms crossed over your chest and glare at me. "We're starting from scratch, Mason. Step one," you say seriously. "What happened in that beach house while I was asleep?" I take a deep breath and run a hand through my hair again. *I don't want to do this, baby*, I think. But I can see you are not going to give me a choice, so I drop my head backward and close my eyes.

"Look at me, Mason," you demand and I frown, but look at you, slightly enraged from under my eyelashes. "It was sex, Emilia. Nothing more." I barely get it out.

"I don't believe you, Mason." You sit down on the table in front of me and cross your bare legs. The white sweater hangs loosely over your knees.

"When did you first fuck her when we were there?" The way you say it, I almost flinch.

"It lasted almost a week," I reluctantly answer.

"Wait a minute! Why was it so hard to be faithful to me?"

"Baby, I didn't mean it like that. Can you please stop turning my words around?"

"Where did you first fuck, Mason, and what time?" What have I done?

"You were asleep. She came into the room and called for me."

"Oh, that's what I call ruthless. Go on." You are so incredibly angry and hurt at the same time, Emilia. I don't like this at all.

"She brought a bottle of gin and we went to the palm tree just off the porch." I don't want to say another word. My heart is racing.

"What were you thinking at that moment, Mason?"

"I believed she was everything I wanted, but when you left, I realized she was not you and nothing more than a beautiful illusion from my youth. You put up with so much from me, I lost respect for you, Emilia, so I thought I wanted someone like Cherry. But I never wanted that. I wouldn't be able to deal with someone like that in the long run. I only want you. Okay?"

"No! Nothing is okay. Go on. So you sat under the palm tree."

"Fuck... Emilia, aren't you tired?" I ask.

"Oh, no, I've never been more wide awake in my life than I am right now, Mason!"

"She kissed me and I tried to stop her, but suddenly..."

"Were you inside her? What? You can go that fast, Mason. How many times? Total?"

"Five times," I growl gruffly and you exhale loudly.

"Fuck!" You get up from the table, dig your hands into your hair, and pace up and down the room. "Five times? Really?"

I don't answer. What do you want me to say?

Until you stop in front of me and break my heart a little. "Why, Mason?" You stare at me like you feel responsible, like you're not enough.

"Fuck," I whisper when I realize something. "I'm to blame, aren't I? That you bounce from man to man all the time, seeking their approval. It's my fault for breaking you and taking what little faith you had left." You snort.

"Baby, it has never been because you're not pretty enough or because you haven't given me enough. I've always received more from you than I deserved. It has never been because I did without something from you. I was merely convinced that Cherry was the one woman who could tear me away from everyone else. But you know what? That one woman is you. The one that gets me away from everyone else in one fell swoop." Tears flow with a silent sob and you sink to your knees as if the burden that has been weighing on you for years has been lifted. You press the back of one hand against your mouth.

"I hate to see you like this, baby, and I hate that it's my fault. Seth broke your arm, but I broke your heart. This is much worse." I slide off the chair, get down on my knees before you, and take your face in my hands. My thumbs run over your wet cheeks. "I never want to fuck another woman, Emilia. I'll never cheat on you again. I don't care about others, I'm not attracted to them. You're all I ever think about, no matter what I do. All these accusations are of no use to us. I know we have done so much to ourselves, but we must now learn to trust each other. You trust me as much as I trust you or this won't work, baby. I never want to be without you again and that's why I want you to marry me!" Your eyes shoot up immediately and you rub your nose with a sleeve. You blink and the tears slowly dry up.

"What?" you ask stunned. I don't even know where that came from. All I know is I want it bad.

I take your hand and kiss your palm gently. "Marry me, Emilia."

"Fuck!" you whisper. Your eyes, baby, they're huge with wonder, like a little kid at Christmas. "Are you serious?"

"You should know I don't say anything I don't mean. Especially not this." You laugh.

"Can I say yes or is it an order?" I smile and wipe the last of the moisture from your cheeks.

"Both," I say gently.

Then you shine like a damn nuclear power plant, Emilia, and I know I did something right for once. You fall around my neck so violently that you knock me to the ground and lie on top of me. I like it, baby.

"Of course, I'll marry you, what do you think?"

"Shit, Emilia!" I'm still gasping and then I can't speak anymore because we're kissing.

There's going to be a sequel in a couple of months. What do you think?

Note of Thanks

Thanks to the best publisher in the world, the A.P.P. Verlag. Thanks to the best editor in the world, who we constantly cause to have sleepless nights, he-he.
Of course, thanks to Marie Graßhoff for her beautiful cover designs.
And thank you, thank you, thank you all who have so far accompanied us on our path. Especially Alex! We would be nothing without him. Probably starving to death, emaciated, and headless long ago. LOL.
But above all: Thank you all! Again and again, you leave us breathless! We love your reviews! We love the heart, soul, and passion you put into them! How do you like Mason's transformation? So, who is as smitten with that little shit and the Rush universe like we are? Who can get enough?
We eagerly wait to find out how you liked it. Please leave us a few lines wherever you want!
A big hug from us!

Yours, Maria and Don <3

Book Recommendation

For those who want to learn more about Keaton and Olivia Rush.

You don't see me, but I'm watching you, Olivia.

I always watch you.

I'm always there — no matter what you do.

I watch when you rub your little hot body against other men and when you serve guests in your chaste uniform.

I know what you think, who you are, and who you would like to be.

I know what you need and I will give it to you. Soon.

Then you will be mine.

The dark prelude to a series that will take your breath away.

Obsessed - Until You're Mine.

Read at your own risk!

https://amzn.to/2DrPEDy

About Don Both

Don Both is 30 years old and lives in Bavaria. She started writing stories at the age of 12 when she wanted to hand in the best short story in school. Her plan succeeded and she recognized she had a talent for writing stories.

During her school years and vocational training to become a nanny, she let her imagination run wild as a hobby author. Initially, she mainly focused on writing romance novels and humorous comedies. However, she also dabbled in drama, fantasy, and horror. Later on, she added more and more eroticism that quickly became her favorite genre.

In 2010, she took the big step, daring to publish a few of her stories on the Fanfiction website for a larger audience. Her fear of them mocking her was utterly unfounded. She quickly amassed a large enthusiastic following with her provocative yet honest stories and won awards in several competitions.

Encouraged by these successes, in 2013, she published her first successful novel *Always on Saturdays* and has since become one of the most widely read authors in the e-book market.

Privately, she is committed to animal welfare and lives, together with her cats, husband and son, in the smallest cowtown in the world.

Recommended reading

Previous volumes – Under Your Skin – A series!

Under Your Skin:

Always on Saturdays – Series (The unholy Book of Tristan Wrangler)

A review, if you want to learn more about Tristan, Mia, and Robbie:

"The story has been told a thousand times — he is young, sexy, athletic, and rich. She is smart, chubby, insecure, from a poor family... Actually, I never expected to be this engrossed — but we're talking about Tristan Wrangler...who is really hot! It quickly becomes apparent that his perfect outer facade is hiding a wonderful person. I really like the writing style of Don Both. She can write as dirty as Tristan grins!"

The Unholy Book of Tristan Wrangler

Constant Seduction

Always Tristan and Mia

Always is not enough

Travel To Luck

If you want to know more about Lilian Price and Vladimir Romanov,
Available only in German, soon to be translated into English:
Mad Love
Bad Love
And especially, Ménage à trois, (This is about Kristov's parents)
The Tower series also includes a part from Kera Jung, but not with the familiar characters.
If you want to know more about Luca Cavalli and his Isabella:
Isabella Parker is thirty-two years old and as a successful public prosecutor, has achieved all she can professionally. Her private life is quite different — she has no need for love, friends, or a family. She likes being a loner until she meets the charismatic Luca on her (forced) vacation, who shows her what it means to live.
On one hand, she has never met such an attentive, charming, and attractive man, and on the other, he does have a dark side — one that could become a fatal attraction. By the time she finds out, it is already too late and she succumbs to the subtle seduction of the mysterious stranger. This concludes the first move of his game.
A slightly different Don Both novel
Available only in German, soon to be translated into English:
Corvo – Game Of Love

About Maria O'Hara

Maria O'Hara was born in 1991 and lives in Baden-Württemberg. Writing for her is the equalizer to everyday life, balancing between reality and fantasy. With the right musicians, she can capture precise moments in her mind and after many cups of latte, it can happen that the night is abruptly over and three chapters have been written. In the foreground, Maria's stories are about drama, the more tangled and profound the better.

Published in German:

Wild Cherry, Sweet Cherry
Ride or die - Obsession, Ride or die - Black summer, Ride or die - Dark Paradise
Beautiful Mess
Rebels – Volume one; Rebels – Volume two
Pretty in White - Emily, Pretty in Black - Emma, Pretty in Red - Ami
Pure Sin:
With Emily Key:
The Plaza Manhattan:
1. Room 666
2. Diamondheart
3. Game of souls
4. White Satin
Una Palabra
With Don Both:
Seducing, Mr. O'Connor
Rejecting Mr. O'Connor
Tempting Mrs. Waldorf
With Kera Jung:

14 Carat
20 Carat
24 Carat

Printed in Great Britain
by Amazon

21408793R00194